New Zealand

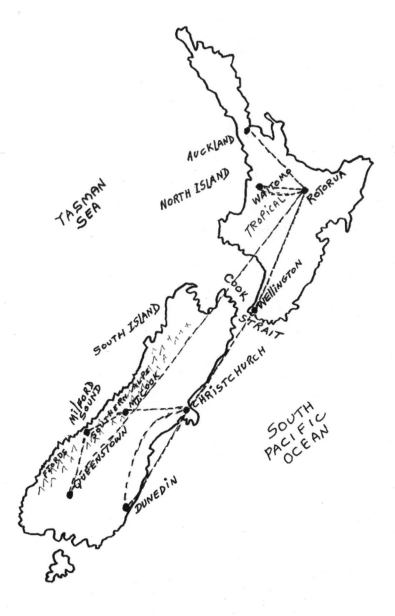

AUCKLAND

NORTH ISLAND

TASMAN
SEA

WAITOMO

ROTORUA

TROPICAL

WELLINGTON

SOUTH ISLAND

COOK
STRAIT

MILFORD
SOUND

SOUTHERN ALPS

MT. COOK

CHRISTCHURCH

QUEENSTOWN

FIORDS

SOUTH
PACIFIC
OCEAN

DUNEDIN

Guardian
of
Innocence

JUDY BOYNTON

Authors Choice Press
San Jose New York Lincoln Shanghai

Guardian of Innocence
A New Zealand Murder Mystery

Authors Choice Press
an imprint of iUniverse.com, Inc.

For information address:
iUniverse.com, Inc.
620 North 48th Street, Suite 201
Lincoln, NE 68504-3467
www.iuniverse.com

Originally published by Dell

ISBN: 0-595-12555-7

Printed in the United States of America

FOR
BOB, ROBIN, GARY,
AND GRANDPA

CHAPTER ONE

I tried to concentrate on my paperback novel, but the words turned their backs on me; I sighed, turned down the corner of the same page again, and tucked it back in my tote bag. The plane was in darkness except for my lone overhead light. Most of the passengers were cramped or sprawled in an effort to sleep, making it eerie being sandwiched in with so many unconscious bodies. I thought of the man who'd been staring at me rudely ever since the trip began. He couldn't be over thirty and was extremely handsome, but his stare wasn't flattering; it was too intense, too curious. It gave me a queasy feeling knowing he was seated somewhere behind me. I fought the desire to look back over my shoulder, afraid I'd find his probing gray eyes still studying me. The thought shivered an unseen cobweb across the back of my neck.

This was a long flight—five hours from San Francisco to Hawaii, six to Fiji, then three more to Auckland, New Zealand. I struggled against my seat belt in an effort to find a different uncomfortable position; when I switched off my light the total darkness telescoped the interior of the' jet into a shrinking cylinder. The shock of my brother's death had left me supersensitive, and a separative loneliness engulfed me, an orphaned feeling that I was no longer related to the world. If only I could sleep like everyone else, but the sharp pain of memories and unanswered questions about the future kept my eyes propped open.

I checked my watch; it was only 1:30 A.M. We'd left Hawaii four hours ago, this meant more than two hours left before our brief stopover at Fiji. I forced my head back against the seat and visualized the airport in San Francisco, where I'd first become aware of that man watching me.

He was the kind of man any girl would notice, especially if he were going on her flight, but he'd caught my attention for different reasons. Something about the controlled defiance in his tall figure relaxed against the pillar, the strange, puzzled way he stared at me through the smoke of his cigarette, the bitter, unfriendly twist to his mouth. Was I exaggerating the situation? But he'd made no effort to speak to me in Hawaii; his expression had remained unchanged each time our eyes met.

I looked past the sleeping form of the heavy man in the seat beside me to the dark mirror of our window. The thought of our jet piercing the black sky thirty-five thousand feet above endless stretches of deep, murky ocean didn't brighten the moment. I couldn't shake my depression, my throat ached with longing, empty longing; Steve dead, in an unreal war in Vietnam. It was cruel irony that the war was expected to end any day. My beloved brother had died two months ago; now I belonged to no one and no one belonged to me.

I imagined Uncle Mitch's soft voice as I'd last heard it. "You're never alone, Marlie. Your faith in the Word of God will always sustain you." My faith was all that I had now, other than David. David would be my whole world. I touched my purse and thought of his letter. David, David, you do want me. You wouldn't have sent for me if you didn't need me. Your little sister was only an excuse to bring me to New Zealand, to meet your family, to be with you. . . .

The elderly woman across the aisle from me was

asleep like the others, her mouth sagging open in her fleshy, round face. I was glad she was asleep; her mouth was open most of the time either way. What had she said her name was? . . . Mrs. Pillan. . . . Mrs. Pilgrim from an Audubon Society somewhere in Wisconsin. She was touring New Zealand and Australia for new material on the New Zealand kiwi and other birds that don't fly. I'd been exposed to an hour of her twitterings on ornithology. "The kiwi has rudimentary wings, dear, and their nostrils are at the end of their long, curved beak just like humans' nostrils are at the ends of their noses." Sitting still another minute was suddenly unbearable. I picked up my purse and walked along the shadowy aisle toward the front of the first-class section.

The cabin stretched ahead of me in darkness. The air had become increasingly rough, and I staggered to keep my footing. Fortunately the lavatory was vacant; I secured the bolt behind me, leaned against the cool door, and sighed deeply. It was a change from the cabin, but not for the better; the tiny cubicle gave me the feeling of being locked in a suction cup, and I couldn't wait to get out. I forced myself to run the comb through my short pageboy, struggling to keep my balance. The captain's impressive voice over the loudspeaker intruded on my locked-in privacy, warning about clear-air turbulence. The big plane lurched again, and walking back was extremely difficult.

Before I was halfway down the aisle, I could see that staring stranger sitting in my seat and the window seat now empty. How would he dare . . . ? I drew in my breath, and my pulse raced. I looked around helplessly for some way out. The steward was bent over talking to the intruder; when the steward noticed me he raised his head.

"Better sit down and strap yourself in, miss," he said, avoiding my eyes. "This may get worse before it gets better." The stranger stood up and off to one side to make room for me to cross in front of him. His hair was a cared-for length, an odd, vital shade of grayed-brown, almost smoky. He'd removed his tie, and his short-sleeved blue shirt was open at the neck. His shoulders were broad and his arms strong and tanned like an athlete. He didn't smile. The steward spoke again, this time as an urgent command, "Please sit down, miss, the captain says. . . ." I had no choice without making a scene. I tried to avoid being thrown against my unwelcome companion by the jolting plane as I climbed across him to sit down. He'd transferred my tote bag under the window seat; he was that sure of himself. My hands trembled as I fastened my seat belt.

He kept his deep voice low. "I'm Parker Brandt." His gray eyes searched my face as he spoke.

The name was like an electric shock. I looked up at him with unbelieving eyes, "You're Parker Brandt?" I repeated. "David's best friend?"

"And you're Marla Creighton."

"Yes, but how did you . . . ?"

"I checked at the airport in Hawaii."

"If you knew who I was, why didn't you say so, instead of just staring like that?"

"I thought you might be meeting someone." It was a weak excuse and it didn't explain his puzzled, unfriendly attitude, but I was so relieved to find out who he was, I didn't care. "Are you on your way to Fiji?" he asked.

"Fiji? Why no, I'm going to Rotorua . . . to David." I felt the heat of color in my cheeks. "That is, David has asked me to be with his little sister. She's been ill."

"Jessica. I should have known."

"Jessica? Is that her name?"

He frowned. "You didn't know? What else didn't David bother to tell you?" he asked bluntly.

I stared at him, angry with his tone. There was a

chill in my reply. "David knew I would come if he needed me. For any reason." I felt my chin go up.

"I see."

This wasn't going right. I struggled to overcome the antagonism between us. "I still can't believe it's you, Parker, after hearing so much about you all those years. To think you grew up with David."

"With David and Estelle."

"Estelle, she's David's older sister?"

His expressive brows drew into a puzzled V. "She was just about your age. You have no knowledge of the Cavenaugh tragedy?"

I shook my head. It was a strange conversation; he had all the answers, I had none.

The muscles in his cheeks grew tense. "Estelle drowned in an accident two years ago."

"And I didn't know. . . ." I could hear the anguish in my own voice. Two years. David had never written in all that time till now.

Parker's voice was filled with anger. "David should have told you. There's a bloody lot he should have told you before he brought you over."

I grew defensive again. "David would want to tell me in person, not in a letter."

He gave an impatient shrug. "How long has it been since you've seen him?"

"Four years. Not since he graduated from Berkeley with my brother. David went home to New Zealand. We had one card from him from somewhere in Europe later. Steve went into the war."

"I met your brother, Steve. He came down to SC with David one week."

"I remember. I wanted to come with them. You're an architect."

"How is Steve?"

I turned my head toward the window and tried to keep my face from crumbling. "He was killed in Vietnam two months ago."

"Damn shame. Sorry, I didn't know."

My words sounded muffled. "I thought David would've told you."

"Haven't seen him this past year. I've been studying motel designs in the States."

His soft New Zealand accent reminded me of David. I turned to look at him again. "Why didn't David tell us about his sister?"

"I'd rather you'd ask him when you get there." The muscles in his cheeks were tense again, and he changed the subject. "You went to Mills. Did you finish?"

"I still had two years to go after Steve and David graduated from Berkeley. I taught sixth grade after that. Isn't it strange that we never met, Parker? I mean" —I blushed under his scrutiny—"we weren't that far away and you and David were. . . . David shared your letters with us. We knew more about you than any of David's family. David talked about his country, never about those close to him. I know his mother died, but what about his father?"

"Aaron Cavenaugh's an importer. He's seldom in New Zealand. He has import houses in both London and Johannesburg."

"Then who lives with David in Rotorua, other than Jessica?"

He hesitated, weighing my question, then as though he'd made an important decision he answered, "I'm out of touch, but his auntie always managed the household. And there's Ariki Meri."

"What a strange name."

"In Maori *Ariki* means eldest daughter, the equivalent of princess. Meri's a foremost historian on Maori art and legends."

"I remember reading that the Maori were cannibals at one time."

His mouth twitched at one corner. "Most Maoris are as well educated and live as well as most Europeans in New Zealand, with full political rights and four seats in Parliament. They also own vast quantities of land and are a strong cultural influence in our country. Ariki Meri is one of the few remaining pureblood Maoris. She's been in Aaron Cavenaugh's employ ever since I can remember. She's somewhere around a hundred years old; no one knows for sure."

"That's incredible."

"Yes, she's incredible in many ways. Estelle was afraid of her. Ariki Meri has a way of seeing right through to what you are thinking."

"I'd better remember that." I smiled. "What was Estelle like?"

His jaw tightened. "She was earthy, beautiful . . . wild. She was. . . ." He stopped and frowned. "Forget it. She's dead." He looked at me with cold, unfriendly eyes. I'd gone too far. I'd invaded his privacy. "Excuse me," he said, "I'll be right back." He reached underneath his seat to pull out a polished wooden cane. As he started up the aisle he evidenced a slight limp in his left knee. I knew he'd played tennis at SC, so he must have been injured sometime during the last four years. He hadn't mentioned being in the war when we'd talked of Steve. I had difficulty picturing him close to David, they were such sharp opposites; jolly, fun-loving Steve had been so good for gentle, shy David.

I pondered again that this was really Parker Brandt, David's lifetime friend. I was conscious of an invisible bond between us; we knew so much about each other though we'd never met. Why was he so antagonistic toward David now? There'd never been any bitterness in his letters at school. He was different from David's descriptions, more serious, more intense. . . . I liked him.

David, Steve, and I had been inseparable. Little Marla always hanging on to their coattails. David and I had never dated, the three of us were always happy together. There'd been such a deep bond of affection between David and me, a sharing of values, I'd always assumed that someday that affection would grow into a boundless love. Now David had sent for me.

The memories disappeared as I watched Parker returning through the shadows. "I told the stewardess we'd enjoy a cup of coffee," he said, lowering himself into his seat. "They literally float you in orange juice, but it's bloody hard to get a cup of coffee." He said nothing about his injury.

"Thank you, that does sound good." I looked at my watch.

"We'll be in Fiji in another twenty minutes. I checked with the steward."

"I can't believe how fast the time has passed," I said.

"Why did you do that?"

"Do what?"

"Lower your eyes, then raise them so quickly."

"I didn't know I did."

His cool, silver eyes scanned my face as though he were memorizing it; he turned reluctantly as the stewardess brought our coffee. She lingered over Parker as though she wanted to crawl into his cup.

"Do you drink it black or white?" Parker asked.

"Black, please." The hot liquid did taste good. I pressed my face against the window to look for lights in the distance, grateful for my window seat. There were streaks of rain like tears on the glass.

"It's a bloody shame you won't get to see more of Fiji than the airdrome," Parker said when we were alone again. "It's beautiful. New Zealanders spend their vacations there." I put my cup back on the tray; it bounced and tried to slide off with the motion of the plane.

The steward's voice woke everyone to attention, "Fasten your seat belts, put your seats in an upright position, we're now landing at Nadi."

"Be sure your belt is tight," Parker cautioned. "We're in for a rough landing."

Fiji. How remote it had always sounded; was I really halfway around the world? Parker watched me with an amused expression as I struggled to see the lights of the airport. I tightened my seat belt against the unsteady air; the metal felt cold against my hand. The mountainous outline of the island was barely visible in the overcast, black sky; then the wet runway glistened just ahead, its border lights dimmed by rain. Our tires skidded with a sickening whine, and the roar of the reversed engines preceded our coming to a halt. I experienced a new excitement as we taxied toward the dark outline of a building blurred by the weather.

The lights in the plane were bright now and sleepy-eyed passengers were stretching. Mrs. Pilgrim pecked her head back and forth to find me after she discovered Parker Brandt in my seat. When she found me, she waved and winked an owlish eye.

I picked up my sweater. "You won't need that," Parker said just before we headed down the aisle.

We stopped abruptly as Parker recognized the man just ahead of us. "Kreska," he said, frowning at the immaculate, black-haired man in his middle thirties. It was a blunt acknowledgment, nothing more.

"Hello, Brandt," the man answered in a cool, articulate voice. "I noticed you at the airport in San Francisco." He glanced past Parker to me, and a sudden coldness prickled my skin. It was his eyes; they were the dead-blue glass eyes of a doll I'd owned when I was six. I'd found them so frightening, I'd buried the doll in the backyard. I could still picture their demanding, unchanging glassiness staring up at me as I'd struggled to push the dirt over them with my small hands. Kreska's skin was too china perfect for a man. His flawless grooming exaggerated the frayed appearance of the sleep-ruffled passengers around him. The two men glared at each other for a brief moment, then without another word Kreska turned and walked on. We followed his unwrinkled back down the aisle.

I forgot him quickly as an unbelievable blast of hot tropical air struck me in the face through the open door of the air-conditioned plane. It was close to one hundred degrees at 3:00 A.M., Fijian time, and pouring sheets of pungent, steaming rain. The stairs from the airplane to the ground and the walkway into the terminal were uncovered.

Mrs. Pilgrim waddled up behind me. "You never know when it's going to be raining, dear, so I always carry my umbrella. Here, it can cover both of us." She pushed her body against me like a damp down comforter. Black soldiers in British-style uniforms, tan shorts and shirts, flanked the palm-tree-lined ramp into the airport. They held rifles with bayonets fixed and ready. "Protection against hijackers," Mrs. Pilgrim whispered under the inadequate umbrella.

The terminal had the atmosphere of a large grass hut. There was no air conditioning and the fans in the ceiling only made the humid heat more oppressive. I was glad Mrs. Pilgrim had gone off in another direction but was disappointed that Parker was nowhere in sight. I asked a Fijian policeman in his knee-length skirt if there was a souvenir section and walked in the direction he pointed. Most of the ware displayed was woven: mats, slippers, rugs. The island salesgirls were colorful in their long dresses. There were several beautiful carved pieces, some ivory, some jade, and all expensive. Parker came up beside me.

"It's bloody hot in here. It always is. They have a new modern terminal planned soon. I hate to see them lose this atmosphere in spite of the heat." He put a cigarette in his lips, lit it, and inhaled deeply. "You're seated in a nonsmoking section," he explained, appreciating the cigarette in his fingers before inhaling again.

"I asked for it specially." I smiled.

"I should have guessed," he groaned.

"I bought a pair of woven slippers as a souvenir." I studied the wide variety of people in the terminal as

I waited for my change. Suddenly I noticed the man called Kreska off to one side, partially hidden by a post as though trying not to be seen; he was in conversation with a thin, dark-skinned native. Kreska gestured in my direction, glaring at me in surprise as our eyes met; at the same time the slender man cast furtive glances at me through the crowded airport. I turned away and listened to the formal English spoken by the native girl counting out my change.

"You must see the rest of Fiji someday," Parker said. "You do get used to the heat in time. It's much easier to take out on the beach. Come on, we'd best hurry; it's time to board again. This is only a twenty-minute stop, you know."

The rain was still pouring down like an unscheduled hot shower. I tied my rain scarf around my head as we hurried along. The metal stairs to the airplane were just ahead. People pushed all around us, trying to get aboard the plane and out of the oppressive moisture. A heavy woman with a large bundle squeezed herself between Parker and me. It was every man for himself to keep from getting soaked. Suddenly I became aware that someone was pulling at my purse. I clutched the shoulder strap tighter and twisted the bag. The edge of the leather bit into my flesh making me wince, but I tightened my grasp and twisted harder. I thought I'd lost it for sure; then I felt it give and I realized I'd thwarted the attempt to wrest it from me. I whirled abruptly to meet the enraged eyes of the native who'd been talking to Kreska. Before I could speak, he wove his slight body into the oncoming tide of passengers and disappeared from sight. I could see Parker ahead of me, unaware of what had happened.

I was alone with rained-on people milling all around me . . . alone and frightened, my heart pounding like a native drum in the tropical downpour. . . .

CHAPTER TWO

"What happened? You look frightened." Parker had a worried frown.

"Someone just tried to steal my purse. It was scary. I saw him; he was a native." I began to search through my bag.

"Is anything missing?"

"Everything seems to be here." I checked my passport and reread my ticket—it still said we'd arrive the morning of the third of April. "Guess I'm getting nervous about going through customs. I've never traveled before."

"I wouldn't have guessed."

He smiled for the first time, and the effect was dazzling. His teeth were very white against his tanned face. I managed a shaky smile at his sarcasm.

From the moment we were airborne it was evident we were in for even rougher weather. My lipstick rolled off my lap to somewhere under the seat, and Parker struggled to retrieve it, trying not to end up in the aisle. Mrs. Pilgrim groaned audibly. She looked a little green even from where I was sitting, like a parakeet I'd almost bought. My stomach stayed somewhere on the ceiling each time we dropped in elevation, but the most frightening sensation came from the sliding motion of the big plane, like skidding out of control on ice. The loudspeaker crackled and the captain's voice broke through, "We're skirting a tropical typhoon. No danger, but keep those seat belts on. No one is to move around."

Parker had his eyes closed as though he were trying to sleep. Suddenly, without opening them, he reached over and laid a strong, brown arm over mine where I clutched the armrest. His hand smothered my tense fingers, and I finally began to relax as a new current of courage surged through me. Soon he was asleep. His arm grew heavier, but I didn't move; the weight of his arm absorbed my fear of the jolting plane. I slipped the earphones on with my free hand, hoping to watch the movie; unfortunately, due to the storm, the dialogue croaked in all the wrong places. I finally gave up. It was raining so hard, I could hear it beat on the metal roof above the noise of the jet engines. The memory of the purse-snatcher at Nadi was still vivid in my mind.

The incident wouldn't have seemed unusual in a large crowd anywhere if it hadn't been for the thief's connection with the man called Kreska. But why would anyone want my purse? I wasn't a likely candidate for abundant cash. I stroked its leather surface with my fingers and shuddered at the thought that I might have lost my passport. I would be a foreigner in New Zealand; any red tape in Auckland could have ruined my connection with my flight on to Rotorua. Why hadn't I told Parker about Kreska? Was it because he knew the man? But they weren't friends; I was sure of that . . . still. . . .

I looked at Parker's sleeping form. A lock of hair had fallen over his forehead; it gave him a boyish look. His face was relaxed; his strong jawline slack with a foreshadowing of beard; his long legs stretched out partially into the aisle. He had arms that could give a bear a man hug. I enjoyed his physical nearness and felt a twinge of guilt at this admission, which I lost the next minute when we lost altitude again. I still couldn't believe our meeting, my uneasiness at the airport in

San Francisco. He said that he'd checked my name in Hawaii. A puzzling thought struck me: If he hadn't known who I was in San Francisco, why had he been staring at me there? Had David shown him my picture at some time? There were still unanswered questions. . . . I was glad I hadn't mentioned Kreska. I must be getting tired; I'd ask him in the morning. In the morning I'll see David. David. . . . I pressed my head against the back of the seat. The wavy lines of the decorative upholstery on the seat in front of me blurred my vision. I was soon fast asleep.

The next thing I knew Parker was shaking me gently. "Marla," he said, running his fingers across my arm. "You'd better wake up, we're almost to the airdrome. Good thing you got a little rest; you'd have been bushed for days."

"I can't believe it," I said, blinking my eyes at the bright sunshine outside the window. The jagged gaudy-green coastline of New Zealand's North Island was very much in view. The restless water was fringed with the morning shadows of shaggy clouds. Suddenly I realized that Parker's arm was still covering mine. I looked up at him, blushing. "I don't think I can move my hand."

"I didn't want to wake you. Here, let me rub some circulation into it."

"That's fine. Thanks." I pulled my arm back, disturbed at his touch. "Just a few more hours and I'll see David," I said half to Parker and half to myself.

He turned his head and adjusted his seat to a higher position, but not before I'd seen his mouth twist into that bitter line I'd almost forgotten. "Yes, it won't be long."

"I hadn't realized Auckland was so large," I said in an awed voice while looking out the window.

"See the two harbors with the city between? That's Waitemata Harbor to the east and Manukau Harbor to the west."

I saw a city wedded to the sea. I saw David's New Zealand. The mysterious two islands he'd told us could fit into the state of Texas, yet held more phenomena than any other country in the world. My heart was pounding as though I'd been running by the time the huge jet made its final turn on its approach and vibrated momentarily as the wheels locked in place for landing. "Please remain in your seats," the steward's voice requested over the loudspeaker, "until the officials from the Health Department are through with their spraying."

"Spraying?" I questioned.

"You'll see," Parker said.

As we taxied to the terminal, two uniformed men walked briskly through the plane, spraying a fog from aerosol cans over all of us.

I put my hand over my nose and mouth and groaned in a muffled voice, "How awful!"

"It's insecticide. Keep your nose covered, they'll be coming through once more. It's the law for plant and animal protection. There, they're through now, we can get off."

The weariness of the long flight followed me into the old, wooden terminal. My heels tapped out every step I took on the bare, plank floor. This was a different world. I was walking upright, but I was really down under.

"You're in an old hangar," Parker said apologetically. "There's a new terminal planned for Auckland too and not before they need it. Most of the terminals are newer in the smaller cities."

Mrs. Pilgrim came up behind us in the line of passengers waiting to go through immigration. She cupped her hand beside her mouth to speak confidentially, but her stage whisper carried remarkably well. "I knew it wouldn't take you long to find a handsome young man, dear. Such broad shoulders, and he's so tall. . . ." She noticed Parker turn his head. "Sorry," she apologized, "I didn't mean to embarrass you. Is your passport in order?" Before I realized what she was doing, she'd plucked it from my hand and scanned it intently. "Good picture of you, dear, you look like a movie star. Such a sweet face. Mine's terrible. I look like I was having a fit or something." I retrieved my passport from her fluttering fingers, grateful as Parker took a firm grip on my arm and maneuvered me on ahead of him.

"She's a tourist bore," he said in my ear.

"She's harmless," I whispered back.

The customs official went through our luggage thoroughly before he waved us on. I tried to keep even with Parker's broken steps as we walked toward the counter to confirm our flight on to Rotorua. My nerves tensed when I saw Kreska already in discussion there. "Let me have your ticket," Parker said.

Kreska turned and faced us. "The trip's on time, Brandt." He raised his black eyebrows and waited for Parker to introduce me.

"Marla Creighton, this is Leon Kreska. Kreska is an agent for Aaron Cavenaugh. Miss Creighton is to be a companion to Jessica."

"How do you do?" Kreska answered. "Then I'll see you often at Blandish House." His speech was too formal while his thoughts were hidden behind his glassy eyes. This man would be part of my new life? The thought was like knowing there'd be a snake hiding under the furniture. I acknowledged the introduction, but said nothing. The pressure of my shoulder bag against my ribs reminded me that I couldn't trust him, and it was hard to mask the way I felt. "Miss Creighton, I'm sorry I won't be able to drive you out to the house, as I have an appointment with the prime minister as soon as I arrive."

Parker ended the conversation. "We've just time for a cup of coffee before the plane leaves. Marla slept through her breakfast." Kreska accepted the rudeness of not being included with a shrug of his shoulders as Parker took my arm and ushered me in a different direction.

We climbed the stairs to the crowded coffee shop. Parker found us a table in one corner. There were structural steel beams in the high hangar ceiling; several tiny brown wrens flew down by our feet, expecting crumbs.

"They've nested in this old hangar since it was built. New Zealand is slow to change."

The aroma of the hot coffee smelled heavenly and its taste was even better. I used the rich cream. Parker drank tea with milk. I bit into a hot scone. "Is Kreska an American?" I asked between bites.

"Yes, originally. He's international now."

"I don't like him," I said.

Parker stirred his tea, slowly weighing his answer, "I detest his damn expertise."

"Why?" I asked, surprised at his earthy reaction.

His face took on a veiled look, the open friendliness between us gone. "There are reasons," he said. "I hope you can avoid him as much as possible. Will David be meeting you at the airdrome in Rotorua?"

"David will come, I'm sure. I'm to call when I arrive, because the schedule was uncertain."

"If he doesn't, I'll drive you out to the house. My car's at the terminal."

"Thank you, but I wouldn't want to impose."

"Someone has to take care of you."

"If I can just get to Rotorua, David will take care of that."

Parker paid the check and started for the flight gate without answering.

We stood in silence until it was time to board the smaller plane to Rotorua. Parker insisted I take the window seat again. I relaxed against the natural yellow sheepskin that adorned all the seats. I presumed Kreska was somewhere behind us. I became completely engrossed in the varied, fertile countryside. There were great stretches of brilliant green fields dotted with hundreds of sheep and cattle. Strange outcroppings of rock and small forests were scattered everywhere. The roads that etched their way across below us must be very narrow, I thought; they looked as though they'd been sketched with a fine pen.

"Leon Kreska called David's home Blandish House, Parker?"

"Blandish was David's mother's maiden name. Old Blandish was a wealthy Scotsman. He had three daughters: Elizabeth; David's mother, Charlotte; and a younger one that died in England. He built the house on Blandish Hill into one of the largest racehorse ranches in the area. After he died, Charlotte inherited the property, and Elizabeth ended up with a lifetime annuity."

It seemed only minutes until, after a brief glimpse of the small city, we landed smoothly at the tiny airport bordering ten-mile-long Lake Rotorua.

I looked for David's lanky figure among the people waiting, disappointed that he hadn't planned to surprise me. Kreska, the first to disembark, walked briskly to a black Mercedes waiting for him beside the small ultramodern terminal. Parker was right, this was a country of contrasts.

A disturbing thought crossed my mind, "Parker, Kreska doesn't stay at Blandish House, does he?"

"Yes, always." It was a nauseous thought.

I could see Parker searching the crowd for David as I had done. "Let's go inside and check," he said when it became obvious David wasn't there. "Wait here in front a minute. I'll call the Cavenaughs and tell them you've arrived and that I'm bringing you out; then I'll fetch the key from the office and pick you up. My car's inside my hangar."

David hadn't come. I tried to shake my disappointment as I waited. There were sheep grazing not far from where I was standing. "My hangar," Parker'd said. He must have his own airplane now. I remembered his letters to David about his flying lessons. He'd wanted David to learn too. In moments Parker drove up beside me in a dark green Rover with the top down.

He stepped out and limped around to help me into the wrong side. "Would you like the top up?"

"No, it's fine. The air will keep me awake." I slipped my coat on and turned up the collar, though it hardly seemed necessary with the temperature close to seventy.

"I'll put your luggage in back with mine." There were sheepskin backs on the seats of the Rover too.

"Everyone uses them here. They're warm in the winter and cool in the summer."

We soon gathered speed on the road. The wind whipped through my hair, and I loved it: a quick combing could make it good as new. I liked the competent way Parker handled the wheel, but I gasped as the oncoming traffic rushed past me on my side of the car. It was all I could do to keep from cringing.

"It takes getting used to," Parker said with a twist of a smile.

As we drove beside the lake, a strong scent of sulfur permeated the air. Steam rose from the earth on the surrounding hills and in several areas right beside us, as in a science fiction movie of another planet, foreign and forbidding. "Does it always have such a strong odor?" I asked.

"Yes, I guess it does. It's stronger in some areas than in others. You'll get used to it in time."

"I knew Rotorua was in the heart of a thermal area, but I didn't realize it would be evident right in the city."

"There's a golf course not far from here with thermal hazards. The sulfur water and the mud are therapeutic too, you know, for rheumatism and arthritis especially. Many of our homes are built on steambeds, and the hot water is piped into them for heat."

My emotions were so scrambled, I had difficulty concentrating on his words; the excitement of seeing David, the fear that his family would find me inadequate for him. . . . Parker must have sensed I wasn't listening. I don't know how long he'd been silent when I looked up at him.

"I'm concerned for you, Marla. Blandish House is a lonely place."

"I learned a long time ago that there's no ceiling on loneliness," I answered.

"You're a strange girl."

I looked at him again; his face was serious. "Strange?"

"How did you manage four years at college without a mark on you?"

I had to laugh. "Guess that does make me strange, but I was never a part of it. For the first two years I was close to David and Steve, after that . . . well . . . I kept pretty much to myself."

"It must have been by choice."

I laughed again. "I guess the fact that I studied karate helped." His words stirred brief memories of the times I'd dated in the last four years. I was always happier with my dreams of David . . . David. Gradually the scenery came into focus again. There were pine, eucalyptus, and palm trees all woven together with tropical ferns. I was really in New Zealand; it looked just like the posters.

"What are the trees that look like madronas?"

"Those are pohutukawa. We call them our Christmas trees. They only bloom at Christmas time; then they're covered with large, flame-colored blossoms."

"How lovely." The scent from the pines was strong in the air.

Most of the scattered houses had small gardens and stone fences, no two alike. The bright sun warmed them with a friendly glow, and I had a feeling I would like the people in them.

Parker started to talk about Blandish House again.

"I suppose the old barn is still out in back. Estelle, David, and I used to play in it years ago. But we were forbidden on the grounds after Aaron Cavenaugh surrounded the house with the high-voltage fence to fry intruders."

I sat up straight in the curved bucket seat. "But why, Parker?"

"He keeps objects of great value there at times. He supplies the New Zealand art museums with. . . . Damn fool!" he broke in suddenly. I could see a small, red sports car coming toward us at incredible speed on the narrow stretch ahead . . . it was coming head-on on our side of the road . . . trees bordered us . . . there was no place to turn off. . . .

Parker's hands tightened on the wheel as he cried out through terse lips, "For God's sake brace yourself, Marla. . . ."

I pushed back hard against the seat. The speeding car was almost upon us. . . . I drew in my breath and filled the very corners of my being with prayer.

CHAPTER THREE

Parker veered sharply to the right just as the oncoming car reached us. In the violent turn my arm struck the door; the pain brought tears to my eyes. I crouched as low as I could away from the open top. . . . *Lord*, I prayed steadily, *be with us. . . . David needs me.* We scraped deeply into the trees, tearing at the branches and foliage that scratched across the windshield with furious, dragging claws. The noise was deafening. Parker cramped the wheel and fought to keep it rigid. The muscles in his arms strained against the sleeves of his jacket as he battled the lurching car. We reeled sickeningly back and forth toward an inevitable crash. It never came. We skidded onto the road in a backward position.

"The bloody fool!" Parker exploded as the car stopped.

"Was he drunk?" I gasped, my hand on my throat.

"Crazy, not drunk. That was a deliberate attempt to run us off the road. He timed his turn perfectly to avoid a head-on." His voice was full of anger. "Are you right?"

"I'm right," I sighed in one long breath of relief, recognizing the expression as one of David's.

He revved up the engine, then lowered the power again. "There isn't a chance I could catch him now."

"It happened so fast."

Parker jockeyed the car around in the right direction again, then turned into a hedged driveway just ahead of us, stopped, opened the door, and stepped out. As he reached around in back for his cane I noticed his face was bleeding.

"Parker, you're hurt!"

He touched the spot with his hand, then pressed his handkerchief against it. "Just scratched, probably a branch." He paused and looked at me with an expression I couldn't read. "When I think that you might have been . . . or worse . . . that you might have ended up with one of these. . . ." He shook his cane at me.

I could feel my cheeks burn under his scrutiny. "Steve and I were raised by our Uncle Mitch. He was a Baptist minister. His teachings go very deep. I'm not afraid to die, Parker, but I don't want to be killed." My voice shook like an overdramatic schoolgirl's. I cleared my throat. "You said 'he'; was it a man in that car?"

"I think so; I'm not really sure."

"You weren't serious about it being intentional?"

"It couldn't have been anything else. He was bloody confident."

"But, Parker, who would want to . . . ?"

"Damned if I know, but I'm sure as hell going to find out."

Someone had tried to kill Parker and he didn't care who was with him. . . . I only knew David's Parker; there must be much more to all of this. "I think it was a red sports car," I said.

"That's not much help. Every other sports car in New Zealand is red. It could have been an MG, an Austin Healy, or even a Sunbeam, which doesn't help much either; they're all common here. But you can be sure I won't let this pass. If you're up to it, they'll be expecting you on the hill. I'm bloody sorry you had to go through that scare. Maybe it was a drunk."

I tried my best to stop shaking. "I'm fine now, Parker, really. If you think there's nothing else we can do about that—that maniac, I am anxious to get to Blandish House."

He turned and walked around the car, poking the tires with his cane and checking under the hood. At last he slid back under the wheel and shifted us into motion. "Not much damage. I'll have to take it to the panel beaters tomorrow; they'll knock the dings out."

I forced my mind on ahead to Blandish House as he drove out onto the road again. What would David say if he knew I'd been this close to death? If Parker didn't mention it, I wouldn't either, not until later perhaps. Parker must be wrong, I thought, it couldn't have been intentional . . . that would have been murder. . . . It was a horrendous thought! "Do they keep quite a staff of servants at the house, Parker?" I asked in an effort to sound under control again.

"Right. Sims, the butler. Estelle was fond of Sims. I'm sure she confided in him more than her own family. Annie, the cook. And a staff of cleaning girls. Dutch is the grounds-keeper. He has a crew of men working for him. He used to be the only one that lived on the premises, but I don't know if that's still true. About David, Marla, there's something you should know before . . ."

I put my hand on his sleeve. "Please, Parker, we're nearly there. I'd rather David told me everything he wants me to know."

Tension twisted his cheek again. "Look, Marla, you can see the house now."

Built high atop a craggy hill, the house was visible for miles. "It's a castle," I said in an awed voice.

"Yes, it is—almost."

The outline of the immense mansion became more detailed as we drove closer. The front of the manor jutted out with long wings on either side at the back.

As we approached, the countryside around us became more rural and hilly. Larger ranches with lovely, sloping green fields and grazing sheep were on every side; above it all, demanding attention like a threatening hawk—Blandish House. Parker slowed and turned into a narrow driveway that wound upward, edged with the now familiar clusters of pines, punga palms, and king fern. I tried to envision all the bloomed madrona-like Christmas trees we had passed like a wedding parade. We neared the high, electric fence; the stone house still loomed above it. A young guard, who looked Polynesian, stood behind the heavy, iron gates. There was a caretaker's cottage in the background. As we drove up, he walked over to talk to Parker through the grillwork.

"This is Miss Creighton," Parker called to him. "She's expected." The guard nodded his head, and the heavy gates swung inward. "He's Maori. He's new," Parker said.

We drove the remaining distance up to the house in silence. I took out my mirror and touched up my hair before Parker brought the car to a stop at the arched stone entrance. "I won't come in with you. I should've told you I'm no longer welcome at Blandish House."

"I don't understand."

"There are personal reasons." He frowned. "You look pale. Are you sure you want to stay? I can get you a place in town."

"I'll be all right. It was the scare we had on the road and being so tired. . . . I'll be all right, Parker," I repeated to his disbelieving eyes.

"Be careful, Marla. In every way be careful." He held my door open for me as I climbed out. "I'll get your luggage."

I dug my hands deep into the pockets of my coat and looked up at the house while Parker got my two suitcases then stepped in front of me to use the brass knocker on the huge carved door. An elderly man in a black suit answered; the stereotyped butler from every English movie I'd ever seen, with the long face, the high, wrinkled forehead, elevated chin, and haughty eyes that looked down a thin but extremely prominent nose.

"Master Parker," he said. "It has been a long time."

"Yes, it has, Sims. You look well."

"Oh, I am, sir, I am." When I stepped into view, the man's eyes dilated and he grasped the door frame with his bony hand.

"Sims, this is Marla Creighton. Are you right?"

"Yes, quite right. . . . It was just . . . thank you, sir, I'm quite right now."

"Is David home, Sims?"

"Oh, yes, sir, he's in the library. I'm to bring Miss Creighton to him as soon as she arrived." He struggled for composure. "Are you coming in, sir?" His eyes never left my face.

"Not this time, Sims," Parker said as he set my

suitcases inside the door. "But I do plan to see Miss Creighton again soon."

I looked up at him. "I'm really grateful we met at last, Parker. I needed a friend." He looked at me intently, not wanting to leave. "I'll tell David how helpful you were," I assured him. "I know he'll be pleased." His lips tightened and he turned to go. As I watched Sims close the door on his receding figure I realized how much I'd wanted him to stay, at least until I was with David.

"This way, miss," Sims's voice was hardly more than a whisper. I wondered if he greeted all guests with such astonishment.

We were in a cavernous entrance hall that suggested suits of medieval armor and coats of arms. The ceiling towered above us two stories high. The walls were lined with elaborate, gold-framed oil paintings, even along the wide stairway that curved up one entire side. I remembered this part of the house protruded from the rest, as I looked up at the narrow stained-glass windows between the paintings along the stairs. The light from the windows, streaming through the intricately carved wooden banister, created a spiderweb shadow on the opposite wall. The foreboding pattern twisted across the heavy doors of the rooms we passed. My feet buried themselves in the plush rugs. There were exquisite pieces of sculpture on highly polished tables, tapestries of ageless beauty. I noticed a billiard table in the gloom of one room. A gigantic, ornate grandfather clock chimed 11:30 A.M.; its beautiful, deep tones echoed in the immense hall. Suddenly I felt a chill.

The figure of a woman stood motionless in a doorway ahead, watching our approach. Threads of shadow streaked her aged bronze face and flowing, shoulder-length, white hair. She was short and stocky, but there was grandeur in the attitude of her body. She wore a floor-length gown of heavy, woven material. It was not until we drew closer that I sucked in my breath involuntarily. Her lips and chin were tattooed in a strange blue design. Her old eyes did not waver, and her seamed face remained expressionless as we reached her.

Sims cleared his throat. "It is Miss Creighton, Ariki Meri."

She spoke in strong, articulate words. "We have been expecting you, Miss Creighton."

"Thank you. Is David . . . ?"

"Of course, child, he is in the library waiting for you. We will meet again later. Take her there immediately, Sims."

"Thank you," I repeated, trying not to show my fascination with her strange appearance.

My knees were weak and shaking as I followed Sims. His steps were slow . . . too slow . . . I wanted to run to David. David would answer my questions. . . . David would allay my fears. I held my breath as Sims paused to knock on a large wooden sliding door, which opened at the sound of a voice inside. "Miss Creighton is here, Master David."

CHAPTER FOUR

It took my eyes a few moments to adjust to the dark, book-lined library, as the recessed lead-cast windows with their ornate colored-glass tops limited the light. I searched for David only to find that I was surrounded by native artifacts and carvings everywhere I looked.

Frightening objects with hideous faces appeared out of the shadows writhing and leering at me in the glow of the fireplace from the far end. Evidently the soft warm air that had brushed my cheeks during my ride in Parker's convertible didn't penetrate this mausoleum. I blinked at one giant carved mask with its tongue extended grotesquely, its eyes bulging in fury from their sockets. I caught my lower lip in my teeth to keep it from trembling. Then I saw the top of a blond, curly head barely visible above the back of one of the massive red chairs facing the fireplace and I knew I'd arrived at the first moment of my future. I hurried forward. A familiar hand placed a half-filled drink on a low table, and David Cavenaugh labored his lean body out of the chair and faced me.

"Hello, Marla," he slurred.

The bleary-eyed, handsome man before me wasn't my David . . . dear, special David. . . . "Hello, David," I said in a choked voice.

"Marla. Glad y're here. Shoulda met you at th' plane, but. . . ."

I must be numb, I thought; the sound of his voice didn't thrill me, but then it wasn't really David's voice. He was smashed at 11:30 in the morning. The air reeked with alcohol. In spite of his condition the sight of his familiar figure stirred such precious memories that my disappointment over his not meeting me disappeared in my joy of being with him.

"It's all right, David." I tried to cover my concern until he could explain. "I came out with . . ."

He brushed my words aside like insignificant lint on a dark sleeve. "God," he said, staring at me closely, eyes squinted as though trying to clear his vision. "Thought 'xaggerated in my mind, but you. . . ." He stopped and ran his fingers through his hair. My heart lurched at the familiar gesture. "Still pretty," he finished lamely.

"David, I'd hoped . . ."

He put up his hand as though to fend off my words. "Would y' like a drink?" he asked.

I sank weakly into the chair across from his, shaking my head. He picked up his glass, staggered to the small, leather-trimmed bar, and filled it almost to the brim with straight Scotch. Tears of frustration burned behind my eyes, and the long hours of the trip settled over me like metal mesh. Was this what Parker had been concerned about?

"Hell 'bout Steve. Sorry. So sorry." His eyes filled with tears. I didn't want his emotions to get out of control.

"I still can't believe it." I spoke the words while my thoughts pushed me away from reality. Maybe when he was sober, he'd be David again and the trouble would be gone from his beautiful eyes.

"Trip okay?"

"Stormy all the way." I tried to smile as I said, "Guess who I met on the plane, David, after all these years? Parker Brandt!"

His thin, sensitive face registered surprise, then sudden anger. "Parker. Damn. Hadn't planned . . . so soon. Was shocked w'n he saw you?"

"Did you expect him to be? David, had you shown him my picture?"

The glass slipped out of his hand and spilled; in the necessary confusion to get a towel and clean it up, my question was lost. Had this been deliberate? He refilled the shorted portion while I watched helplessly, then he staggered back half falling into his chair.

"You haven't changed, Marla."

"You've changed, David."

"Still the direct approach. Face the fac's 'n' truth'll go away. Things happen to people, Marla. Unchangeable things happen. Sorry didn't meet you." For a moment his misty, blue eyes had the soulful depth of the old David, but there was a new element—was it fear? I wanted to reach out and touch him, and he knew it.

"You're pretty as I 'membered you . . . prettier. Four years . . . long time, Marla."

My cheeks were flushed. I didn't want to reminisce while he was too far out of it to know what he was saying. "Parker drove me here from the airport."

Anger twisted the corners of his mouth again. "Sims'd instructions to . . ."

"Parker told him that he'd bring me out. He must have been coming this way."

He shook his head, "Parker lives 'n th' other d'rec- tion." He sobered momentarily, thought better of it, and took a long drink from his glass. His last answer had startled me. Why had I been so accepting of every- thing Parker had said?

"I can't wait to meet Jessica, David."

"Jeshica doesn't know you're here. Haven't told 'er." He ran his fingers through his curly hair again. His words were becoming thick and garbled.

"Was she happy about my coming?" I asked.

"Happy? Hard t' tell with Jessica. Doesn't show feelings ver' offen." He became serious. "She—she needs you, Marla. She needs friend. You're only one I trusted . . . only one with . . . thought you'd share. . . ." His words weren't making any sense. My heart ached to help him, but something in his manner had changed so drastically, I felt uncomfortable; as though he were reaching out for me but he didn't want me to take his hand. He turned his head and stared into the fire as if trying to smoke out something he wanted to tell me. "Did y' know I'm married?" he threw at me without any warning.

His words hit me like a medicine ball; I almost crumbled under their weight. I fought the tears that wanted to wash them away. I looked down at my hands as though they belonged to someone else . . . anyone else. "No, David, I didn't know," I struggled to say aloud, while an inner voice kept saying, It can't be true! I couldn't have heard the words. David married! "Did Steve know? Did he forget to tell me?" He faced me again.

"Don't know 'f I told him or not." He rubbed his forehead, "Maybe not. Happened 'bout a year ago. Name's Andrea."

Oh, David, why didn't you tell me? my heart wept silently. Why did you let me hope? Parker hadn't mentioned David's wife. He must have avoided it purposely, but why? Why hadn't David met me? What could possibly have made him drink himself into this shape . . . ? Could it have been his wife? Was drinking only an excuse so I wouldn't know? But she must have known I was coming. The jigsaw was spread all over, and I couldn't find any of the right pieces. I searched David's face for a clue; his eyes haunted me with their tortured expression; they were pleading eyes. I knew now I'd read into his letter what I'd wanted to hear. His need for me had been there, but not beyond friendship.

"I'm very tired, David. I'd like to rest before meeting anyone else." I had to get away by myself.

"Jessica won't show up 'til dinner. Andrea's in town."

"Is your father home?"

"Father?" He looked at me closely, as if suspicious of my words. "Father'll come home, don' worry 'bout that. He's always here when you don't need him." Anguish swept over his face. "Why're you so interested in Father?"

"I guess because he is your father."

"Forget him. It's Jessica I'm worried 'bout. Bett'r get some rest." He pulled a velvet cord on the wall by his chair. Sims appeared instantly in the doorway. "Take Mish Creighton to 'er room, Sims. I'll see you a' dinner at eight, Marla."

With leaden feet I followed Sims out into the hall

and back toward the curved stairway, grateful Ariki Meri was nowhere in sight. It took forever to reach the top of the steps and another forever to proceed down the long hall. Finally Sims opened a door and announced it was to be my room. He mentioned lunch and tea, but I told him I'd rather rest until dinner. When he'd left, I felt like a prisoner beginning to serve an unjust sentence. It was a large room, very feminine, with floral wallpaper and Colonial furniture. My suitcases were already on the luggage racks in one corner next to a four-poster bed that looked as if it would swallow me. No use unpacking now. I'd get away as soon as I could. I didn't want to think. . . . David was married. . . . David had a wife . . . my David. What was she like, this Andrea? David's wife . . . David's wife. . . . I picked up the mirror of a delicate, mother-of-pearl dresser set on the dressing table. It was initialed in gold leaf: E.C. Estelle Cavenaugh. This was Estelle's room. I was only to be a stand-in for a dead sister. Something pushed at my memory, something important, but I was too overcome with self-pity to pursue it. I would catch the next plane home. How could I have been such a sentimental fool. Parker must have realized. . . .

I took mechanical steps over to the window and pulled the lace curtain to one side. That must be the barn Parker had mentioned. Parker, who had grown up with Estelle and David and was no longer welcome in this house. There were beautiful green grazing fields surrounding the barn. The hydrangeas were clinging to their last bit of color. Of course, I'd left America with azaleas blooming in April, but April in New Zealand was October weather for me. I wasn't conscious that my cheeks were wet with tears until I needed to find a Kleenex in my purse and blow my nose. I'd thought I was out of tears, but someone had wrung them from my heart again.

A small lamb ran out of the barn, a spindly little girl in ill-fitting jeans in fast pursuit. They scampered around in circles as if playing a game of tag. I forgot myself for the moment and half-smiled through my tears at the child's brown pigtails flying behind her slight figure. She's small for her age, I observed as I sniffed and blew my nose again. More like eight than eleven, and so thin. She didn't act ill. She caught the lamb in her arms and held on to it with difficulty, finally tumbling over on her back with its weight. Glasses with dark, heavy rims monopolized her tiny face. They gave her an odd, old-fashioned look. As if compelled, she looked up at the window where I was standing.

I'd expected her to be surprised at my presence, but I was aghast at the terror on the girl's blanched face. I realized no one had prepared her for my arrival and I was in her sister's room. How heartless, David, how mean! My partial smile froze on my lips. We stared at each other for a minute or more; then, still staring, she staggered to her feet, the lamb clutched in her arms. I struggled to open the window and call to her, but it stuck. She ran back into the barn as fast as the lamb's weight would let her. I knew there was nothing more I could do just then. I let the curtain drop back into place, but one area stayed in wrinkled pleats from the tenseness of my grip.

I kicked off my shoes and sank onto the bed, pulling the comforter up over me. It had seemed so right for me to come to New Zealand. *Why, Lord? Why had I been so sure?* I sobbed into the white starched pillow. Uncle Mitch's voice came back to me as though he were in the room: "Give the tragedies in your life to the Lord, Marlie; He'll change them into victories." But this is too much. . . . I can't cope with this, I cried from the depths of my despair. "You're stronger than you think you are. . . ." The voice went on and on, and his words laced back and forth through my mind until they wove a merciful web of exhaustion and I slept. . . .

CHAPTER FIVE

When I woke the last bit of light was dwindling. The arm I'd bumped in the car ached all the way up to my shoulder, but it was nothing compared to the pain in my heart that revived the memory of my meeting with David all too clearly. I didn't move for a long time, as I tried to sort out my thoughts. My eyes were swollen from crying. I would have to meet his wife . . . see them together. They would be expecting me for dinner, David said, at eight. I reached over and switched on the lamp beside the bed; my watch said six o'clock. Clawing, active fingers in my stomach reminded me I hadn't eaten since the airport in Auckland. I can't go to pieces, I told myself. I have to care, even knowing David can never be. . . .

I forced myself to my feet and away from my thoughts. The sheer curtains were blowing gently in the breeze as I stood at the window and took several deep breaths of the sweet, autumn air. The shadowy barn looked deserted, like a neighborhood street when the children have all gone in to dinner. I walked slowly into the bathroom, conscious that the light switch worked opposite to what I was used to at home. I turned the hot water on full into the old-fashioned tub with its claw feet, then forced the plug into place. I noticed the water spiralled strangely in the wrong direction, clockwise, not counterclockwise as it should have. I'd walked through the mirror with Alice; everything was turned inside out.

The leisurely, warm bath relaxed me. After I shampooed my hair and dried it, it felt fresh and clean under my brush. My eyes were less swollen; hopefully the family would credit what redness was left to my being tired from the long trip. Just as I finished tucking my white satin blouse into my long, tailored, navy skirt, there was a sharp, quick rapping at my door. Startled, I walked slowly across the room and opened it.

She was just a little taller than I was, slender but voluptuous, with glowing, shoulder-length red hair. Her porcelain neck was graceful all the way down into the plunging neckline of her long, silk jersey dress, which echoed the intense green of her eyes. Her sultry voice matched everything else. "I'm Andrea. David said that you had arrived." Her accent was decidedly British. "I'll walk to supper with you if you like. David may be late. You met him when you came in, so you know why." Her eyes were cool and calculating, the green irises a little too large. I knew they were categorizing me for size, weight, appeal—but for what? Opposition, competition?

I was too stunned at being face to face with David's wife to say anything for a moment. We just stood and looked at one another. I sensed every woman was her natural enemy. Somehow I couldn't picture her with David. I knew she recognized the brand of schoolmarm in my navy skirt and white blouse. Finally I stammered, "Thank you, I'd like that. I—I guess I'm ready. Has Jessica gone down yet?"

"I'd be the last to know," she shrugged. "Her room is across from yours; we can check." She turned with the precision of a model and knocked on Jessica's door. When there was no answer, she rapped harder. "Jessica,

are you in there?" There was still no sound. She tried
the doorknob. It was locked. "Jessica, I know you are
in there. You might as well come out, it's time for
supper. Miss Creighton is here. Come out now, Jessica,
or I will call your auntie."

I heard a stirring in the room. The lock snapped and
the door handle began to turn. Jessica had changed into
a pink dress, and it hung on her bony little shoulders
like an empty sack. The smocking around the neck increased my impression that she looked years younger
than eleven. Her long brown braids had been brushed
neatly. The dark, heavy rims of her glasses emphasized
the pallidness of her complexion; the deep, brown eyes
that stared through the glass were locked with fear on
my face.

"Why are you acting so foolishly, Jessica? What will
Miss Creighton think of you?"

"I think I know," I said gently. "Jessica didn't know
I was arriving. She was shocked this afternoon when
she saw me in the window of her sister's room. I'm
Marla Creighton, Jessica. I'm from America. David
went to school with my brother, Steve." Though she
didn't speak, the color crept back into her cheeks.
She didn't move, however, and her expression remained
the same.

"How like David to have forgotten to tell her," Andrea said.

I tried to keep the criticism in my voice to a low
key. "It was a cruel mistake. That's not like David."

"We may be talking about two different men," Andrea answered, then her voice rose impatiently. "Don't
just stand there, Jessica; that's rude. Miss Creighton is
a guest. Come along now; we'll be late for dinner."
Andrea took her arm and forced her forward. Once
the child was in motion and Andrea was sure she would
follow, Andrea walked on ahead of us.

We moved slowly down the hall: first Andrea with
her effortless glide; then I followed, Jessica behind me,

down the curved staircase, past the gallery of paintings in their ornate, gold frames and the stained-glass windows muted by the darkness behind them. The deep, melodious chimes of the grandfather clock followed our descent. It struck eight just as we came to an open doorway. The large carved sliding doors I'd admired earlier had been opened to reveal an immense dining room. The table stretched out long enough to seat thirty people, but it was formally set with silver service for seven. The remaining chairs stood like sentinels along the walls beside the enormous china cabinets and vast dark mahogany sideboards. Elaborate, heavy silver pieces dominated the room, and the chandelier above the table glowed majestically with a million fragile teardrops of crystal.

I recognized the short stately figure in the brocaded robe as Ariki Meri, her white hair flowing as wildly as I remembered it. She bowed her head just a fraction to acknowledge me, a stoic expression on the wrinkled, mocha face. Standing next to her was a tall wraithlike woman dressed in long black chiffon. She was so blond there was no contrast between her hair, skin, and pale amber eyes; as though a few hours in a bright sun might bleach her away to nothing. She was extremely nervous and after her first almost frightened acknowledgment she avoided my eyes. Her thin, colorless mouth curved into a forced spasm of sweetness, and she brought one frail hand forward from the soft fullness of her black sleeve to greet me. "I am Elizabeth Blandish, David's aunt. Forgive me for not being here to welcome you this morning, but I wasn't feeling well. We must rest when we don't feel well." The hand I took in mine was bone cold and gave no welcoming response. Maybe the chandelier was in reality ice and not crystal, too. Miss Blandish pulled her hand back into her sleeve and looked with relief over my shoulder. "Leon, Meri is planning on your business discussion after dinner, but now you must meet Marla Creighton."

I could feel my body tighten as I heard his smooth voice. "Miss Creighton and I met on the plane coming over. Parker Brandt introduced us." Icy silence accompanied his words. Miss Blandish covered her mouth in shocked surprise.

Andrea was the first to speak. "You flew over with Parker Brandt?"

As I answered I turned and faced Leon Kreska. He'd obviously hoped to put me at a disadvantage. In his dark green suit, his thinning black hair brushed flat away from his receding temples, he reminded me of a lizard. "Parker Brandt introduced himself on the plane. I was very grateful. It was a long trip."

"How did he know who you were?" Andrea persisted.

"He asked in Hawaii. Evidently David had shown him my picture at some time. David had talked a great deal about Parker at school. It was a pleasant surprise to meet him after all this time." Why were they all so hostile?

"It was most fortunate for Parker, I'm sure," Leon Kreska said.

"What an unusual coincidence," Miss Blandish said skeptically.

Leon Kreska extended a small package to Jessica. "I brought you this from Austria, Jessica."

"How thoughtful you are, Leon. You spoil her. Jessica, take the package. Jessica!"

Jessica reluctantly took the gift.

"Well, open it, silly," Andrea admonished.

Jessica tore off the wrappings. It was a little hand-painted music box. She raised the lid, and the tiny bell tones of a Strauss waltz wafted around us. Jessica gave a quick, defiant look at Kreska and closed the lid. She doesn't like him either, I thought.

"Will David be down for dinner, Andrea?" David's aunt asked to smooth over the incident.

"There's no use waiting for him, Auntie. He won't make it tonight."

"I'm here," David's voice said from the doorway. There was fire in Andrea's eyes as he came toward us. "Have you all met Marla?"

"David, how nice." His aunt fluttered. "Yes, we've met Miss Creighton. Now shall we all be seated? Miss Creighton, please sit over there between Ariki Meri and Jessica," she directed. Kreska seated Miss Blandish and Andrea before taking his place between them as though he were quite at home. David held my chair for me, then sat at the head of the table. He was a bit unsteady but not as far gone as he'd been when I'd arrived. Perhaps this morning had been an exception. I started to pull the heavy, tall-backed chair from the table to help Jessica, but she made it obvious that she could do it alone. She might look eight, but she had eleven-year-old independence. My sixth-grade class had quickened my perception. I sipped the water from my goblet during the awkward silence that followed.

"What's new in London, Leon?" Andrea asked eagerly, turning her head to look at him through half-closed eyes. She was born seductive, I decided. It was difficult for me to watch her without prejudice. I looked over to David. He met my eyes in such a knowing way, I quickly dropped mine.

"I think the pace is getting faster all the time," Kreska answered. "I'm afraid it's an American influence, if you'll forgive my saying so, Miss Creighton."

"I imagine you would know, Mister Kreska," I said crisply. "I understand you were an American at one time." He looked surprised, as if he hadn't expected me to fight back.

Andrea's eyes were wide open again. David had a smile in his eyes for the first time. Miss Blandish's eyebrows rose high with disapproval. I was sure she'd considered my rude retort in bad taste. "We were sorry to hear about your brother." She tactfully changed the subject again. "David was very fond of him."

I swallowed hard before I spoke. "I'm afraid I'm still adjusting to his being gone."

The silence was so thin, we could hear the clock ticking in the hall. Just then a stocky teen-age girl came through the swinging door carrying a tray of steaming food. Even though I hadn't eaten since the scone and coffee with Parker, I found I had no appetite after all. The delicious aroma from the platters didn't entice me. Andrea and Kreska talked endlessly of London during the next few courses. It was obvious she was homesick.

"Your shipments arrived today, Leon," Ariki Meri spoke during a lull.

"Excellent," he answered.

"More crates. Every day more crates. We'll soon be the museum you've always wanted, Meri." Miss Blandish's tone was peevish.

"Remember the crates are always from Aaron, Elizabeth," Ariki Meri told her.

"I do wish he'd come home. It's been so long." David's aunt's hands fluttered nervously; they were never still. She looked directly at me. "He should come home. Della, serve Miss Creighton more of the roast lamb."

"Thank you, no, Miss Blandish, I've really eaten all I can. It was marvelous."

"Annie is a superb cook. We do know how lucky we are," she answered.

David poured himself another glass of wine. I couldn't blame him; if I were a drinking person this would have been one time I'd join him. He'd hardly spoken a word, and not at all to me. Jessica had been ignored by everyone. New Zealanders might believe in a child being seen but not heard, but this was over-doing it.

"Where do you go to school, Jessica?" I asked her.

Andrea looked across at me obviously puzzled. "Didn't David tell you?" I looked back questioningly. "Jessica hasn't spoken since her sister's accident two years ago. She has some type of trauma." I could see Leon Kreska studying me carefully for my reaction.

I turned quickly to David. "David, what . . . ?"

Miss Blandish didn't give him a chance to answer, "It is a most unusual case," she explained. "Jessica can understand every word that is said to her; she simply cannot speak. She has a special tutor who comes twice a week to keep her abreast of her schoolwork. We do what we can."

How unfeeling of them to discuss this in front of Jessica, and how embarrassing for me not to have known. I could feel the humiliated anger in my eyes as I looked again at David. I couldn't trust myself to speak.

"Meant to, but. . . ." He ran his fingers through his hair as though it would help the cobwebs in his mind.

I looked down at Jessica. She stared at her plate, and her food was hardly touched. I cleared my throat. "Jessica, I'm sorry I didn't know. Let's start over. Is your lamb a pet?"

She nodded without lifting her eyes, pushing the glasses back up on her nose. So she did communicate, I thought, instantly relieved.

"I've never petted a lamb. My brother and I used to have a dog we loved. I still miss him very much. Will you show me your lamb sometime?"

She nodded briefly.

"You mustn't count on it; Jessica is very changeable. That lamb will be the death of her," Miss Blandish said. "The hours she spends with it in that barn. We can't understand it."

Ariki Meri spoke out in strong tones, "A child must first give love to know what love can be."

Jessica raised her head and looked past me to the

ancient Maori woman; a strong current of affection passed between the two of them.

Miss Blandish scowled at them, then turned to me. "As a matter of fact, Miss Creighton . . ."

"Call her Marla, Auntie," David said unexpectedly.

"As you wish, David. I was about to say Jessica's tutor, Geoffrey James, will be here in time for coffee in the parlor before Jessica has her lesson. If you are not too tired, it might be a good time for you to become acquainted with her schoolwork. We do want her to keep up."

She was treating me like an employee. I'd planned on being a companion to David's sister as a gift of love. But then I'd planned on so many intangible things. "Yes, of course, I would like that." Anything to kill the time until I could be alone again to finalize my plans to leave. It was obvious Miss Blandish doted on David and his father.

Ariki Meri addressed Kreska: "Leon, we have more business than usual to accomplish during your stay." He donned an immediate official air and placed his napkin on the table; the others followed his lead. I was grateful when we adjourned to the parlor.

Andrea was pouring tea and coffee for the rest of us as Geoffrey James entered the room. He was like a breath of fresh air, under six feet, husky, and he wore his English tweeds well. His hair was the color of nutmeg, and his hazel eyes danced with bright yellow highlights when he smiled. "Good evening, everyone." He acknowledged each person in the room from where he stood; when he came to me, his appraisal was flattering. Miss Blandish took him by the arm and brought him closer to where I was sitting. "Marla, this is Mister James. I've been telling Miss Creighton about you. We think you will have a great deal in common, both of you teaching school and all."

"I was very pleased when I heard you were coming," he said, echoing his words with his eyes.

At least one person felt that way. I smiled back at him in spite of the way I was feeling. "I'm looking forward to observing Jessica's lesson tonight," I told him sincerely.

He looked over to where Andrea was still pouring tea. "If the family will forgive me, I'll forego my tea tonight. I do have another engagement after I leave here, and if Jessica is ready, I would like to get started on our lesson right away."

Andrea smiled at him as he bade them all goodnight. He took Jessica by the hand and I followed them from the room. David gave me a pleading look as I passed him, as if he expected something from me that I didn't understand. Mr. James ushered us into the now familiar library.

Jessica drew her brows together slightly and sat down at the huge desk that stretched across one side of the room. She opened a drawer and drew out some books and papers.

"Jessica spends most of her time reading," Geoffrey James began. "She has a flair for writing. I've encouraged her to write compositions for most of her subjects as a substitute for oral work. History and geography can be very dull subjects until you involve them with your own imagination." He sorted through several of the pages in front of him and chose one to hand to me. "Read this," he said.

I read and reread the paper as he went on to explain Jessica's future homework to her. "King George the Third ruled without knowing the needs of his people," I read. "He was a selfish, arrogant man involved only with his own greed, and the people lived in the shadow of his dark thoughts."

It was not the usual paper of an eleven-year-old. I still burned inside when I remembered the cool, thoughtless manner in which Miss Blandish and Andrea had treated her. What a dreadful atmosphere for a young child. David said she needed me. She needed someone, that was sure; this family was enough to give a child a trauma, not overcome one. What did David expect of me?

"There, Jessica." Geoffrey James's voice interrupted my concentration. "Why don't you take this up to your room where you won't be disturbed. I'll stay here and talk to Miss Creighton for a bit. I do have to leave early tonight."

Jessica gathered her homework together. As she turned to leave I handed her the paper I'd been reading. "That's excellent writing, Jessica. Please knock on my door in the morning. I'm not sure I can find my way down to breakfast alone." I realized now that before making arrangements to go home, I would have to stay a few days to save face for David.

Jessica pushed her glasses back up on her nose, nodded quickly, and was gone.

"I'm impressed," I said. "She's extremely talented. Her writing has a Victorian charm."

"She's read everything Charles Dickens ever wrote." He smiled.

"I'd have thought someone fifteen or sixteen had written it. You've obviously done a fantastic job of tutoring her."

He seemed pleased. "It has its difficult moments. You will probably be the best thing that has happened to her since her sister died. The average child would perish of loneliness in this house." He began to wander about the room, picking up sculptures and artifacts here and there. "God, there's a fortune locked up in this room alone. Look at this jade war club. What a fancy way to die that would be."

"That horrid mask with its bulging eyes and its tongue extended gave me a real scare when I first saw it."

He laughed at my reaction, "You'll get used to it. The Maoris trained their warriors to exercise the muscles in their tongues and eyes to grimace at their enemies in this way. It was a secret weapon. Their dancers still use it to depict their legends."

"Mister James . . ."

"Geoff, please, and may I call you Marla?"

"Of course. Geoff, has Jessica been under a doctor's care, a psychiatrist or psychologist?"

"I understand she was for a time. Evidently she was so close to complete withdrawal that the family decided it was best to keep her away from questions demanding answers. She's so damned smart. I can't help feeling she's smarter than any of the rest of them, the doctors included."

It was obvious Jessica had one real friend. I liked Geoff James. There was vibrant energy in his movements and in his voice that brought life into this room of relics.

He crushed his cigarette into the already full ashtray and grinned at me like a schoolboy. "I'm sorry I made other plans for tonight now. I wish we could talk more, but at least I'll have you to look forward to in the future."

"Thank you," I said, not committing myself one way or the other. "How often do you have lessons?"

"Twice a week. I'll see you again on Friday night. Good night."

By Friday I may be gone, but no use going into that now, I thought. As he left I heard voices in the hall, then a moment later David walked in. He leaned against the doorframe. The heavy scent of wine was on his breath as he said, "We're lucky we found him. Shims went t' school with his father. Andrea's gone t' League meeting 'n' town." His speech was disjointed and thick.

His blue eyes once so clear and confident were veiled and uncertain. It was no time to tell him my plan to go home. "Why didn't you tell me about Jessica, David?"

"Just wanted you here. Don't do anything I should

anymore." He walked to the bar and fixed a drink. What had I read somewhere, "Both self-pity and alcohol create their own appetites"?

"You could change that, David."

He slammed the glass down on the bar so hard, I was surprised it survived the shock. "Damn it, Marla, don't you know the hell I'm going through? Kreska says Father's talking 'bout coming home."

"I'm glad, David. Your aunt will be pleased."

"You're glad." He laughed without humor, and I was shocked at the pain in his eyes as he said, "You can't 'magine how ironic that is." Jessica and Andrea were only part of David's trouble, I realized that for sure now. There was something more that was causing his tortured expression. Something to do with his father that was kin to dread.

"Then I'm not glad. Either way, you can't drink yourself out of a problem."

"If problem can't be solved . . . then y' got t' ease th' pain any way ya can."

"Would it help to talk about it, David?"

"Never!" There was anger again in his voice. This was the friend I'd known so well. Well enough to know he wasn't given to fits of temper. "Sorry, didn' mean to fly off like that."

"David, what do you want of me? I'm not trained to help a child in Jessica's condition."

"Just be her friend. She needs a friend . . . not easy to come by here—friends aren't friends at all. I've needed you, Marla. God, how I've needed you. . . ." His large sad eyes were pleading.

His need disarmed me. My heart ached to respond. Didn't he understand how I felt at all? How could he beg for my help after crushing all my dreams? But I knew our friendship would always be there and he was asking for help from me just as he would have from Steve if he were alive. I had to find some way to salvage the David we'd known, keep him from destroying himself. I would love to have asked him the multitude of questions that chased back and forth in my mind, but I wanted answers, not blurred evasions.

"Forgive me, David, I'm very tired. I'm going to my room." Suddenly I'd had enough for one day.

CHAPTER SIX

I felt much better after a good night's sleep. I was still sick with the shock of David's marriage, but my sympathy for Jessica's needs had eased the pain somehow. Andrea was not the wife I'd envisioned for David, but then David wasn't the husband I'd pictured either. I was haunted by a deep sense of trouble threatening David, something I didn't understand, or perhaps didn't want to understand.

Jessica sat self-consciously on the edge of the chintz chair, her hands clasped together tightly in her lap, never raising her eyes. She was dressed again in the oversize jeans and a faded shirt. Her brown eyes followed my every move through the windows of her glasses, nodding or shaking her head when spoken to directly but with never a change of expression on her face.

"There," I said, giving the pillow a final pat, "Let's get some breakfast. Thanks for waiting, Jessica."

The hall was dark and quiet as though there were a conspiracy in the house to keep out the bright outdoors. No doubt Andrea and David slept late. I wondered who occupied the rooms we passed. Was one Kreska's? I suppressed a shudder. How was I to entertain this silent child for hours at a time? David had said in his letter that we could sightsee throughout New Zealand, but first she'd have to like and trust me. As we walked down the curve of the stairway I asked, "Did I notice a billiard room downstairs?"

She nodded, obviously puzzled. I plunged on, encouraged that she'd reacted at last.

"Can you play pool, Jessica?"

She shook her head. I knew I had her full attention.

"Would you like to learn?"

She hesitated as though she hadn't understood my question, then, with the puzzled expression still on her face, nodded.

"When I was just about your age," I told her, "we lived in an apartment-hotel that had a billiard room just off the lobby. There were never any adults playing in the afternoon, so my brother, Steve, and I used to play pool after school. It's fun."

We walked through the long, empty dining room toward the swinging kitchen door. Jessica pushed her way through and held the door timidly for me. It was a gigantic kitchen with endless counters, chopping boards, hooded cooking areas, and immense ovens. There was a large square worktable in the center, and off to one side a round table set for eating. The morning sun was pouring in the windows, and my heart lifted with its brightness. David's aunt sat holding her coffee cup poised in midair, watching our approach with her pale eyes. She still wore black. How fragile she was, like the top of a dried dandelion that can be blown away with one breath.

"Good morning," I called to her, determined to do everything in my power to make her like me. After all, she was David's aunt and she had every right to be unhappy about my rudeness to Leon Kreska last night. I was the only one who knew about the purse

snatching at Nadi, so how could anyone else understand my revulsion for the man. I'd always found it
difficult to camouflage my true feelings, but I'd have
to try.

A heavy woman with gray-streaked hair wound into
a knot at the back of her head smiled at us from the
stove. "You're late, little Jessica, now my clock will
be mixed up all day." I gravitated toward her warm
voice.

"Jessica waited for me," I said, smiling back at her.
"I'm Marla Creighton."

"Call me Annie," she suggested. "I can usually set
my clock by Jessica, she's always that prompt. Come
sit down. What can I fix you to eat, Miss Creighton?"

"After tasting your dinner last night, most anything.
What does Jessica usually eat, Annie?"

"Glory, nothing, that's for sure. Not even a wee bit.
Jessica just walks through the kitchen on her way to the
barn. Sometimes I can get her to drink a glass of
orange juice, but usually she just picks up her apple
and walks right on through."

"I don't like breakfast either, Jessica," I confessed,
"But I make myself eat. Tell you what, I'll squeeze
down a boiled egg and a piece of toast if you will."

Jessica looked over at her aunt, hesitated, then
nodded her head.

Annie clapped her hands together and started for
the stove. "Will wonders never cease," she said.

The strained scowl appeared on Miss Blandish's
brow and I wondered what I'd done to make her so
hostile toward me. Perhaps I was only adding fuel to
a resentment already existent between Jessica and her
aunt; the thought made me more determined to make
every effort to be pleasant.

"Your country is beautiful, Miss Blandish," I said.
She looked up surprised. "It was a rough trip over.
After Fiji the plane skirted a typhoon."

She expressed no interest and I had the feeling I'd

embarked on a long monologue. Annie came to the rescue with, "Glory, weren't you scared spittin'?"

I smiled and called over to her, "I would've been if it hadn't been for Parker. . . ." I caught my words in midair as I realized my mistake too late. My reference to Parker had frosted over any further chance for communication. Miss Blandish's thin lips became a hard, sealed, straight line.

During the awkward silence, I picked up the pitcher of fresh orange juice on the table, poured two glasses, and set one before Jessica. We drank them together slowly.

Annie placed egg cups and hot buttered toast before us. The white bread was fragrant and sliced very thin. "Is this home-baked, Annie?" I asked in an effort to breach the quiet for Jessica's sake.

"Yes, miss, I bake all our breads and pastries. Nearly all New Zealanders do. I'm Irish, but my James was a native-born New Zealander, a typical Kiwi. We were married twenty-seven years, bless his soul, so I learned to cook to please a Kiwi. Glory, you probably don't know New Zealanders call themselves Kiwis. It's the national bird."

Jessica watched me take my second half-piece of toast before doing the same. She matched me bite for bite. At least she was trying, even if it was without enthusiasm.

"Are you a 'typical Kiwi' too, Jessica?" I asked.

She gave a short, sober nod.

"That was delicious, Annie," I said, pushing back my chair. "We'll take our apples with us, but we'll be in for lunch. Now I want to see the barn."

Jessica looked startled.

Miss Blandish broke her silence in a patiently tolerant voice: "As I said last night, Miss . . . Marla, we let the barn be Jessica's private domain. Only Dutch goes in there to clean out the lamb's pen."

"I've done it again. I'm sorry, Jessica, I didn't realize. I was only thinking how much fun it would be to pet a real lamb."

She pushed her glasses back up on her nose and looked at her aunt, then back to me. She gave an impulsive nod of permission and started for the door at the rear of the kitchen. I noticed the frequent frown was again firmly entrenched on Miss Blandish's face as I followed the child.

The air outside was as fresh as I remembered it. A lovely autumn day stretched out over the bright green fields dotted with rocky outcroppings. We were dwarfed by the huge barn once we'd entered through the large, open doors, like Lilliputians in jeans looking up at the high, vast loft.

"They must've had many cattle here to need such a gigantic barn," I said.

Jessica shook her head, pointing to a long passageway of stalls jutting out from one side.

"Racehorses, now I remember. Parker said your grandfather raised racehorses. I'd forgotten."

She nodded, and we headed in the direction of the stalls. I'd noted with relief she'd shown no adverse reaction to Parker's name.

"Do you keep horses now, Jessica?"

She shook her head no.

As we walked past the empty stalls their vacant stillness gave me an uneasy feeling. Maybe even horses have ghosts, I thought. I gasped, then shuddered as a gray body slithered across the floor in front of us, its long tail a giveaway as to its identity. I knew rats were familiar occupants of barns, but the thought didn't cheer me. Jessica hadn't reacted at all. Were they that common to her? It wasn't a pleasant idea. I was glad we were almost to the end, surprised to see that the last section wasn't a stall but boasted instead a heavy dutch door with an inverted horseshoe mounted on a plaque above it.

"Do they keep that room for storage?" I asked just to make conversation.

She started to nod yes, then changed her mind and shook her head. I could tell she was making a decision about something very important to her. I said nothing. It had to be her choice, and I didn't want to influence her either way. She studied me carefully before she walked toward the unusual door. I followed her silently. She motioned for me to follow her. Once inside, she ran across the room to a pen filled with straw. The minute she opened the bars a wooly bundle of white lamb bounded into her arms. As she sank to her knees to hold him I looked around me in disbelief.

It was a beautiful room paneled in knotty cedar with a fireplace on the far side above which there hung a wood-framed painting of a racehorse. A thick, faded rug covered the floor. There was a comfortable couch, two straight chairs, and one oversize rocker by a large window that would give light enough to read even on a dark day. It was an appealing, cozy room. On the wall opposite the fireplace were rows of shelves stacked with beautifully bound books. I walked over and sat on my heels to look at them. Shakespeare, Poe. So this had been Jessica's private, lonely world. No wonder her compositions were learned and Victorian. I opened a well-read copy of *Tom Sawyer*. It was a first edition.

"You've read about America, Jessica?"

She nodded and buried her head in the lamb's back.

"Does your lamb have a name?"

Her head came up slowly and she peered at me through her outlandish glasses; then she released the lamb reluctantly and searched through the shelves until she found a particular book and handed it to me. It was a worn, leather copy of *Oliver Twist*.

"His name is Oliver Twist?"

She nodded.

"Mister Dickens's Oliver Twist, Jessica, that's a wonderful name." I looked over to where the lamb was standing, "Oliver Twist," I called, "Oliver Twist!" He came running to me and nuzzled into my knees. "He's adorable," I said, running my hand over his wooly back, conscious of a strong smell of lanolin. I leaned over and put both arms around his neck and hugged him to me; it was then I realized the lamb had come to me when I'd called him. He knows his name. Jessica talks to her lamb. . . .

CHAPTER SEVEN

I didn't look up, afraid Jessica would realize I'd guessed her secret. I continued to pet Oliver Twist until I was sure my face would not give me away. When I finally raised my eyes, I found Jessica staring at me, her brows knitted into a frown. Her attitude had changed completely; she was remote and unfriendly as she edged toward the lamb's pen. It wasn't the reaction I would have expected if she'd thought I knew her secret; something else had made her resentful and hostile. Why she's jealous, I realized with a sudden flash of clarity. Sharing is new to her. I released the lively bundle of wool from my arms. Jessica snatched him up instantly and tumbled him back into his pen, then ran to the door and waited impatiently for me to follow.

As we walked in silence back past the ghostly stalls she darted just ahead of me, consciously avoiding any close contact. Don't let yourself get too involved, I told myself. But I knew this child had touched a hidden part of me, a fragile thread of common loneliness, as no one else ever had. Jessica stopped suddenly and gestured for me to wait. She ran back, I presumed to be sure she'd secured the lock on the lamb's pen. I walked on ahead very slowly, lost in my thoughts, knowing she could catch up with me. How long had Jessica been able to talk? Had she been fooling the doctors and her family all the time; or had her voice returned recently and she was reluctant to let them know? She'd been existing in a private world for so long, she might not want to change. A lamb is not demanding, a family is.

When I came to the end of the stalls, I paused and looked back over my shoulder. Jessica was still all the way down at the end, headed toward me. I waved and started forward again. Just before I entered the barn, there was a sharp, scraping noise up above somewhere ahead of me. I tried to ignore the cold, prickly needles that crept up my spine to my hairline. The slinking body of the rat flashed across my mind, making my steps more hesitant. I entered the barn to hear the ratching sound again, this time directly above me; a sprinkling of hay showered down. At the exact moment I stepped back to keep the hay out of my hair, a heavy pitchfork whirred past my body with terrifying force and lodged its tines deeply into the dirt floor a few inches in front of me.

The cold metal had almost brushed my face with death. A terrified scream tore at my throat, and I crushed my hand against my mouth, struggling for control as I watched the fork vibrating where it was embedded in the dirt. The horror of what might have been engulfed me. Jessica came running up behind me, her eyes wide with fear. My throat ached from the violence of my scream, and I found it hard to swallow. I looked down at Jessica's frightened face.

My voice sounded strained and husky. "That was too close!" I tried to stop shaking as we gaped up at the

loft suspiciously. "It must've been left near the edge
and slipped off. It's such a long way up there, that
would account for the force of its fall." I cleared my
throat and said, "I think I'd better see if there's anything else up there that could fall and hurt someone."
Jessica followed me as I started for the ladder to the
loft. "Wait for me down here," I commanded as I
started to climb.

My legs wobbled on the steep, narrow rungs that
stretched up in perspective like vanishing railroad ties
above me, but my determination to know what had
happened kept me climbing. Supposing Jessica had
been ahead of me when I'd entered the barn? I shuddered, moving hand over hand, up the endless rungs.
When at last I reached the top and stepped off, I
realized the rungs were a far better choice than what
I still had to do.

Why had I always thought that haylofts were cheery-
sounding places? This was the spookiest expanse I'd
ever seen. There was the overpowering, heavy musti-
ness of aged hay and, I imagined, of accumulated
spiderwebs. The only light was from the open hay door
at the end, which cut a ten-foot shaft of sunlight
through the center of the gloom, leaving me in gray
shadows facing an almost pitch black area on the other
side of the swatch of sunlight. It could hide anything or
anyone. I must be crazy to be up here alone, I told myself. My body didn't want to move, then the anger over
the fact that Jessica and I might have been hurt or even
killed spurred me on.

I walked gingerly over to the hay door and leaned
out. It faced our bedroom wing. There were shuttered
windows below, so the barn was not exposed to any
watchful eyes. A ladder on the outside of the barn
reached to the ground, but there was no sign of life,
other than the movement of the pulley on the extend-
ing beam, which swayed innocently back and forth in
the windless air. I drew in a deep breath and pulled

back inside. It looked blacker than ever in the far area after I'd had the bright sun in my eyes. I crept along the shadows of the outer edge of the light, keeping as far from the blackness as I could. I made my way among scattered bales of loose hay, broken crates, and empty beer cans, then my foot caught and I plunged forward on my knees; something moist and round slithered under my hands.

"Ugh!" I groaned in horror. I snatched my hands back only to see it was a coil of old rope I'd tripped on. Get hold of yourself, I scolded, if you're going to do this get on with it. Deeper shadows of objects hanging on the wall of the darkest area revealed themselves to be old harnesses and yokes. I shivered with revulsion as another gray form zigzagged across the floor in front of me. It paused for a long moment to stare with defiant, rodent eyes, before it darted under a pile of hay.

I took wary steps to the far wall. It must have been from about here that the pitchfork had fallen. A few old farm implements were hanging from large nails. I reached over to touch one to see if it was secure and jarred a spider in the web that coated the handle. The sticky substance clung to my fingers. I wiped them vigorously on my jeans. The straw at my feet had been disturbed as if someone else had shuffled it not long before, the dust still sealed the rest. There was a vacant nail not far from the edge that might have held the pitchfork. A torn piece of black cloth caught my eye where it had been snagged on the scythe next to the empty space. I removed it and put it in my pocket, then leaned over the edge and called to Jessica, "I'll be right down."

I was through. No way was I going to search the spiderwebbed blackness on the other side. My mission completed, I ran back to the ladder, my foot slipping several times in my haste to climb down. I wished suddenly that I had Parker to talk to. I needed his calm reasoning.

Jessica was waiting for me at the foot of the ladder. I swallowed over the lump in my throat. "I'm sure it was a rat that knocked it off its nail." I tried to make my voice reassuring. "I saw one while I was up there."

She nodded, but there was disbelief in the eyes behind the glasses.

As we walked back out into the fall sunshine, the stocky, broad-shouldered figure of a workman was striding toward us. "Hello," he called out to us in a loud masculine voice with a heavy Dutch accent. Then as he came closer he said, "What's this, Missy, you found yourself a friend at last?"

"I'm Marla Creighton," I told him, trying to regain my composure. "I'm Jessica's new companion."

"That's good, that's good," he said heartily. "My name is Dutch." He held out one red, rough hand and gave me a painful handshake. "You'll be good for Missy. She been too much alone. You been in the barn?"

"Jessica gave me a tour." I watched Jessica walk over and sit on a rock. She stared at the ground. "Did you fix up the room for her, Dutch?"

"Yah, Missy's father said it would be good thing to do, so we fixed up the old tack room together, didn't we, Missy? A little girl has to have a place to play, and her lamb, he likes it too. I will go let him out to graze now."

"Dutch," I said, unable to hold it in any longer, "just now in the barn, a pitchfork fell from the loft and almost struck me." An instantaneous reaction of alarm registered on his broad, florid face. "I wasn't hurt, Dutch," I hastened to assure him, "but it frightened me. I left the fork right where it landed, then I searched the loft and I could only guess it was laying near the edge and a rat knocked it off."

"I hang them up," he said, scowling and shaking

his grisly head. "I always hang them up, so they won't never hurt Missy. Too many bad things happen to suit Dutch."

"What kind of things, Dutch?"

"You better forget about what I said, Miss Creighton. I'm just a worrying old man."

"You worry about Jessica's safety, Dutch, and so do I. Do you mean there have been other accidents?"

"Accidents? Well, more like funny kinda things that don't make sense. Missy had a cat. It got drowned in a rain barrel. Cats don't kin to rain barrels. Sims gave Missy a puppy, nice little collie feller. Got poisoned. Wasn't no reason we could find. Now Missy's got another special friend and a fork almost hits her. I don't like it, Miss Creighton, I just plain don't like it."

"It's probably just a series of coincidences, Dutch." I could almost hear Parker's voice saying, "Be careful, Marla, in every way be careful. . . ." We started back toward the house.

CHAPTER EIGHT

Annie made a clucking sound at our refusing a bowl of the aromatic soup heating on the stove. I'd mentioned lunch to Jessica before we'd entered the kitchen and was relieved at her negative headshake. My own stomach was still tied in a knot from my brief brush with death and the fear-provoking conversation with Dutch. The many coincidences had taken on nightmarish proportions, and now Jessica was maintaining a distance between us. I struggled to think of some way to bridge the separation before it widened, then I remembered the interest she'd shown in learning to play pool. Hopefully, concentration on the game might ease the tension. When I suggested that we play, she agreed with a shrug of resignation. I wondered where David was. We stopped as we heard conversation in the hallway ahead of us. I recognized Leon Kreska's voice.

"That should satisfy Aaron, Meri," he was saying. Ariki Meri was standing beside him. He looked up from zipping some papers into his briefcase. "Good morning," he said. His ice-blue eyes met mine with a haughty challenge. He was dressed in a black blazer with an ascot and black-and-white checked slacks. He looked freshly ironed, even the whites around his eyes looked bleached, emphasizing their glassy look.

Jessica walked to Ariki Meri's side. "Leon was just leaving," the Maori woman said, her round figure hidden in the native muumuu. "We've been working most of the morning. Please visit with me in my study after he leaves."

I looked at Jessica and she nodded. "We'd love to," I said.

"I will catalogue the items we discussed, Leon."

"I'll be calling Aaron in Antwerp tonight. I should have the answers you need by tomorrow afternoon."

"Then shall we say after dinner tomorrow night?"

"Of course."

He acknowledged us with a curt nod of his head as he left. Had he been with her all morning, or had he managed a few moments away to visit the barn? I remembered the threads of black cloth in my pocket and wished I'd checked his jacket for a tear. There'd been no other telltale evidence on his clothing.

Ariki Meri motioned us across to the door directly opposite the dining room. "Come in, please. Jessica spends many hours in here with me. I hope that you will too, child."

We entered a pleasant room, a combined workshop and office filled with metal file cabinets and floor-to-ceiling shelves broken in a few areas by cabinet doors. Every shelf was filled with sculptures, pieces of jade and jewelry, and strange, braided costumes, some with feathers.

Ariki Meri noticed my interest in them. "They are woven of our native flax and dyed with colors from the earth and fruit and berry stains."

Across the end of the room in the light of the windows was a large desk flanked by several inviting chairs, one a rocker. Jessica immediately fitted her small body into its familiar contours. I felt comfortable with this amazing Maori woman. Somehow the blue tattoo on her lips and chin gave her dignity, and there was such strength of character in her carriage and the regal way she held her head, such pride in her heritage.

"Sit down, child, I will fix us a cup of tea. Annie brought these little biscuits in just a few minutes ago."

She carefully slipped a tea cozy over the china pot and arranged napkins and milk on the tray in the now exposed tiny kitchen that had been camouflaged behind the cabinet doors. "Did you meet the young boy at the gate?"

"Yes."

"He is my great, great, great grandson. A fine young man." There was a rhythm in her movements that was fascinating to watch. I could see a bedroom through an open door beyond where she was preparing tea, and I realized this was an entire apartment. I sat in the chair next to Jessica and accepted the fragrant cup. It rattled against the saucer, and I realized how shaken I still felt. I set the cup on the table beside us. My head was aching slightly, no doubt a part of the aftershock too. Jessica was still aloof. I was still too tense from the pitchfork to swallow a biscuit. It was unreal

to be drinking tea with a Maori princess, surrounded
by priceless pieces of art.

"Did you show your lamb to Miss Creighton?"

Jessica nodded.

"He's adorable," I said. "And he's crazy about
Jessica."

Ariki Meri smiled at my diplomatic effort. "He has
been good company for Jessica."

"It's too bad her little dog and her other pets didn't
last," I said, hoping for a reaction.

Her face remained stoic, but her reply surprised me.
"You must not let Dutch frighten you. He is given to
being too protective of Jessica."

Parker had been right. She could see right through
you to the truth. "A pitchfork fell from the loft just
as we were returning," I said impulsively. "It just
missed me, but it could have struck Jessica."

"No wonder you are shaken. Barns are not the
safest place to be. Did you explain this to Dutch?"

"Yes." I hoped my eyes would say the rest. I didn't
want to alarm Jessica.

Ariki Meri knew I'd said all that I could for the
present. "Are you interested in art, child?"

"Sculpture intrigues me. The beauty of those carvings is haunting."

"The skill of Maori carving has been handed down
through many generations." She picked up a wicked-
looking little knife from the desk. "This is one of the
very sharp tools they use. However, for the most part,
they use chisels with a wooden mallet.

"Until they visit our country, few people have knowledge of the native art beyond the welcoming *tiki*, which
is only a trinket, a token of good fortune. Notice the
intricate static design of this *tecteco*." She took an
ornate carving from the shelf and handed it to me.
"This was done by one of our contemporary carvers.
Now compare it to this older masterpiece with its fluid
movement, so simple and free. Here is real value." She

chose a manuscript still in rough form from her desk-top. "This might be of interest to you. It is a brief sketch that I am compiling of several legendary phenomena that exist today." She stopped my hand on a particular page. "That is an area near the Bay of Islands that the Maoris call *tapu*, or you would recognize the word as 'taboo.' It is a small section of the bush country not over one hundred yards square. The temperature inside its limited boundaries drops sixty degrees for no reason. It has defied scientific explanation."

I shivered at the eerie thought, as she flipped over several more pages.

"You must see Lake Wakatipu at Queenstown on South Island. It is called the Breathing Lake. The water level mysteriously rises and falls about three inches every fifteen minutes." Her aged hands rose and fell with her words. "We have a legend that offers an explanation for the lake's strange behavior. It seems a *tipua*, a giant demon"—her eyes grew large—"kid-napped a beautiful girl and took her to his moun-tain lair. Soon the girl's lover followed and when he found the giant asleep, he set him on fire. The giant drew up his great knees in pain," she exaggerated the action for Jessica's benefit. "The flames fed on the fat of his huge body, eating deeper and deeper into the earth, carving out a great chasm." I could feel the hairs tingling at the base of my scalp. Her melodious voice was chantlike, spellbinding. Jessica hadn't moved, and I was sure now she was steeped in Ariki Meri legends. The moving voice went on: "Rain began to fall, the chasm filled with water all the way to the top, and the lake was born. The fire consumed all of the giant but his heart, which still beats far beneath the waves, thus causing the rise and fall of the water."

A breathing lake, a sinister, taboo area of sudden, unexplained cold. This is what David had meant by a land of mystery. I set my cup on the table and stood up. "I would love to visit again, Ariki Meri, and hear more of your legends. Thank you for the tea. I'll return the booklet as soon as I've read it. I've promised to teach Jessica how to play pool and I think we should get started."

A flicker of amusement responded in her eyes. "Do so with my blessing, and please come and see me often. There is no hurry about the booklet; I will have to complete my inventory with Leon before I can resume work on it." I could feel her penetrating eyes following us down the hall until we entered the billiard room.

The pungent, masculine smell of deep leather chairs permeated the room. Jessica waited for me beside the huge table, its emerald-green felt illumined by the octagonal fixture above it. She looked diminutive standing there. I took a deep breath. "First we'll choose our cues, then I'll show you how to rack up the balls." I found the small cue used for tight shots and showed her how to chalk the end.

I was amazed how quickly Jessica learned the game. Her powers of concentration were hungry for challenge, but she didn't know how to play for pleasure. She was attacking the balls, then suffering her errors in tense silence.

"Relax a bit, Jessica, it's not the end of the world if you miss." Gradually she lost some of her tenseness and enjoyed the game in her own reserved way, never smiling, but a few shoulder shrugs over a failure were encouraging. Strange little girl, I thought. All corked up inside like a bottle of Coke, not to be jarred for fear it will explode, yet no one seems to know how to uncap the pressure.

I looked up from a lucky play to see David watching us from the shadows bordering the table. My heart contracted with the awareness of the affection in his beautiful, sad eyes. "I'd forgotten how well you played," he said. "You never did help Steve's ego, or mine."

"Your egos didn't need help then," I answered,

carefully watching Jessica pocket the ten ball. "Jessica's a natural, David, she's fun to play with already."

"So I've noticed. Odd, I've never thought of teaching her. It isn't common here, you know."

"Oh?"

"For girls to be accomplished at pool."

I remembered Ariki Meri's smile when I'd told her I was going to teach Jessica. "Will your aunt mind?"

"Probably. But don't let that stop you." I watched him cup his hands to light the pipe he'd been filling. In his voice, his manner, he was almost the old David. If he'd been drinking, it was not in excess. The soft green turtleneck and the smooth fitting gray slacks flattered his lithe figure. My heart was aching again. It was as though Steve might burst around the corner at any minute and join us.

"David, you mentioned in your letter that I might travel throughout the islands with Jessica."

He studied me closely before answering: "I meant it, Marla, just don't rush things." He discarded one match and lit another.

"We'll have to fill our days some way. For instance, we could start close to home. I've been reading about the fabulous Glow Worm Caves. . . ."

I stopped talking abruptly as David jerked his body to attention, almost burning his fingers with the match. He stared at Jessica. Her powder-white face made the dark rims of her heavy glasses look almost black by contrast. Her mouth contorted into an ugly spasm, as though she didn't know whether to scream or cry.

"What did I say, Jessica . . . David . . . what did I say . . . ?"

Jessica dropped her cue as though it were capable of an evil spell. It crashed and rolled across the table. With one long, agonized look at me, she turned, stumbling in her haste to run from the room.

CHAPTER NINE

As I started to follow Jessica, David caught my arm
and whirled me around with unexpected force. I winced
in pain as his fingers bit into my flesh. "You mustn't
follow her, Marla. Let her calm down by herself." I
struggled to free myself from his viselike grip. "Believe
me, I know." He shook me to emphasize his words,
then released my arm. "Sorry, I didn't meant to hurt
you."

"David, I must explain . . . I must tell her . . ." I
pleaded. Then I realized how foolish my words were.
What could I tell her; that no one had told me what
I could or couldn't say to upset her, that I was
stumbling in the dark of some diabolical family secret?
"I must know what happened, David, before I can
help Jessica. Please, you must tell me." I rubbed my
arm where it still hurt from the pressure of his grip.

He ran his fingers through his hair. "Not here. Come
on, let's go back to the library. You're right. You have
to know."

I followed his long steps down the hall. He closed
the doors behind us, then hesitated before heading
for the bar.

"Wait, David. Let's talk first."

He set the glass down and spoke with his back to
me, "I didn't give you much of a greeting yesterday,
but don't go self-righteous on me."

"You're wrong, David. I'm worried. You've changed. I still believe in righteousness, but don't confuse the word with self-righteousness—that's not like you either." I walked weakly to one of the fireplace chairs. David followed and seated himself across from me.

"I need your friendship now, Marla, more than ever." His soft, blue eyes spoke the truth.

"Then tell me what happened to Jessica."

"Estelle drowned in the river beneath the Glow Worm Caves. Jessica was with her."

"Oh, David," I moaned. "Poor Jessica, but how . . . ?"

He stared into the cold ashes in the fireplace as if trying to fade the picture his memory had conjured. "Jessica worshiped Estelle, maybe because of the eleven years age difference. Estelle had only one thing on her mind—Parker. She'd always loved him, even when we were kids." I remembered the tenseness in Parker's cheek when he spoke of her. "She wanted to follow him to the States for college. Father wouldn't hear of it and insisted she go to school in England like Mum. Estelle gave 'em hell in England, and gave it to Father, too, every chance she had." He chuckled without mirth. "She was good at that."

"What was she like, David?"

"Estelle? Beautiful, impetuous, headstrong . . . the dark hair and eyes of a gypsy."

I visualized her with Parker, surprised that it bothered me.

With shaking hands David refilled his pipe before he continued. "My God, I've had to go over it all so many times the last two years I sound like a tape."

"I'm sorry to put you through it again, David, but I must know.

"I'll try to keep it short and to the point," he said, lighting the pipe in his hand. "Estelle wanted Parker to marry her. He refused until he was earning a living as an architect. Estelle wouldn't listen as usual. She begged Father for part of her inheritance so that they could be married. They clashed violently. Then Estelle—" He cleared his throat and moved restlessly in his chair.

"Well, it really started when Father acquired the amulet. It was a Celtic periapt, a religious amulet, encrusted with precious gems. Father said a Druid priest had hung it around the neck of the lost Dauphin as a talisman after his father, Louis XVI, was executed. The jewels alone were worth over a million dollars, but its historic significance made it priceless. Father stood to make a fortune from it. He brought it to New Zealand where he could take ultimate precautions to keep it safe while he negotiated its sale to the French government."

"What a responsibility, David."

"It was insured. Father'd handled many transactions worth fortunes. En route to New Zealand, one agent was shot through the head during an attempt to steal it. The thief didn't know that the agent had transferred it to Leon Kreska as another precaution. Leon has always been one of the best in the business."

It was difficult to picture Kreska not involved in intrigue; he always looked like he'd invented it. I reverted to an old habit and kicked off my shoes, tucking my feet up under me in the chair. I could concentrate better in this position. David half-smiled and I knew he remembered. "Go on, David," I urged.

"When Leon arrived with the amulet that night, Father didn't show it to the family. We were seldom permitted to know anything about his art dealings. I suppose for our own safety and all that. Then it all began. . . ." He was becoming emotionally involved in remembering. I wished there was something I could do to make it easier for him. It twisted my heart to see him suffer. "Someway," he began again, "we still don't know how, Estelle took the jeweled piece from the safe during the night." I sat up straighter in my chair. "She left a note for Father that he could consider it her inheritance." He gave a bitter, dry laugh. "You had to know Estelle to appreciate that. By the time Father found the note she was already—" He cleared his throat.

"But, David, why would she . . . ?" He raised one hand in helpless acceptance, then gripped the arm of his chair again as if making a decision. He met my eyes, then stood up and walked deliberately to the bar and poured himself a full drink. I made no effort to stop him. He took several long swallows. "God, this is hell telling it like this. . . . Estelle wasn't all bad. I know she didn't realize the value of what she'd taken. She'd have known she couldn't fence it without established contacts. It could have been just to spite Father. I loved her, Marla; she was my sister. I don't want you to think . . . oh, damn." He drank deeply from his glass. "She knew Father would never prosecute."

"Please go on, David."

He ran his fingers through his hair. "Estelle used Jessica as a ploy, needing an excuse for a trip to the caves the next day. Parker worked the tour boats there every summer. She knew he'd be leaving the following day for the States. She planned to be there waiting for him. She'd made a reservation for herself that very afternoon one hour before the French government officials were to arrive here to negotiate for the amulet. At the last minute Auntie decided to go with them. I'm sure this wasn't in Estelle's plans, but it didn't stop her. Sims drove them."

"Would Parker go along with stolen jewels?" I asked. This didn't fit the Parker I'd met.

"No. He denied any knowledge of the theft, only that she was running away from home to meet him in the States. He was against the whole idea and I believed him. Kreska was never sure."

So this was what was behind Parker's dislike of Kreska.

"Anyway, Sims stayed in the car and Auntie glued

herself to the girls. Estelle anticipated the darkness at the river beneath the caves. We figured she must've recognized Parker at the helm of the next boat and pushed others aside to get herself and Jessica into the front seat that accommodated three people. As she hoped, a man stepped in beside them, leaving Auntie to scramble into a back seat at the last minute before Parker oared the boat from the dock."

"Are they large boats?" I asked, shivering as I pictured the dark, underground water.

"Quite large. Thirty-some feet. It takes a strong arm to manipulate them in the swift current of that underground river."

"How many people?"

"About twenty. Remember, Marla, we had only the confused versions of what happened; from Auntie, the other people on the boat, and Parker, of course. Parker said he had difficulty bending down to hear Estelle's desperate explanation and maneuvering the boat at the same time. Several passengers testified that they were arguing. Parker had stood up and was concentrating on keeping the boat on course when Jessica screamed his name. He saw Estelle struggling with the man beside her. He laid the oar across the bow and grabbed the man. As they fought, the boat crashed into the side of the tunnel time and again until it finally wedged itself in the rocks. The frightened people in the boat were yelling and screaming at this point, and the worms were snuffing out their lights by the thousands."

My legs had stiffened from being in the same position beneath me too long, but I didn't dare move for fear he wouldn't continue. "Somehow," he said, "Estelle crawled out of the boat onto a ledge, dragging Jessica with her." He stared into the bottom of his empty glass, trying to capture his mirrored thoughts. "She squeezed Jessica to the back of the ledge. Protected her with her own body. Somebody grabbed the bottom of Estelle's jacket and pulled her back. She lost her balance and just as she fell into the water . . . Oh, God, Marla, it must've been ghastly . . . the man who was fighting with Parker picked up the oar and swung it at him. The man couldn't have planned it, but he swung the oar back for leverage and, before it struck Parker in the knee and knocked him overboard, Parker saw it strike Estelle in the head." I gasped; the pain in his eyes was almost more than I could bear. "She must've been unconscious when she hit the water. She didn't have a chance, Marla. Everyone saw Parker fall because he was silhouetted on the bow, but in the darkness no one except Parker knew Estelle had been hit."

"David, how dreadful!"

His words came faster. "Some kind woman helped Jessica into the boat while other passengers fished Parker out of the black water. His knee was a mess. He asked for Estelle first thing, but by the time the rescue boat arrived, it was too late to find any trace of her. It would've been too late anyway." He ran his fingers through his hair again. "When they found her body later, her skull was crushed. . . ." His eyes were swimming with tears.

I walked over to him, set the glass from his shaking hand onto the table, knelt, and took both of his hands in mine. "David, she didn't suffer. She never knew. It doesn't make it right, I know, but it should make it easier to bear. I only know one way to help you, David. You're always in my prayers."

"Thank God, you haven't changed, Marla. That's what I wanted for Jessica."

"Poor Jessica, she's been through so much."

"There's more," he said looking down at me, his eyes tender. "They never found the attacker or his accomplice, and they never found the jeweled piece. Empty pouch was on the ledge." His words frightened me. "Jessica was petrified. She couldn't speak. . . ."

I almost blurted out "But Oliver Twist comes when

she calls him." Fortunately I held my tongue. I didn't have enough proof. For all I knew Dutch could have taught the lamb his name.

"Poor li'l Jessica." David was beginning to slur his words. "Doctors think slight shock might make her speak again, but it could plunge her into permanent condition. Jessica hates doctors." I kept picturing Jessica alone on that ledge in a state of shock. David must have read my mind. "Never had chance to thank th' woman who was so kind. Auntie lost track of her after they docked."

"And they never found the amulet?"

"They closed the caves. Dragged th' river for months. Almost killed the tourist trade. Lotsa problems with treasure-seekers. Combed th' entire tunnel, Marla, with detection devices. We were all under suspicion. It was hell!"

"Could the man in the boat have taken it?"

"Police never thought so. There's a chance Estelle hid it in the wall of th' tunnel while that man fought with Parker. Might never be found."

"What a horrible thing for your father to go through, David."

His face changed visibly as his mouth drew down at the corners. He gave a short, bitter laugh before he picked up his now dead pipe and clenched it in his teeth. "Father got insurance for the necklace. Far's he's concerned, it ended there."

"David, you mean—"

"I mean Father didn't give a damn 'bout anyone but Estelle. What li'l love he had for Jessica dried up with his tears. But hell, who needs him . . . ?"

"Jessica," I said softly, "and you, David."

"That's why I needed you, Marla. I needed someone I could trust, someone Jessica could trust."

"What about Andrea?"

"Yes, you'd wonder 'bout that. Met Andrea last year in London. I wasn't sober much. She was a beautiful, available woman." He dropped his shoulders in an expression of hopelessness.

"David, the man in the boat, are they still looking for him?"

" 'Course. Not much chance. Confusion, darkness, all the people . . . had a perfect getaway. Police're sure there was more than one involved."

The amulet . . . Jessica . . . a new thought struck me full force in the stomach. . . . Suppose the thieves thought Jessica knew something about its whereabouts. They couldn't force her to tell them anything or she might flip out for good and the million dollars with her; but if they could threaten her subtly by destroying the things she loved most around her over a period of time, she might be forced to confide in someone. Could this be why death stalked the little Kiwi, yet never touched her? Was I a threat? Of course, I had to be. If Jessica turned to anyone, they couldn't let it be me. That car with Parker . . . they weren't trying to kill him, it was me. The pitchfork was real. The purse-snatch hadn't been a coincidence. Kreska, was he one of them? Supposing his bringing the jeweled piece had only been a front to stealing it. He knew the safe, and with his expertise. . . . Only his plans went awry and now he had to get the jewels back. He made obvious efforts to make Jessica like him. A clammy cold swept over me.

"What is it, Marla? You look terrified."

"I was just reliving what you told me." I lied. How could I burden him with the thought that I was in danger. Not now. Not until I had time to think. The threats on Jessica were too fragmented. David probably didn't know they were happening. He was only half aware most of the time. Who else would know? They were all only halfhearted, part-time guardians of Jessica. Someone had been counting on this, until I arrived, now they were threatened. . . .

David called "Come in" to a knock on the door.

Andrea's eyes blazed when she saw me. "I thought you were with Leon," she said to David.

I realized suddenly I was still holding David's hands. I dropped them as though they were on fire.

"I've been telling Marla about Estelle," David explained.

"With the door closed? It's not a secret."

David stood up, walked to the bar, and poured himself a glass of straight Scotch. "It's not something I felt like sharing with the servants either."

My face grew even hotter as I slipped my feet back into my shoes.

Andrea faced me in cold fury. "You would have been the perfect wife for David. You don't exist in this world any more than he does. You could both go through life perfectly happy just holding hands."

I caught my angry tears in time as the sound of the phone filled the room. David answered it, his face white and his eyes full of fury. "Just a minute," he said coolly. He gave Andrea a hard stare as he said, "It's for you, Marla. It's Parker."

My hands were shaking as I picked up the phone. "Parker?"

"Is something wrong?" His deep voice gave me strength.

"I'm glad you called."

"Look, Marla, ask David if it would be all right for you and Jessica to do a little sightseeing with me tomorrow. I'd have you back in time for dinner. That is if you'd like to?"

"I'd like to very much," I said, looking at David as I spoke. "Parker would like to take Jessica and me sightseeing tomorrow if you approve. We'd be home in time for dinner." He frowned. "It would be good for Jessica, David."

"All right," he said, "if that's what you want."

"Yes." I told Parker. "What time shall we be ready?"

"Ten. I wish it were now."

"Yes, Parker, so do I," I said, meeting Andrea's hate-filled eyes.

CHAPTER TEN

"I hope you're hungry," Parker said as we reached the arched entrance to the *pa*, Maori for "native village." Steam rose from the ground everywhere on the sloping hills behind the compound, giving it a mystical appearance.

"That's the Meeting House," Parker said, pointing to a large A-frame. Huge, bright, red, carved Maori totems towered like sentinels all the way to the steep rooftop and across the wide doorway. "We'll see a Maori concert there after lunch. Speaking of lunch, the *hangi* takes place over there." He pointed to one of the smaller A-frames just ahead of us. His limp was barely noticeable as we walked toward it. Several groups of small children were playing tag or digging happily in the dirt. "It was great you could come today, this is the last *hangi* 'til next summer. I didn't want you to miss it."

"Another strange word, *hangi*," I said.

"Means a celebration, a feast. The Maoris use it for everything from weddings to funerals. In this case it's their way of welcoming you to New Zealand."

Jessica had knelt to put her arms out to one of the little dogs that were running freely everywhere. It was good for her to be away from Blandish House. Had she forgiven me for my blunder about the caves yesterday?

"Where do you live, Parker?"

"On Lake Rotoiti. There's an island in the middle of the lake that's a Maori burial ground. They wrap the bodies and put them in caves there, like a natural mausoleum. I grew up with a lot of Maori friends. The lake is full of black swans."

"You went completely out of your way to drive me out to Blandish House."

"I enjoyed it. All but our encounter with that damned red sports car. I haven't gotten a single line on him yet."

Jessica didn't want to leave the little dog when we reached the restaurant.

"Hello, Parker." A smiling native girl with long, black hair and flashing eyes and dressed in Maori costume greeted us, "We haven't seen you for months."

"I'm trying to change that." He smiled in return. "Timi Kara, this is Marla Creighton and Jessica Cavenaugh."

"David's sister?"

"Yes," he said.

She looked down at Jessica. "Say hello to him for me. We went to school together."

Jessica nodded.

"Marla is from the States," Parker told her.

"I've an uncle and two cousins there," she informed me. "It'll be a few minutes before your table is ready, Parker. I reserved one by the window as you requested. Perhaps Marla and Jessica would enjoy the curio shop while you're waiting."

"Why not," he said, turning us toward the small enclosure off the entrance. "Timi and I used to ski together at the Chateau."

"I'd forgotten there was skiing in New Zealand."

"Great skiing."

There were all the usual souvenir items in the gift

shop; I realized Ariki Meri had already enriched my cultural knowledge. The sculptures were mostly the busy, static work of the contemporary carvers; there were none of the older, more valuable pieces with their simplistic flowing movement. Parker was watching Jessica, who was enchanted with a stuffed koala bear. She would courteously notice the items I pointed out, but in seconds her eyes returned to the bear.

Timi Kara called to us from the doorway that our table was ready.

"We'll be right there," Parker told her. He pulled out his wallet and motioned for the Maori saleswoman. "He's yours, Jessica," he said, putting the koala bear in her arms.

The little girl in Jessica was evident in her pathetic look of gratitude. She pushed her heavy glasses up on her nose and hugged the bear as though she'd never put him down again.

"What a nice thing for you to do," I whispered to Parker as we walked toward our table.

"There are so damn many times we can't have what we want," he answered.

I looked up at him to find he wasn't smiling and I knew he meant David and Estelle. I quickly dropped my eyes.

Our table was perfect, set with a woven cloth, lovely, heavy silver. Out the window we could see Maori women in their native dress, cooking over steaming rocks. The room was filled with people. The high-peaked roof and the blazing fire in the stone fireplace gave a wonderful friendly atmosphere.

"There's thermal heat underneath that cairn of rocks." Then Parker explained, "The women wrap the food in leaves, then cheesecloth bags, and drop them into the rocks to cook. Let's go to the buffet table and try some. Here, Jessica, this plate's for you." He guided us with the same well-bred ease and courtesy I'd always admired in David.

"It all looks so good," I said contemplating the gorgeous display of food. "What would you recommend, Parker?"

"Try the venison and wild pork; and here, definitely some *kumara*, the Maori sweet potato." He served a portion of the pale yellow vegetable onto my plate, then Jessica's. "New Zealanders are vegetable happy. Everyone has a garden and eats very little frozen or packaged food. I think the American stomach is born in a package." It was good to laugh and forget the threatening clouds that hung over us. "If you two are gourmets, you might try some of this."

"What is it?" I asked cautiously.

"Smoked eel." I could have sworn Jessica wrinkled her nose.

"And this?"

"Mussels."

I passed them by and concentrated on the fabulous salad and fruit selection. "I'll try one of these instead."

"Kiwi fruit. You'll like it. Just scoop it out of its green skin."

Jessica filled her plate sparingly. I thought it best to let her make her own choices. She'd refused to leave her new bear at the table and managed her plate amazingly well with the bear under one arm.

"It tastes as good as it looks, Parker," I said between bites back at our table. "I love the Maori colors, the way they use bright red with brown, black and white; it's so different, so Maori."

The white turtleneck shirt flattered his tan skin. He laughed in his quiet way, and the expression in his gray eyes made me blush hot pink. "Your blush looks good with those blue-green eyes of yours." He grew serious. "I'm glad you can smile, Marla. I know it hasn't been easy."

"It's been full of surprises." What else could I say in front of Jessica?

"I just hope David had a bloody good reason for

not telling you about Andrea." He kept his voice low.

"Yes, he. . . ." I looked self-consciously at Jessica, but she hadn't heard a word we'd said. Her attention was held captive by a little girl seated with her father and mother at the next table. She looked to be about Jessica's age.

"They're Aussies, I think," Parker said.

Jessica devoured with her eyes the little girl's pink pants suit. Jessica exuded dullness in comparison, in her drab brown coat which she'd refused to take off. The outlandish heavy glasses and the old-fashioned braids were in sharp contrast to the pink, blondness of the girl that held her spellbound.

I had already seen Jessica's brown coat when I'd chosen my navy pants suit instead of my yellow one. I sighed without realizing it until Parker said, "I was shocked when I saw her hollow cheeks. She didn't look that way when her mother was alive. You'll be good for her, Marla."

"I really hope so."

He crushed his cigarette into the ashtray and cleared his throat to get Jessica's attention. "If you girls are through eating, I'll pay our account and we'll head over to the concert."

Timi Kara called, *"Haere ra,"* as we left. I knew it meant "good luck" before Parker told me.

The sky was overcast as we walked toward the Meeting House. Jessica looked about for the little dog, disappointed when he was nowhere in sight. We followed the people going to the concert. Parker managed somehow to find us seats up in front just as the show began.

The twirling motion of the poi balls never wavered from the beat of the plaintive native music, over and over, under, to the side and back with magnificent precision. The lovely Maori girls swayed in their colorful flax skirts flashing reds and yellows, while swinging with perfect control and rhythm the soft little balls connected by a fiber cord. The men performed with flying sticks. Humor had been woven throughout the hour-long program, while their melodious voices rose and fell as they sang and danced their love songs and legends for the dancers. Young and old, they were a happy people.

I stole a glance at Jessica; her body was alert, her expression rapt. Parker placed his arm lightly across the back of my chair, and I was pleasantly conscious of his nearness. I wanted to savor each moment of this day and dreaded the thought of going back to Blandish House even though David was there. Was it because Andrea was there too? No, I knew it was more than that. This was only a brief escape from the danger we had to face and somehow conquer. When had I stopped thinking of rushing right back home? When had I committed myself to Jessica, to bringing her back into the world of normal, active people with little girls who laughed and played for the sheer joy of living? There were so many virgin areas in Jessica's mind that had never been touched by experience. I thought of Andrea's words, "You would have been the perfect wife for David. You don't exist in this world any more than he does. You could both go through life perfectly happy just holding hands." Though my face still burned when I thought of her insult, I had to admit there was a strong element of truth in what she'd said. It was not a physical love I had for David. I knew that now. Being with Parker again had made me face this truth. Holding hands with Parker would never be enough, I was more than aware of this. But physical attraction wasn't enough either. Andrea was proof of that. But she's David's wife by choice, I reminded myself.

"This is the finale," Parker whispered in my ear. "Their war dance." I looked up at him, the strong line of his jaw, the unmistakable lines of tragedy in the twist of his mouth. Estelle's death had hurt two men so deeply; no, three, there was David's father. How could it have warped his father so completely as to estrange him from his other children? Or was there more to this too?

The music swelled loud and savage. The warriors extended their tongues to incredible lengths, rolled their eyeballs ferociously, making guttural cries as they beat their chests in mock fierceness. The lights dimmed, and suddenly their costumes were iridescent in the dark. Jessica was glued to the edge of her chair, the bear squeezed out of shape in her arms. I was sorry when the dance ended; my heart was still pounding to the music as we left the Meeting House.

We followed a small pebbly path toward where steam rose out of the ground on every side of us and the air was more oppressive with the smell of sulfur. Maori women were washing clothes in some of the pools of steaming water. Parker waved to them as we passed, and they called his name and waved back. There was a rash of small houses up on the hill behind them. The vapors increased as we walked on, making it easy to envision weird shapes through the changing sulfuric colors. I thought of elves and magical pixies.

We stopped by a fenced-off area where small wisps of steam puffed from swirling gray mud. "Stand here a minute," Parker instructed. A low rumble shook the earth beneath our feet. The growl rose gradually to a steady roar. The intensity built until the guardrail under our hands shook violently as plumes of boiling vapor burst into the air at least thirty feet. It took my ,breath with it. The guardrail stopped shaking as the vapor subsided again, but I didn't.

"How frightening and thrilling!" I said.

"We timed it just right. I wanted you to feel the buildup. It's the Pohutu Geyser. There's something over here that Jessica will like." He led us on to a boiling pool of pale apricot to terra-cotta mud. "Iron oxide creates the color, graphite makes the others gray. This is called the Frog Pool. Watch!" Unbelievably clots of boiling mud jumped in the air looking ever so much like an army of leaping frogs. "I'll be right back," Parker told us. When he returned, Jessica didn't want to leave the frogs, but he urged us on.

He used his cane expertly on the uneven, rough ground as though he knew it well, climbing over the small rises in the earth that were like upside-down gravy boats. There were guinea hens and Chinese pheasants walking over the hot earth, the peaceful and the turbulent so close together. This is David's beloved country, I kept telling myself, as I remembered his poetic descriptions. Parker was a realist, David a poet. I had a sense of oneness I'd never felt before, with the earth, the sky, the mysteries of nature, and with the Maori people. I was in love with New Zealand.

We crossed over a small hand-carved bridge where the steam almost engulfed us. It was hard to see where we were going. I should have told Parker of my dread of fog. Now it was too late. The warm, damp fog enveloped us completely with its choking sulfuric fumes. Vivid pictures of the fatal car crash that'd torn our parents from Steve and me reached out from the mist. The crash . . . the sound of breaking glass . . . the waking up with strangers. . . .

"The Devil's Bath is out there," Parker said, pointing with his arm. "Eighteen feet deep with boiling mud. They've had several *huritinis* there—suicides."

"Dante must have been a Kiwi," I commented with a shiver.

I slipped on a small rock, and Parker took my elbow to help me get my footing. I leaned against him, conscious again that the strength of his arm flowed through me, the glow warmed every nerve in my body. He gave me a knowing look and would have tightened his hold, but I tried to stand on my own again as soon as I could.

"We're almost in the clear now," he encouraged me.

"This only lasts for a few hundred feet. It's perfectly safe here on the path."

"Parker . . . where's Jessica?" We both looked frantically through the steam. "She was right beside me a minute ago . . . just before I slipped. Oh, Parker . . . help me find her. . . ." I was close to tears. "Jessica . . . Jessica . . ." I cried into the blinding fog.

I was surprised at how quickly Parker moved as we retraced our steps back to the jumping frogs, hoping to see her there. But no Jessica. We asked the women washing their clothes if they'd seen her. They shook their heads, promising Parker they'd watch for her and help him search if he needed them. We turned again into the deepening mist. I raced on ahead of Parker. My shoes slithered on the pebbles. I could hardly see.

"Jessica . . . Jessica," I called again and again as I ran. Suddenly out of nowhere a strong arm grabbed my waist from behind and pushed me off the path. A hand covered my mouth. I made strangled sounds as loud as I could. The steam was growing hotter and hotter . . . burning my skin. I kicked back hard with my heel but struck only thin air. My captor was strong enough to propel me ahead of him as though I were weightless. I clawed at the hand over my mouth. I could hear the blurbs of boiling mud just ahead of us and I knew I was to be forced into its turbulent, scalding midst. . . . "The Devil's Bath is out there," Parker had said. My smothered prayers were lost in its terrifying hiss of steam. . . .

CHAPTER ELEVEN

I brought my arms back suddenly in a karate action and took him by surprise; at the same time I kicked and struck solid flesh a nasty blow. He uttered a flow of four-letter words and staggered back, giving me time to lurch off to one side away from the pit. I bruised my hip on a large rock, then followed its contour with my hands until I was sure I was behind it, praying all the time that the heavy steam would hide me. My attacker searched through the blinding mist to find me, while I almost choked on my own breath to keep from making a sound. Jessica, I moaned inwardly, lost in this dangerous jungle of boiling mud—the thought was unbearable. I waited, trembling, expecting another assault any moment, then I heard an unintelligible oath and diminishing footsteps. Was he trying to fool me? As much as I dreaded it, I wished I could see his face, identify him—was he tall or short, heavy . . . ?

I didn't dare move, and the waiting was excruciating, the moments dragged interminably. It was impossible to see my watch in my cover of steam; how long had it been—ten, twenty minutes? Then I heard Parker's voice somewhere in the distance, shouting through the fog.

"Marla, are you there? Marla, answer please. . . ."

If I answered, my assailant would know right where to find me, but if I didn't . . . ?

"Here," I screamed, knowing it might be my only

chance. "I'm over here." Oh, Parker, I prayed, please find me first.

"I've found Jessica," Parker called again. "Can you follow my voice to where we are? Be careful of your footing; it's dangerous to get off the path."

Was my attacker really gone, or could I expect another encounter the moment I moved? Parker mustn't leave Jessica alone. It was up to me to reach them. But where was the path? I was surrounded by the sputtering red-hot mud, like boiling pudding. Parker kept talking to me as I slowly moved back in his direction. His voice was getting stronger. Surely my assailant couldn't see me any more than I could see him. The ground scorched the soles of my sandals. Slowly now, slowly. . . . Suddenly my foot slipped and I felt the burning of the sticking clay on the side of my sandal, just a few inches more and it could've. . . .

"Are you still moving?" Parker called.

"Yes," I cried, "but I have to be careful, the mud is all around me."

"Don't hurry . . . take your time . . . Jessica's fine." He kept talking in a steady voice, like a welcoming beacon.

A form loomed ahead of me out of the fog. . . . I stepped back in terror, but it was only another large rock. My hair clung in wet tendrils against my cheeks and my sweater felt clammy on my arms; then the wonderful scratch of gravel was under my feet and Parker's voice just beyond it. Tears choked my throat. I could still feel the pressure of the arm around my waist, my bruised hip, my burned foot. I tried to keep alert for any new attempt on my life. Then I saw their familiar forms just ahead of me.

"Jessica," I cried in relief, "where were you?" My own terror dissolved at the sight of her standing beside Parker, shrouded by fog; her body shaking with dry sobs, knees scraped and bleeding, the new bear in the dirt at her feet, and in her hand the lifeless body of a small brown bird. "Oh, Jessica, how did you ever find it?"

She pointed to her ear.

"You heard it crying?"

She nodded.

I picked up the bear and brushed him off. Parker looked at me with a shocked expression. "What happened to you? Are you right?"

"I fell," I stuttered, avoiding his eyes. "I couldn't see." If I told him about what had happened, I would have to explain so many things and I couldn't do this in front of Jessica; she was frightened and worried already.

He sensed why my answer was so vague; I saw him look at Jessica again. He wet his handkerchief in a nearby pool and handed it to me. I washed the blood from Jessica's knees with the warm square of linen, conscious all the time of the tenderness with which she held the limp, feathered body. "Please, Parker, could we find a place to bury the poor little thing?"

He looked from my face to Jessica's. "Of course." He found a suitable spot next to a large boulder a few feet from us and scraped out a small hole with his hand. "This should do." I took the cold, rigid body from Jessica's unresisting fingers and placed it gently in the tiny grave. Suddenly my hands shook. Cold, rigid . . . this bird had been dead for hours. . . . Jessica couldn't have heard it cry. . . . It'd been a trap to lure her away from me. Parker pushed the dirt back in the hole, unaware of my discovery. He picked up a nearby twig, broke it in two, then laid it across the fresh mound of earth in the shape of a miniature cross. It was an odd ceremony in the eerie, sulfur mist.

Jessica took the bear from me and held it close to her chest. I clasped one of her hands tightly in mine with the feeling I would never let it go again. "I think we should go home now, Parker."

"Just one more stop that will only take a few

minutes. Please, Marla, it's special for you. I saved it purposely for last."

I knew he was still concerned about me; his searching eyes made me uncomfortable. I must be a frightening spectacle, I thought, with my limp hair, my muddy shoes. I agreed, too weak to protest, depleted by the terror of the last hour, and more than anxious to leave this steaming lair. Who was here? Who was following us and knew our every move? I almost stumbled as a shattering thought came to me. Where had Parker gone when he left Jessica and me at the Frog Pool. He could have planted the dead bird. His arms were strong enough to have dragged me off the path. He'd had ample time to find Jessica and call to me while I'd crouched in terror waiting. . . . He was no longer welcome at Blandish House. . . .

We were no longer surrounded by capricious pixies, only vaporous tongues of fiery steam thrust forth in warning from the faceless dragons sleeping in the moorish bogs of Rotorua.

As we neared the compound, dark clouds mushroomed in the sky and the wind began to blow. The calm surface of the lake boasted white caps in the distance. I searched the scattered people we passed, looking for my assailant. He would be strong. . . . There'd be mud on his shoes as there was on mine and Parker's. But there was no one answering that description, just tourists and the little brown faces of the Maori children.

"The cross you made for the grave, that was a nice gesture, Parker," I forced myself to say.

"I'm not a heathen, Marla. David, Estelle, Jessica, and I went to Sunday school together at our Episcopal Church. After Jessica's mum died, David's auntie let that part of their life die with her. David's father never—" He was interrupted as we neared the small A-framed church bordering the lake. I didn't know what to expect next with Parker. "Let's go in," he said.

"There's something you must see and from the looks of you the timing's perfect.

"This is a Maori Anglican church," he told us. "Most Maoris are Christians, Marla; that is, most of them are married or buried in the church." He made us walk on ahead of him into the main sanctuary. The walls were covered with a designed native matting. The sound of his cane followed us past the carved wooden pews. It took a moment before I could swallow again. Jessica pushed her glasses up on her nose, struggling not to drop her bear as I still held her other hand captive. We slowly walked forward up the aisle.

"Stop about here," Parker whispered, coming up close behind us.

Bigger than life, the form of Christ was walking toward us on the stormy waters of the lake, one arm extended lovingly. The figure was etched on the glass of the cathedral window at the far end of the chapel beyond the altar. It had been positioned to give the perfect illusion that he was actually walking on the white caps of the blue water behind the window. It was magnificent. Tears blurred my eyes.

"He loves us, Jessica," I bent to whisper in her ear. "Always remember he loves us." I thought I felt a slight squeeze from the small hand in mine, but it could've been my own wishful response.

The Christ etching was strong and masculine in the Maori warrior fashion. "His flowing robe with the feathered neckpiece is the *korowai*, the cloak of a Maori chieftain," Parker said softly. We stood silently, each in his own thoughts looking at the window. How could I have doubted Parker?

"Thank you, Parker," my voice was barely audible. "I needed this just now. . . ."

We rode in silence after leaving the church. Jessica curled into a corner of the backseat with her bear.

"I'm sorry Jessica gave you such a scare, Marla." He kept his voice so low, I could hardly hear him. "Aren't you getting a little too uptight about her? You were all in pieces when you found us."

I shifted closer to him in my bucket seat. "I was frantic," I whispered. "She's so vulnerable."

"She's not the only one. What else happened to you at the thermal area? You looked like you'd seen a ghost."

I fought the desire to unburden all of my fears, to tell him everything, to pull on his strength again; but I knew David would never forgive me if I confided in Parker first. I could never hurt David that way. Parker would be a man of action; if anyone took any action, it would have to be David. Parker would understand that when he knew the whole story, and I'd tell him for sure the next time I saw him without Jessica. I knew all my doubts about him had not dissolved with the church window as I had wanted them to. "My mother and father were killed in a car crash in the fog when I was five. Steve and I were asleep in the backseat. We weren't hurt, but fog terrifies me still." I tried to sound convincing.

He frowned. "You should have told me."

"It's all over now." I looked up at him. "Parker, why didn't you tell me David was married?"

"I figured David must've had a damn good reason for not wanting you to know. He's not telling you everything, Marla, even now. Are they treating you right?"

I wanted to ask him in the worst way what he meant by "everything," but once again it seemed disloyal to David. "It's not as I hoped it would be. Parker, why does David's aunt always wear black?"

"She has ever since David's mum died. She was devoted to her sister all through her illness. I don't think they were that close before."

"It's a strange household," I said.

"Just don't judge New Zealand by Blandish House."

"No. Whatever is haunting them has nothing to do with this beautiful country."

"Haunting them?"

It gave me satisfaction to tell him, "David told me about the caves, about Estelle, how you were hurt. . . ." He didn't answer, and I noticed the familiar tenseness of his cheek muscle. "It was a dreadful experience for all of you, Parker, but it's Jessica I'm worried about." I was beginning to sound just like David.

"Of course," he answered finally.

We rode the rest of the way in silence until the menacing outline of Blandish House rose above us. I was still trembling inside from my attack at the *pa,* grateful that Parker had accepted my temporary explanation as to why I'd been so upset. It was beginning to rain when we reached the gates of the electric fence. There was a flash of lightning and a roar of thunder as we pulled up in front of the house.

Jessica seemed reluctant to climb out of the car. "We've had a wonderful day, Parker. I know Jessica would like to say thank you for her bear."

He looked at me long and hard. "You know I don't want to leave you."

There was so much feeling in his words, I didn't know what to say.

"I'll be away for a week or so on my motel location. I'll call you as soon as I get back."

I nodded. Jessica and I watched the little green Rover from the archway until it disappeared in the rainy dusk of the tree-lined driveway, then we entered the house.

We barely had time to freshen ourselves before dinner. As we walked back down the stairs I noticed Jessica had left her bear in her room, afraid of inappropriate comments no doubt. She'd changed into a green dress with a wide taffeta sash. It was much too long, but it covered her bruised knees, which were red with the Mercurochrome from my travel kit. The average child would have asked for sympathy. Was she protecting herself from the inevitable questions, or was she afraid I might be criticized as an inadequate chaperon?

The deep chime of the grandfather clock struck for the eighth time as we reached the bottom stair. We were almost late. I quickened our pace toward the dining room to find we were the first to arrive. Puzzled, I pushed open the kitchen door. Annie bustled amidst delicious aromas emanating from the ovens.

"I was afraid we were late for dinner, Annie."

"Mercy no, not tonight, Miss Creighton. Sims left me that note that Miss Blandish won't be down for dinner. The others are all in the parlor having cocktails and canapés. 'Scuse me, can I get at those plates?"

I picked up the piece of paper she indicated. It was in bold, sprawled handwriting:

Miss Blandish has a severe headache and will be unable to join the others for dinner.

Sims.

"It's easy to see you don't need our interruption," I told her. I'd rather have stayed in the warm kitchen, but reluctantly we turned back into the dining room to the sound of approaching voices, and I remembered it was Thursday night, the night Ariki Meri would be discussing business again with Leon Kreska.

Dinner dragged interminably. I didn't have to look at Jessica to know that she was as bored as I was, but then Jessica was used to this. Andrea plied Kreska with questions about London again until she'd drained the city dry of even fog. David refilled his wineglass from the cut-glass decanter each time it was empty. He'd made only a few comments, and Andrea ignored even those. He'd asked Jessica if she'd enjoyed her day; after her brief nod, he forgot she existed. He ignored me completely, and I felt a deep, inner hurt. I wondered how much of this I could attribute to the wine and how much to Andrea? Parker's name was never mentioned. I knew my best course of action was to keep quiet. I had such a penchant for saying the wrong name at the wrong time. Kreska took a phone call while we were eating. Several times after he returned to the table I found his eyes studying me. Jessica and I were both tired and asked that we might be excused. Jessica went straight to her room.

The storm had really broken now and a flash of lightning lit up my window, followed by a long peal of thunder that sounded as if it were on the roof. I'd just kicked off my shoes when there was a loud pounding on my door. I undid the lock to find Jessica, her face contorted, holding her precious koala bear out in front of her for me to see. It had been slashed into long strips of fur, its stuffing gruesomely disembowled, its black bead eyes gouged from the head and hanging by their threads.

CHAPTER TWELVE

"Oh, Jessica," I cried in despair. "Who could have done such a cruel thing?" I pulled her sad, little figure into my room and shut the door. That this could have happened during the brief time we'd been downstairs had a shocking significance. Someone here in the house was definitely involved. A monster with easy access to Jessica's room. And mine. I shuddered.

"You'll spend the night in here with me," I said,

wedging the dressing table chair underneath the door-knob. "There'll be no more surprises tonight." I found a pair of yellow pajamas in my drawer and tossed them to her. "You can wear these; just turn up the legs a bit."

I sat on the bed and inspected the mangled bear as she slowly undressed, almost in a state of shock. "He isn't too bad, Jessica. See his eyes push right back into his head." I noted upon closer inspection that the slashes must have been made with a razor or a very sharp knife. I remembered the wood-carving knife in Ariki Meri's desk. I looked over at Jessica. "The strips are cut so clean and straight I'm sure I can stitch them up again. He may be a little lopsided when I'm through, but he'll know he's a bear."

Suddenly my lap was full of yellow pajamas and two very small arms encircled my waist in a tight grip. The sound of her sobs crushed my heart, then I realized they were sounds. The slashed bear had brought about the first break in Jessica's silence. My sympathy pains gave way to grateful thanks. I let her cry it all out as I undid her tight braids and ran my fingers gently through her hair, listening to the storm inside and out. At last she was calm. I helped her curl up on the far side of the bed, and before long her steady breathing told me she was in a sound sleep.

My own eyes refused to close, and I stared into the darkness while my tangled thoughts tripped through my mind. I was sure now my calculations were correct, that whoever was after the precious amulet was convinced Jessica knew its whereabouts, and they must have a good reason for thinking so. I tried to go back over David's account of the tragedy. He'd said while Parker fought with the man, someone else pulled Estelle from the shelf into the water. . . . Backing up from this, that someone else could have seen Estelle hide the necklace in one of the areas where the boat had scraped the side of the tunnel. Jessica would have seen this too;

perhaps Estelle had made sure she had. I looked over at Jessica, so peaceful in her sleep, yet carrying the burden of such a heavy secret.

If only I had my brother to talk to. Steve would know just what I should do. But Steve was dead. . . . This was all for real; coincidences no longer existed. My assailant at the steam pit had not been imagined; my waist still ached from his strong arm. There's no other way, I must tell David everything—the knife on Ariki Meri's desk; the pitchfork; the mud pit; and the car incident with Parker . . . and now the bear. I must convince him that Jessica should be away from here. I must take her somewhere else . . . anywhere else. I needed to get away, too, not only because of the danger, but Andrea had made it impossible for me to stay. Somewhere else . . . I repeated it over and over. . . . *Help us find a place, Lord . . . anywhere else. . . .*

I woke at seven thirty. Jessica's side of the bed was empty. The bathroom door was ajar. "Jessica?" I called, but the room was vacant. I rushed to the window. Dutch was standing by his truck, Jessica beside him with Oliver Twist in her arms. She was trying her best to convince him of something. He kept shaking his big head as though he didn't want any part of whatever she was trying to tell him. I wondered how long this had been going on. Finally Dutch gave a resigned shrug, took Oliver Twist from her arms, and placed him in the back of the pickup. After the truck drove away, Jessica stood with her back to me, her arms hanging limp at her sides; then she clutched at her stomach and ran stumbling into the barn.

I stared down at the vibrant green grass sparkling in the after-storm sunshine. Suddenly the full import of the dramatic scene I'd just witnessed hit me and I could hardly breathe. Jessica had given up Oliver Twist to protect him. Was there greater love than such a sacrifice? I was torn between pity and pride. Jessica, you're just wonderful, I told her silently, wiping my eyes. I would comfort her as soon as I could. I didn't want her in the barn alone, but I knew it would be best to let her cry it out. They had nothing to hurt her with now but me. It was time for action, to find David and make plans for our future, if we were to have one.

The library doors were closed. I knocked gently, grateful when David answered. His soft, blue shirt open at the neck made his eyes even bluer.

"Marla," he said without too much surprise. "I rather thought you might be down early. I've been going over some accounts for Father, a job I don't relish."

"What happened to the engineer I knew?"

"I haven't felt like holding down a job. I guess Mum's inheritance took away what little incentive I had."

"You should get back to it, David. You were very good, you know."

He smiled in appreciation. "You're good for me. You always were."

"David, I have to talk to you. Seriously. About Jessica."

"Come on in." He hesitated, then closed the doors tightly behind us. So much for Andrea, I thought.

"Trouble is, I don't know where to begin and I won't enjoy burdening you with what I have to say."

"Let's sit down. That's a beginning."

"I'm frightened for Jessica, David."

"In what way?"

I sat on the edge of the chair and detailed as well as I could remember everything that had happened right up to the koala bear. David lit his pipe and listened without interruption, though his frown had deepened into worried furrows when I'd finished.

"My God, Marla, how could I have been so blind? If Steve knew you've been in danger. . . ." He ran his fingers through his hair. "I didn't know Jessica was being threatened. Oh, I knew about her dog, but that dead bird and the bear. It's diabolical. I can't believe it." He stood up and looked down at me. "Do you know what that means?"

"Yes, David. Someone in this house is part of the original conspiracy."

"And you suspect Leon?"

"Yes," I said, my heart beating rapidly.

"Leon's spent the last two years working on the crime with the police. Losing the amulet was his only black mark for the insurance company in an otherwise perfect record."

"Could he be taunting Jessica to find the jeweled charm and clear his spotless record?"

"It's not his style. He'd know Father would blacklist him forever."

"Then why did he hire that man to steal my purse?"

"I'll ask him."

"No, David, please don't. Let's not involve anyone else until we know what to do."

"I'll have to tell the police." He walked to the phone.

I rushed after him and held his hand to the receiver. "If Kreska is involved and he's working with the police. . . ."

"I see what you mean. It's one hell of a mess."

I took a deep breath before I spoke. "David, if Jessica and I could just get away for a few weeks to give me a chance to really get close to her, she might confide in me."

"She likes you. I'm sure of that."

"Please, David, we could lose ourselves on your South Island, where she has no memories to haunt her. It would be good for her, I know it would."

"I want you here, Marla. I'll devote all my time to watching over you here."

"Andrea would love that," I said bitterly.

"She'll have to understand."

"David, I'm serious. I must get away too. Surely you know that."

"Was this Parker's idea?" His eyes were stormy.

"David, Parker knows nothing. I blamed my being upset on my fear of fog due to my parents' accident. He seemed to accept it."

"And the chirping dead bird?"

"He never touched it. He believed what Jessica told him. David, what happened between you and Parker? Why are you so bitter toward him?"

"It's personal." He poured himself another drink.

"Yet you trusted Jessica and me with him?"

"Yes."

"David, we must go. If no one knows our schedule, not even you, we'll be safe." I knew I had my trust fund to draw on. "I can afford to pay my own way."

"Money's no object, you know that. I'd want you to go first class in every way, take advantage of every opportunity, see it all."

"Then we can go?"

"When did you—"

"Tomorrow morning," I interrupted eagerly. "Very early."

He grew thoughtful as he emptied his pipe on the ashtray. "What would you think of staying at a sheep station for a start?"

"That would be perfect." I told him about Oliver Twist. His eyes grew misty and he headed for the bar. The ice sounded metallic in his glass during the silence before he answered, "It would be hell not knowing where to reach you after you left there."

"I promise no news would be good news. In that way you'd know we were all right without endangering us."

"I'll call the Crookshanks. They have a station in the Canterbury Plains just out of Dunedin."

"Thank you, David."

"I don't like this, Marla, any of it. Maybe you should go home—even take Jessica with you."

"It wouldn't solve anything, David, and you know it. They'd follow us. The solution must come through

Jessica, the way to discover the truth of what really happened."

"Marla, your eyes are beautiful, so caring. . . . My God, think what could have happened to Jessica if you hadn't come, but I can't buy Jessica's freedom at the price of your—"

"You haven't a choice now, David. They could never be sure whether or not Jessica had confided in me. I'd always be a threat to them."

I knew the truth of my words had reached him. "I'll call the Crookshanks first, then make your plane reservations. I'll drive you to the airdrome in the morning myself."

"Tell everyone we're taking the bus and please don't tell them about the Crookshanks, David. Just that we'll decide on a place to stay in Christchurch after we get there."

"If that's the way you want it."

"I want to tell Jessica about our plans now. I don't like her being in the barn alone, but I had to get this settled with you first." I turned to leave.

David set his glass on the bar and put his hand on my arm. "How can I ever thank you, Marla? You've made me come alive again."

The gesture blew on the small spark of hope that remained in my heart. I left still feeling the pressure of his fingers and his unanswered question.

I dreaded going into the barn again, but I knew I'd find Jessica still there. The loft looked innocent and foreboding; I trembled with vivid memories. The empty stalls were even worse. I expected a boogeyman behind each opening, sure that it was stalking my back no matter how many times I looked over my shoulder. My heart was pounding in my chest by the time I reached the tack room. The door had been flung open. Jessica was huddled in the straw of Oliver Twist's pen, still shaking with sobs. I shut the door behind me and slipped the bolt against uninvited company.

"Jessica," I said, putting my arms around her. "I'm so proud of you. Oliver Twist has to grow up a little, just as you do. Then you'll see him again, I know. You wouldn't have been able to be here with him for a while anyway, because we're leaving tomorrow morning—we're flying to the South Island for a few weeks.

She raised her head and pushed the glasses up on her nose to hide her tear-soaked eyes.

"We're going to run away from everything and everybody, just the two of us, Jessica, with David's consent. Will you go with me?"

She nodded slowly.

"Come on then, let's get to packing. We've lots to do."

We spent the afternoon sorting Jessica's clothes. There weren't too many decisions to make. I took the sashes off several dresses and shortened them, using the material I'd cut off for quickly made belts. They weren't perfect, but they'd do. Fortunately I'd always been fast with a needle. I pinned an ornament, a little bunch of red cherries I'd brought with me, onto the collar of her drab brown coat, setting it aside to be shortened after dinner. My own things were so newly unpacked, it was a simple task to organize what I needed. We put everything together in my room, ready to go in the morning; even the mutilated bear was packed along with my needles and thread. David had made our arrangements with the Crookshanks, and our plane reservations were for eight A.M.

"You'll sleep in here again tonight, Jessica. I'm not going to let you out of my sight."

Dinner was grim once David told them we were leaving. His aunt was beside herself. Her pale blondness made her look white-hot.

She had difficulty controlling a tremor in her voice, "We hope that you realize the responsibility you have accepted. We can see it would be impossible to counteract your influence over David. I'm very opposed to your traveling alone with Jessica."

"David knows that I am capable, Miss Blandish."

"Capable of many things I'm sure," she sniffed with a knowing look at Andrea. So Andrea had told her about the scene in the library. How she must have relished that.

"That's enough, Auntie. It has all been decided."

"Jessica will send you a postcard every few days, Miss Blandish."

She sniffed again significantly.

"Where are you going on the South Island?" Andrea demanded.

"I really don't know, Andrea," I said. "We're just going to be vagabonds and decide from day to day."

Leon Kreska watched and listened without any comment, his unreadable eyes contemplative. I writhed under his continual scrutiny. I wished he hadn't known even our proximity to Christchurch.

"It will be good for both of them, David," Ariki Meri said with confidence. "There are healing influences in the land of the South Island."

"We must excuse ourselves," I said at the first opportunity. "Mister James is waiting for us in the library."

My thoughts kept wandering while Geoff reviewed Jessica's history lesson with her, stressing what she was to accomplish on the trip. He'd changed his schedule in order to outline the work she would have to do while we were away. She would still pass her grade.

No wonder Jessica liked Geoff. There was a fun quality about him that was a plus to his teaching ability. His infectious grin was good for her, though tonight she gave even less response than usual, and sadness drooped her thin little shoulders. He was so patient with her, going over each lesson again and again, trying to evoke her interest. I had my shoes off and my feet tucked under me, hemming the brown coat, watching them with their heads together at the desk. It helped to have a stranger near, someone who was completely detached from Blandish House. Geoff had given me his telephone number to call if we needed any added information or "just a friend," as he put it. He would be just the friend I'd call too, I thought, if the need arose.

"Marla, she's doing fine," he said, shaking me from my thoughts. "She has a real grasp of it now."

"That's wonderful," I answered.

"When did you say you'd return?"

"It's indefinite, no planned schedule. Maybe three weeks."

"Wasn't this a bit sudden? I don't recall your mentioning it last Tuesday night."

"Yes, it was, but Jessica and I think this makes it all the more exciting, and I promise we'll do our homework."

"I'm not worried." He laughed. "Just enjoy yourselves. School doesn't take all my time," he added. "When you get back perhaps you two could join me in some local tours."

"We'd like that."

He stood up, put his work case under his arm, and thrust his hands casually into his pockets as he came toward me. "I really must go. I still have papers to grade for tomorrow."

I slipped my feet back into my shoes. "Come on, Jessica, we'll see Mister James to the door."

Sims stood formally in the hall, patiently waiting to let him out. He always looked like an undertaker in his black suit. Parker'd said he was Estelle's confidant. I found this hard to believe. He'd hardly speak to me unless I spoke to him first, though I'd gone out of my way to be friendly. However, he was kind to Jessica, which made me like him.

Andrea came walking toward us from the vicinity of the parlor. "Leaving so soon, Mister James?"

"I'm afraid so, Mrs. Cavenaugh." He looked back at us. "I hate to leave such lovely company. Have a wonderful trip, you two. I'll look forward to seeing you when you return." His tone underlined his words.

After he left, Andrea said with sudden anger, "You can't leave soon enough for me." Then slipping into the leather jacket she carried over her arm, she too left through the front door. Sims closed it behind her.

Her remark hadn't pleased Jessica; she watched for my reaction, but before I could answer, David came up behind us.

"The bitch! I could kill her!"

Sims coughed discreetly and walked swiftly down the hall.

I took Jessica's hand and started up the stairs. "Come on, Jessica. Tomorrow is a new beginning for both of us."

CHAPTER THIRTEEN

Jessica pressed against the window of the airplane for our takeoff to watch a forlorn, diminishing David in front of the small terminal. We'd agreed that I wouldn't call him unless it was an emergency. I would post Jessica's cards to her aunt just as we were leaving an area so that no one could know for sure where we were at any given time. The thought of David's anxiety for us in the chill of Blandish House dampened my adventurous spirit, but a new spark kindled when I

looked over at Jessica engrossed in a new world un-
folding with every mile. She never ceased to amaze
me with her reactions, or lack of them. She was a
complex child.

We stayed in the plane for the short stop at Wellington and again at Christchurch. As we neared Dunedin
airport, I became more and more excited. This really
was a new beginning, and it met a longing I'd always
had to spend time on a farm. We were to be met by a
hired hand named Quint, whom we spotted almost
immediately from David's description: short, ruddy
complexioned, eyes deeply set into his head, wiry, with
muscles like wide bands of heavy rope. He twisted a
sheepherder's hat in his hands as he watched us approach.

"Would you be Quint?" I asked him.

He seemed startled to hear me speak to him. Had I
made a mistake? I was the only person to get off the
plane with a little girl, and he must have been watching
for us. He broke into a tooth-missing grin. "Blimey
now, sure I'm Quint and I'm that glad to see you.
Land-Rover's over here. Just let me pick up yer luggage
and we'll be on our way." He led us toward a beat-up
four-wheel-drive wagon, its orange paint scraped to
threads of color by the fingernails of time. "Here we
go." He helped Jessica into the backseat, where he had
placed the suitcases, amidst coils of fence wire, rope
and tools. "Don't hurt yourself on that bleedin' para-
phernalia," he warned her. Jessica fastened her seat
belt, but the one in the front seat was broken, so I
decided to keep my tote bag on my lap until I knew
how rough the going would be.

"Mrs. Crookshank said I was to put you wise to the
'Edinburgh of the South,'" he said, heading toward
the City Centre. "I'm a bleedin' Limey, but Dunedin's
home now."

I looked back at Jessica. She was spellbound with
the unique surroundings and didn't even see me turn

my head. I felt the spell, too; we really could be in Scotland. A lovely, small green park, ablaze with flowers, loomed at the end of the street.

"That's the Dunedin Octagon," Quint said proudly. "A bleedin' garden reserve in the heart of the city. See how all the streets shoot out from here like bleedin' wagon spokes? And right there in the middle big as life"—he pointed to a large statue in the center of the park—"Robert Burns himself. His nephew was the bloke that helped form Dunedin."

I could vividly imagine the strains of bagpipes sifting through the scene.

"Hear the skirl of the pipes? They're practicin' for the field trials next Sunday. Bands are made up of amateurs: mill workers, students, bankers, clerks, and the like."

I noticed the names on some of the quaint, old-world shops circling the perimeter road: TOBACCONIST, LTD., BUTCHERY, NEWSPAPER HOUSE, TYRE CENTRE, FIRE BRIGADE, and CITIZEN'S ADVICE BUREAU. Above the city now, we could see a panoramic view of Otago Harbor, filled with ships and large sailboats.

We turned onto a rural road bordered by native brush and trees, already saffron and red. The terrain was mostly flat with only occasional small hills and gullies banked with gorse and pines. In the far distance jagged, snow-clad alps rimmed the west. We bumped and wound around sudden outcroppings of rocks, all dotted with sheep through endless miles of desolate, narrow road. This was the outback, tremendous parcels of land sparsely populated with ranch houses, the acrid smell of smoke from their red brick chimneys curling upward against jade windbreaks of pines. The neat farms of Rotorua didn't have this smell of "country." And everywhere a sea of sheep.

"We'd better not count them all, Jessica, or we might never wake up." Still lost in the scenery, she didn't even hear my voice. Wherever we were going, it was definitely isolated, I thought, as I watched a lonely hawk soar into the brilliant blue sky.

At last a wide gate greeted us on the left-hand side of the road. Above it in large letters it stated simply CROOKSHANK STATION. Quint stopped the car to check the large rural mailbox. A rabbit frisked across in front of us. Jessica jerked her head to follow it out of sight under the fence. Sheep crowded against the gateway. "Move yer asses, you bleedin' fools," Quint yelled. He gestured and kicked with his foot until there was room to drive through and close the gate behind us. I strained to see a house, but there were only miles of fence and hundreds of sheep in every direction. "Five thousand acres of it," Quint told us as we rattled over small bridges he called cattle stops, past "timber bungalows for our shepherds and musterers and their families," down stretches of chalk-white road blocked with sheep, all the while hearing Quint blow his horn like a trumpet. I held fast to my jolting seat, noticing Jessica was still secure.

"The shearin' crew just moved in." Quint nodded toward a string of shanties. "Ever seen 'em shear a sheep?" he asked Jessica. She shook her head. "Takes a heap of doin'."

After the fifth gate we reached the fruit orchards. "Mrs. Crookshank keeps the finest cellar in the South Land. She's mad keen on cannin'. Can't rubbish anything, just puts it in a bleedin' jar and stores it in the cellar."

We caught the first sight of the house. It was everything a ranch house should be: weathered-white, two stories, with tieback white curtains in the green-shuttered windows. A screened porch covered the lower front section and a wide veranda in front of that. The house was nestled into a backdrop of pines. Flowers, mostly roses, bordered the walks, spilled out of buckets and boxes in every window, on every step. A tall, gaunt man, his thinness accentuating his height, and a slight woman were standing on the veranda waiting for us. They came down the steps as we climbed out of the Land-Rover. Quint set our luggage on the ground and drove off.

The man, his weathered face topped by a mad mop of fading red hair, offered one big raw-boned hand to me and put the other on Jessica's head. "Couldn't ken it was David when he called. It's been so long, hasn't it, Emmaline? And Jessica here, she was just a wee baby. Fine godparents we've been. . . ."

"Now, Charles, don't forget Miss Creighton's here too." There was great kindness in the small sun-baked face etched with fine lines of humor and toil, the faded blue eyes, and the warm timber of her voice. Her short brown hair looked as if it were naturally curly. She wore what I was sure was a blue "company dress," but her tanned legs were bare and there were old rubber beach thongs on her feet. She came toward me, but before I could take her outstretched hand, she stopped and let it fall to her side. She looked puzzled and a little hurt.

"Is something the matter?" I asked, immediately concerned.

"I'm sorry. It's just that no one told us. . . . It is a shock. . . ."

"Please, you must tell me . . . I don't understand . . ." I pleaded.

"You look—you look just like Estelle with blond hair and blue-green eyes. It's so strange I can't believe it. . . ."

"Emmaline's right." Mr. Crookshank squinted his eyes for a closer inspection.

There it was, the memory that had been taunting me. David had gone on and on about my resemblance to his sister the very first time I'd met him, but he'd never mentioned it again and I'd forgotten. Jessica was frowning when I looked at her. She'd known all along. Everyone at Blandish House had known. Andrea was the only exception because she'd never met Estelle. It explained so many things. Sims grasping the doorframe at the first sight of me flashed across my mind. Jessica's shocked reaction. David hadn't forewarned them, or me. . . . Parker had seen the resemblance at the airport in San Francisco, that's why he'd been staring at me. But why hadn't he mentioned this? I wasn't the first person that by some strange coincidence looked like someone else. Why had no one been honest with me . . . even David . . . most of all David . . . ?

Mrs. Crookshank had her arm around Jessica's shoulders, gently propelling her toward the house. "Come you over here with me," she said. Her husband put one suitcase under his arm so that he could take hold of my elbow and follow us. "We're that glad you're here. Jessica will be so good for Emmaline. She gets a wee bit lonesome out here with our own children all off and married now. Of course there's Barth. He's a blessing." He stopped and looked toward the house. "Come on, Barth. Come out, you, and meet these folks." A shadow moved from the side of the house and took the form of a chunky young boy not much older than Jessica. "I'll warn you now, Barth has a wee problem with his ears. He's to have surgery soon, then he'll be back at boarding school." The words were spoken just loud enough for Jessica and me to hear. The sun made the freckle-faced boy's bright red hair look like it were on fire as he shyly came slowly forward. A small black-and-white collie-type dog preceeded him, then stopped and barked its greeting from a safe distance.

"Here, Kanapu, you stop that," Charles Crookshank ordered. Kanapu came timidly forward with just an occasional bark. "I want you girls to meet the champion border collie in all New Zealand," he said proudly. "Kanapu has a whole wall full of ribbons from sheepdog trials, all blue. He's twelve years old now and still thinks he's a wee pup." As the dog came closer he said, "You can pet him, Jessica. He makes a lot of noise to keep us all in line, but he loves everybody once he knows them." Jessica bent down to pet the pointed collie nose, but the dog's head darted past her hand and licked her face before she knew what had happened. "All sheep dogs make those quick darting moves; it's born in them." He laughed. "That's the way they guide their sheep and cattle."

Barth came up beside Jessica and Kanapu. "This is our grandson, Barth."

"Hello, Barth," I said.

He kicked at the gravel on the path and mumbled a hello of sorts. Just then Kanapu turned and jumped into his arms. Barth grinned all over and hugged the dog close, and we started again toward the house.

"Here, Emmaline, let me get that for you." Charles Crookshank opened the door for his wife though his own hands were already burdened with our luggage. "They're here, Mack," he called out as we entered.

An elderly giant of a man in a wheelchair rolled his way toward us, his tanned face radiant beneath a shock of silver-gray hair. Emmaline Crookshank went to his side. "David didn't tell us she looks enough like Estelle to be her twin, Father." She turned to me. "This is my father, name's McNaughton. Estelle was his favorite whenever she was here." I knew she'd warned the man in the chair to spare him. He wheeled up closer and studied us from beneath his bushy gray eyebrows.

"They call me Grandfather Mack. You do look like my Stella, lass, but you're more fragile. She was an orchid; you're more of a yellow English rose." There were bagpipes in his voice. He looked over at Jessica. "And you, lassie," he said, contemplating her gravely, "what shall we call you? Aye, I think I know, you are a chameleon, that clever little upstart that can change its colors to match its environment. Are you a chameleon, lassie?"

Jessica thought about his question seriously before nodding.

"You'd best rustle up some food for these girls, Emmaline," Mr. Crookshank interrupted. "You can bet they are starving."

"And you too, Charles, it's my guess. Barth, show them up to Pamela's room. I'll hassle the food I ken fine they'll want it."

My first impression of the living room was one of comfortable orderliness and scrupulous cleanliness. There was a waxed patina on the old furniture that showed years of loving care; a stone fireplace covered the far side. An extremely large off-white sheepskin rug lay in front of it. Roses were everywhere; yellows, pinks, reds, and whites. They were in every imaginable type of vase and pot, and under each was a starched, crocheted white doily. Crocheted doilies covered the arms of the old sofa and the variety of comfortable-looking chairs. They gave the room a Victorian charm. It was comical to watch Barth struggle up the stairs with our heavy suitcases, Kanapu at his heels. The wood on the spool-work banister felt like satin under my hand. I wished I knew what Jessica was thinking. Not that I regretted my decision to get away from Blandish House; just being with the Crookshanks for these few minutes had told me how right it was, how free of threat. Barth took our bags into a front bedroom and placed them on the floor.

"Thank you, Barth," I said, smiling. When he didn't answer, I realized he hadn't heard me. I walked around to where he could see me. "Thank you, Barth. We can take it from here. Please tell Mrs. Crookshank we'll be down as soon as we freshen up."

He nodded and with a self-conscious grin ran out of the room, again Kanapu barking at his heels.

I paused to look around me. It was a soft, old-fashioned room with big windows overlooking the front yard and the orchard. Pink floral wallpaper matched the dust ruffle under the crocheted spreads on the twin beds.

I touched the neatly folded, thick comforters. "Choose your bed, Jessica, then we'd better wash and go back down. We wouldn't want to keep them waiting. Besides, I am hungry"

I knew at once what had been missing from my life as we bowed our heads for the blessing at the luncheon table. A gentle breeze from the open window blew over the simple prayer given by Grandfather Mack, like a healing balm to my turbulent thoughts. They all talked around and about Jessica in a way that made her an unspoken part of everything. How kind they were.

The Crookshanks told endless stories of the past. How David and Parker treed a squirrel for Estelle. Parker was the one that finally boxed it for her. When she told him she wanted him to skin it for a muff, he let it go. She pouted for days.

"She was a willful girl," Mr. Crookshank said. "David always did what was right, but he tried to avoid friction whenever possible. Parker always met it full on."

"Estelle was full of ginger," Grandfather Mack chuckled. "Some days she was a real mischief-maker." There was affection in his tone.

"You shouldn't talk about her that way, Father," Mrs. Crookshank objected, "now that she's. . . ."

"Dead or alive, memories don't change," he told her.

"And how do you like our New Zealand, Marla?" Charles Crookshank asked.

"I can't believe the contrast between the North Island and the South," I said. "Two different worlds."

"Yes. Would you believe there are North Islanders who've never seen the South Island? They've been to Fiji and Europe and even the States. The same is true here. They think of us as primitives." He laughed. "There's a strong rivalry between the two islands. Our climates are completely different. You'll know when one morning soon the heavy frosts begin and before long it will snow. They have snow on their Mount Ruapehu for skiing, but that's all."

"Isn't Mount Ruapehu an active volcano?"

"Yes, but it boasts one of the most beautiful ski lodges in the world."

"I remember Parker said he skied there."

"I'm sure he did. Parker did every sport well before his knee injury. That was sad. He's a fine boy. He's skied the alps with our children many a time." He looked over at Jessica and Barth. "Now that our plates are all empty, Barth, why don't you show Jessica around?"

"Want to?" Barth asked, without looking at Jessica. In answer she stood up and followed him.

"They'll do right," Mrs. Crookshank said, noticing my anxious expression. "Barth's a wee bit backward, but he's a lovely boy. A reliable boy." She hesitated a moment, then said: "It hasn't been that easy for you has it now, Marla? With Jessica I mean."

"I'm afraid I'm becoming overprotective of her. She's so—so vulnerable."

"I'm grateful David ken the need at last to have someone care for her. We've worried about her. You might as well know, dear, we were very close to Jessica's mother, Charlotte, but Elizabeth never liked us. When Charlotte died, we no longer felt welcome at Blandish House. Estelle and David, and Parker too, still spent part of every summer with us just as they had when they were wee ones, but then at Estelle's funeral—"

"Emmaline, we mustn't burden Marla with our problems," Mr. Crookshank interrupted.

Tears welled in my eyes. I looked down at the crocheted tablecloth, and suddenly words seemed to spill out of me. "I'm so grateful to have someone to talk to that understands. I love Jessica. I needed her as much as she needed me. I've just lost my brother, Steve, in the war. He was the last of my family. Then David wrote, and it all seemed so right for me to come to New Zealand." I raised my eyes to theirs. "But there are so many things that I don't understand. Why didn't David tell me about my resemblance to Estelle? Everyone I've met has had such a shocked reaction to meeting me." I went on to tell them of my meeting with Parker on the plane and those at Blandish House. "Most of all it was so cruel to Jessica. That's not like David."

"Not to blame him 'til it's all fair out," Emmaline Crookshank advised. "We can't answer your question, dear; we're puzzled ourselves. David has changed so since he married. We don't even know Andrea."

"Why not say it right out," Grandfather Mack said. "David married a filly he can't handle and now he can't stay sober and face his mistake."

"Father!" Emmaline scolded.

"Don't fash yourself, Emmaline. He couldn't tell his wife that Marla looked like Estelle. Andrea knew Estelle was beautiful, she'd never have let Marla come. He couldn't tell anyone else 'cause it would've been bound to slip 'round to Andrea. It's a pert explanation for the whole thing. David should have kenned to his engineering. He knew a whole parcel more about that than he ever will about fillies."

My face burned with embarrassment as I looked from one to the other. "I'm sure David will explain it all when we go back."

"I'm sorry Father's so outspoken, Marla, but you must admit what he's said makes a wee bit of sense. We're so sorry about your brother." There was definite sympathy in her eyes. "Was Andrea friendly toward you?"

I shook my head. "You do have a point, Grandfather Mack." What else could I say? Perhaps they had found an explanation. David had felt Jessica needed me and that had had first priority. I wanted to believe Grandfather McNaughton, and he was no doubt right as far as it went; but deep inside I knew the deception had begun back in our college days with Steve, when David didn't want me to meet Parker. . . . Of course there was a reasonable explanation but . . . ? "Would you mind if I go upstairs and unpack while Jessica is with Barth?"

"Of course not, dear."

"Just remember, Marla, the truth will never hurt you, only lies," Grandfather Mack said as I left the room.

Out of my window I could see Jessica and Barth sitting on the fence. Barth was talking and Jessica nodded or shook her head in answer, her braids bobbing. Kanapu sat at their feet. I sighed a deep sigh of relief. Hopefully the loving warmth surrounding me now would help blot out the ugly happenings of the past and point my mind toward a logical solution for the future. If only David had . . . but I mustn't judge David until I know the whole story. I will force him to tell me. . . . He must realize how much it means to me. . . . He had sent me to the Crookshanks, knowing they would expose my resemblance to Estelle. . . . That was a beginning.

I unpacked our things into the big, roomy drawers of the old dresser and put the suitcases in the closet. I took a deep sniff of the roses on top of the chiffonier and ran my fingers over the crisply starched doily under them, hoping they were symbolic of the future, then I went back downstairs.

The Crookshanks and Grandfather McNaughton were sitting in the screened porch, drinking tea. "Charles has to give the shed a go in a minute. Have some tea, dear. Black or white? And here's a wee biscuit." Emmaline Crookshank served as she talked.

"Mister and Mrs. Crookshank, Grandfather Mack, I must talk to you, and it would be best while Jessica isn't here."

"Come, lassie, sit by me," Grandfather McNaughton ordered. "We ken hoped you'd unwind and trust us."

"And please, Marla, call us Emmaline and Charles."

I swallowed hard before I spoke, "You're all so kind. I feel we can't stay here unless you know we might have put you in some kind of danger."

"You'd better tell us all about it, girl," Charles said, "then we can best judge."

They listened quietly as I told them incident upon incident. When I finished the story of the mutilation of Jessica's bear, Emmaline exploded.

"It makes my heart quake. It's daft and all, that it is. It was right that David should send you here where he knew you'd be safe."

"Emmaline's right, girl. You couldn't be safer than with us. Look over there." Charles pointed his arm toward the hill in the distance. I could see a man on horseback. "That's one of our six musterers. They patrol our borders day and night. Each has his own guard dog. No one wants to tangle with the likes of them. You're safe here, girl, and we want you to stay."

"Poor little bairn," Emmaline said, looking out at Jessica. "It's no wonder she's pale and poorly. We'll have her grown a wee more cozy in no time at all. Why don't you fash yourself a nap, Marla. I'll keep an eye on the children and I'll wake you for dinner." I was surprised how quickly I agreed.

"Can Jessica watch the shearing tomorrow, Grandfather?" Barth asked Charles after dinner.

"I thought of that, Barth," Charles answered. "Would you be interested, Marla? It's quite a sight if you haven't seen it before. A wee bit odiferous, but if you don't mind. . . ."

"We'd love it," I told him. "What time?"

"Probably about six will be best."

"I'll set my alarm."

"And I'll have breakfast ready for you at half-past five," Emmaline said.

"Oh, you needn't. . . . It's so early," I protested.

Charles laughed, "She'll have fed six people an hour before that. Barth here is going to be sweep-up man this season. He has to be to work at five."

We said good night and climbed the stairs to our room. I folded the bedspreads and put them to one side, then covered the beds with the comforters. Jessica answered a knock at the door. Barth came in with Kanapu. He snapped his fingers and Kanapu jumped up and settled his body on the foot of Jessica's bed next to where she was sitting. "Stay," Barth ordered, then he turned and left the room without another word. Jessica flew into her nightgown and crawled into bed. I could see her rubbing her toes on Kanapu's back before she fell asleep.

Before I turned out the light, I picked up my Bible for the first time since I'd arrived in New Zealand. It fell open to Chapter 54 of Isaiah. I was drawn to verse 15. "If anyone fiercely assails you it will not be from God. Whoever assails you will fall because of you." I closed the pages, darkened the room, and curled up hugging my pillow, feeling the warmth of the down comforter steal through my body, listening to Kanapu's heavy breathing. I knew I would sleep soundly without dreaming of Blandish House. . . . Only of David.

CHAPTER FOURTEEN

The sharp sound of the alarm startled me awake. Kanapu jumped down from Jessica's bed and wanted out. "Come on, Jessica," I called to her. "We've just time to dress and be down by five thirty." I turned on the bed lamp as it was still dark outside. We scurried into our jeans and down to the kitchen.

"It's pork chops and porridge for breakfast," Emmaline called to us from the stove.

Charles was already seated at the table. "Good morning, girls, I hope you slept snug. We'll get cracking soon as you've eaten."

I was pleased to see Jessica accept a bowl of porridge, though she refused a pork chop. We ate hurriedly and soon we were walking down the path with Charles to where the Land-Rover was waiting. Far off to the west the snowy alps ran like a narrow chain from north to south.

"It's an anticyclone day and a hot one," Charles said, shading his eyes with his hand as he looked up at the sun. "It'll be a scorcher in the shed, that's for sure." He looked out over the acres of grazing fields. "We need now to bring the feed away." I must have looked puzzled. "Rain." He laughed.

"How long will the shearing go on, Charles?"

"Three weeks or more usually. Fall is the most important muster of the year. Shearing gang goes from station to station on contract for mustering and shearing season."

Even as we parked and walked toward the door of the shed, we could hear the loud sound of machinery beating out a metallic dirge. I don't know what I had expected, but the ceaseless, frenzied activity that greeted us was unbelievable. I automatically put my arm around Jessica's shoulders as Charles motioned us off to one side where we could climb up on the stacked bales of wool to sit and see everything. The steaming sweat from the bodies of the men, some naked to the waist, combined with the nauseous lanolin odor peculiar to sheep, was almost suffocating in the heat of the big high-raftered shed. The shearers handled the giant animals with practiced expertise, perspiration running down their tanned necks and bare backs as they bent low over the animals from which they were shearing the fluffy wool. At the end of the long shearing board stood what sounded like a gasoline-driven engine that generated the power relayed through the flexing wires to their electric clippers. It seemed incredible that the men could work at such speed despite the intense temperature. We watched the scene repeat itself again and again.

Every few minutes there'd be a cry of "sheepo" and another sheep would be brought in to one of the shearers. A Maori worker tossed the shorn fleeces, which lay in high stacks everywhere on the oil-smeared floor, into the press, where another man leaped up and down, ramming the wool into place. He would jump out just in time for the pressing machine to finish the job for a wizened bald man who sewed up the filled bales and marked each one with the name CROOKSHANK—DUNEDIN in black stencil.

Jessica watched Barth, who was in the midst of all the activity. With his giant broom, he was sweeping away the endless small unusable pieces of wool that cluttered the slippery floor. I saw him look at us once, his face and sweat shirt soaked with perspiration.

After an hour of watching the men's powerful muscles straining to the utmost every second, the heat and the odor plus the constant roar of the machines began to get to me. I didn't want to move and spoil it for Jessica, she was so engrossed, but I didn't want to get sick in front of the men either. Just as I felt forced to make a decision, the shearer's engine went berserk. It danced crazily across the table, out of control, pinning two of the shearers against the wall. Boiling water from somewhere shot all over the shed. I pulled Jessica to the floor and protected her body with my own. We could see what was happening from between the bales. The men pinned at the shearing table climbed free, grabbed the sheep they were working on, and dove for the doors on the heels of the other workers, to keep from being scalded.

"Keep down, girls," Charles screamed up at us. At the same time he made sure Barth had gotten outside. "Pull the bally cutout plug, you fools," he yelled at the men. He didn't wait for them to act, but snatched up a fleece and held it in front of his face for protection as he dodged back and forth, trying to find an opening to cut the power to the crazy machine. The Maori imitated his action and joined him in the frenzied, darting dance.

"The gov'nor's jammed. It's gonna blow!" a deep male voice bellowed from the doorway.

Crookshank Station was no longer a retreat from danger. We were vulnerable no matter where we were, I realized now. Jessica trembled and I was sure her thoughts echoed mine. I wasn't sure my heart was beating. The taste of fear and lanolin rose in my throat like bile. Then, just as quickly as it had gone out of control, the erratic monster stopped. Charles must have gotten to the plug in time. The noisy pressing machine stopped too, and the silence was beautiful.

"Might as well take your 'smoko' now," Charles called to the men in a calm voice as though nothing had happened. "Somebody plug in the water."

The men filed back in, snatching towels off the hooks by the door and mopping their sweaty shoulders. Some plunged their entire heads into buckets of water. After they dried off, they dropped and sprawled on the filled bales. Jessica and I tried to brush ourselves off as we watched a misshapen, gnomelike man enter the shed, carrying a huge basket from which he produced large aluminum tea pots and promptly filled them from the big electric water jug. He passed out sandwiches and scones. Most of the men smoked. Charles brought a few sandwiches and some tea up to us. I declined the sandwiches, but accepted the strong black tea gratefully. It helped settle my stomach. Jessica refused everything. Barth stayed down with the men.

"I'm damn sorry we fetched you a scare," Charles apologized. "This hasn't happened in years. You girls look like you've had enough. You've stuck it out longer than most could. We'll head back to the house now."

I tried to pass off the terrifying incident as we climbed down off the bales by asking, "Do they work like this all day?"

"Every day while they're here. They have a 'smoko' break in the morning and afternoon and time out for lunch, that's all."

I felt better almost immediately. When we walked out of the shed, I noted how good the fresh air tasted and how modified the usual stench of the sheep became when contrasted with the smell of the fleeces. I hoped Charles didn't realize the extent to which my fear had been renewed in the shed. I noticed he glanced frequently in his rearview mirror at Jessica in the backseat as we bounced along back toward the house. She had reverted to her withdrawn, frightened image. "Jessica," he said fondly, "don't blow that scare all out of proportion. It was a wee bit dangerous, but things like that happen at a sheep station, and no one was hurt, praise the Lord. Machines get sick just like people." He chuckled. "This one even threw up from its sump just like our kids used to do. We'll have it fixed right in no time."

She nodded, and we drove on in silence, but I was sure she was still shaking inside as I was.

We came to where Quint was chopping wood. Charles stopped the car and yelled out the window, "Generator's gone loco, Quint, better get down to the shed and give 'em a hand."

We reached the orchard to find Emmaline and several small children picking apples. "Come you over here a wee bit," she called. She wore a ragged old sun hat and her feet were brown and bare in the thongs.

"Those are some of the shepherds' children," Charles explained.

"How about picking a few apples with us, Jessica?" Emmaline shouted.

Jessica hesitated and looked at me. It would be a good cure for getting our stomachs unknotted, I thought. "May I help too?" I called back to Emmaline.

"Of course, dear, every wee bit helps. That's lovely of you. Just pick up a basket, the two of you."

It was the beginning of a daily chore, and for the next few days Jessica and I picked apples all morning, every morning, then I'd help Emmaline with the canning. Charles taught Jessica to ride a horse. She gained weight, and for the first time there was color in her cheeks. Several times I almost thought she was going to speak to me, then the moment would pass. Late afternoons she would be with Barth and Charles working out Kanapu for the field trials that were to be held on Sunday. While they were together, I had long and precious talks with Grandfather McNaughton.

It was no wonder the furniture had the glowing patina I'd recognized that first day. "My father learned the art of French polishing and taught it to his four sons," he told me. "I enjoy working on this old furniture. Gives me something to do. Did you know, lassie, I came to New Zealand with Gregory Blandish? He settled for Blandish Hill in the North Island with his mind on raisin' his racehorses and high and mighty ideas for his house. I loved this wee bit of Scotland here. I used to own twice the acreage you see now. Sold half to a neighbor and gave half to Charles and Emmaline. They've done me proud in their care of it."

"They're so beautiful together," I said, "so respectful of each other."

" 'Tis said, lassie, that respect is to love what sun is to plants. When the love of God is first in your heart it spills over into every area of your life."

Saturday morning Emmaline surprised me with, "Do you ken what lovely day this is, Marla?"

"Just one more of many," I said.

"Not a wee bit; it's Jessica's birthday, 'tis."

"And I didn't know," I said miserably.

"That wee one probably doesn't know it herself, but we're her godparents, you see. I'm baking her a birthday cake and I thought if we each had a wee gift, we'd surprise her tonight."

"I'll have to think of something."

"Anything will do I'm sure; she'll be that surprised."

"You're so loving with her," I said gratefully.

"She has a way of getting into one's heart."

"Does your father know?"

"Yes, he knows."

"I'm going upstairs and see what I can find," I said.

I searched through my drawers for anything she might really like. Jewelry? No, it was all too old for her. Perfume? Not Jessica. The yellow pajamas she'd worn that first night she'd stayed in my room. The mutilated bear seemed so far removed, but the pajamas were more symbolic of our present closeness. I folded them carefully and went to find Emmaline to borrow some wrapping paper.

"We'll have dessert in the parlor with our cuppa tea tonight," Emmaline announced at dinner, "after Father's story." She crocheted and I sewed on the wounded koala bear while we listened.

It was a short but beautiful story about a dog that God loved especially. Quint was with us and we all knew Grandfather Mack was thinking of Kanapu and the dog trials he was facing tomorrow.

Emmaline disappeared into the kitchen when the story was finished, and Barth followed her. Jessica stayed on the sheepskin rug in front of the fire, alternately hugging and petting Kanapu. Emmaline came into the room with a beautiful cake on a tray with the tea things, twelve small candles blazing their greeting. Barth followed with his arms full of packages. They set everything on the low table in front of the sofa, as we all sang "Happy Birthday" to Jessica.

Jessica raised herself to a sitting position. She looked puzzled and a bit stunned, as though she didn't know what was expected of her.

Emmaline served the delicious cake. "All birthday cakes are fruitcakes in New Zealand," she said. She didn't make an issue that Jessica hardly touched hers. When the rest of us had finished, she said gently, "Come open your wee packages, dear."

Jessica's lips were trembling, "Come on Jessie," I said, "I can't wait to see what's in them."

She opened them one by one with shaking fingers. Barth couldn't stand it and a couple of times he said, "Oh, here," and untied a bow or ripped off the paper to the laughter of us all; it helped Jessica relax a bit too.

She liked my yellow pajamas and I knew she remembered wearing them. "You'll just have to grow into them," I told her.

Emmaline gave her a darling blue pinny, Charles a sheep-currying brush for when she retrieved Oliver Twist, Quint a tanned black rabbit skin.

"It's just bleedin', small beer," he said, "but I thought it might look pretty on yer wall at home."

She took forever to open Grandfather McNaughton's tiny package. She finally lifted the lid of the box and drew out a delicately carved cross that couldn't have been over a half an inch long. The wood was so glowing, it semed to have a life of its own. It hung on a delicate gold chain.

"Come you over here and I'll put it on for you," he told her. She bent down and he pushed her braids to the front and fastened the clasp. She held the tiny cross in her hand and looked down at it, turning it back and forth.

"You've one more package to open, Jessie," I reminded her.

Barth's gift was the last and the largest. She pulled a good-sized book from the wrappings. It was worn from being read. *Bible Stories for Teen-agers fully illustrated* it said.

"It was Barth's favorite," Emmaline whispered in my ear.

Jessica picked up all of her gifts one by one and hugged them close to her body. She pushed at her glasses and ran from the room without looking at anyone.

"Being loved takes a wee bit of getting used to," Emmaline said softly.

Jessica needed time alone. I helped carry the empty cake plates into the kitchen.

"You'll soon get in the way of it." Emmaline encouraged me. "Here's a pinny to keep you clean while we get washed up."

I tied the apron around my waist and took up the dish towel. "That was a wonderful birthday cake."

"Thank you, Marla. Tomorrow night let's let Jessica help wash up; I think she'd like that."

"That's a wonderful idea. She needs to be needed."

"Charlotte, David's mother, was a spoiled darling who never had to work in her life. She would have been happier if she had. I've been wont to think she just wasted away from lack of use."

"Jessica has spent most of her time reading, locked away by herself in the barn."

"Is that right now? They never were a close family, especially since Charlotte died and Aaron and Estelle started going at it ding dong. Too many acrid exchanges can damage a young child. And those outlandish clothes. They must have found them in a service rubbish bin. Poor wee thing."

"I don't think David would mind if I bought her a few things later."

"Not to worry. Aaron is a wealthy man, and David too since his mother died. I'm sure it's why he needed you, to put Jessica right."

"Miss Blandish will resent it."

"Pah, she's a wee bit twisted."

"What kind of a man is Aaron Cavenaugh?" I asked impulsively.

"Aaron is a fine man, but he was never right for Charlotte. She took to demanding too much sympathy from a busy man. She was a bit of a martyr, bless her soul, for all her goodness. She'd get well enough to have another child, then slip back again to being an invalid. Elizabeth fancied him too. Maybe she still does. She has a cool cheek." I tried to imagine Elizabeth Blandish loving anyone and found it difficult. "Charlotte told me once Aaron kenned toward her younger sister, the one who died. I know she fretted about it. Three sisters all in love with the same man. It's no wee wonder he isolated himself."

"How can he be so indifferent to Jessica now?"

"For all their differences, Aaron worshiped Estelle. He'll find his heart again someday. There now, let's get away out of it. Hang your pinny on that hook; we want to be rested for the trials."

As we started to open the door we overheard Quint talking to Charles in the parlor. "Damn, Charles." Quint's voice was exasperated. "He dropped that bleedin' knife in on purpose, the others saw it."

"Why would he do such a thing, Quint? Did you fire him like I said?" asked Charles.

"With pleasure, the bleedin' assassin! Might have been a personal grudge, but the men swear they didn't know of one. One did say he had an extra wad of money on him when he left, as though he'd been paid to sabotage the machine."

"That's really farfetched."

"It's all bleedin' crazy."

Emmaline and I exchanged a look, and she knew what I was thinking.

"Don't jump to conclusions now, Marla."

But I knew even as she said it, she was as sure as I was that we had brought our enemies with us.

CHAPTER FIFTEEN

"Listen to me babble like a brook out of sheer nervousness. I'm all at sixes and sevens this morning; you'd think I'd never been to a Field Day before." Emmaline packed a jar of pickles into the picnic basket as she talked. "Of course I worry a wee bit about Kanapu, he's so far past the age for giving it a go. There, I think it's a lovely lunch for sure."

I looked out the kitchen window. It had rained hard during the night, and grape-colored clouds still stained the sky. "Will the rain spoil any of the trials?" I asked.

"Not a bit."

"We're saying our thanks to God this morning, Marla," Charles said as he picked up the basket. "That dry spell was going to put us on Queer Street for the next mustering. Come on, girls, we'd better get cracking."

I struggled not to dampen their spirits with my fear churning full tilt again in my stomach. I'd slept fitfully all night, and my dreams had had a nightmarish quality.

"You'll not see a nor'west arch over the alps tonight," Grandfather Mack said as he wheeled his chair up next to me at the window.

"I wish you were going with us."

"Don't mind, lassie, there's too much rough ground there for me now."

"Everything's ready in the oven for you, Father."

"Not to worry, Emmaline. Just have a good time and bring home the ribbons."

"Come away now, Emmaline; we're all packed and ready to go," Charles called in to us.

Emmaline had given Jessica a red-and-blue-striped T-shirt that Barth had outgrown. It looked cute with her jeans. I wore a blue-and-green-checked shirt with mine and comfortable loafers that could take the mud. I climbed into the back seat of the Land-Rover with Jessica and Barth. Jessica, holding Kanapu on her lap, sat with her feet braced on the picnic basket. She looked sober, but her cheeks were flushed with excitement. Charles revved the engine impatiently and Emmaline climbed in beside him. She wore her blue dress, and even though the shoes she wore looked comfortable, I was sure she missed her thongs.

She handed me a sun hat that was in amazingly good condition. "I wouldn't want you to get a sun jag," she explained.

Charles laughed as we splashed through puddle after puddle down the sheep-crowded road. "She's an incurable optimist." I held the hat on my lap, trying to control a desire to hold my nose at the same time. "If anything smells worse than a dry sheep, it's a wet one," Charles laughed again as he caught sight of my telltale expression in his mirror.

Barth jumped out and opened and closed the gates until we were driving on the main road. It had been five days since we'd arrived, and I'd not been away from the station in all that time. I'd been lulled into believing the past was asleep outside the gates, until Quint had made it all real and close again last night. I knew Miss Blandish must be beside herself not hearing from Jessica, but this was one time when a postcard was impossible.

The trial grounds were nestled up against the hills on the outskirts of the city. Banners and flags were waving everywhere. We had a difficult time trying to find a place to park amidst the jam of vehicles. There were several other Rovers with deer antlers strapped to their bonnets.

"You girls go ahead and find us a picnic table. We'll get Kanapu settled in," Charles said.

Emmaline knew everyone we passed. "I'll introduce you later, dear, right now we'd best find a place to sit. Charles does so enjoy this."

We weren't the only hungry ones; the picnic area was crowded already. We lucked into a table without too much trouble. "Will Quint be joining us?" I asked.

"He'll be with his buddies. I hope he kens to beer and not hard slog."

When Charles and Barth arrived with the basket, Emmaline gave Jessica and me the task of setting up while she prepared the food on the plates. It looked and smelled so good, chicken and scones and cheese and fruit. I dropped a spoon on the ground and was cleaning it carefully on the edge of the tablecloth when something made me turn my head toward the back of the buildings. The spoon froze in my hand as a frightened numbness paralyzed my body. The familiar smooth black hair, the immaculate clothes, out of place in this setting, the quick catlike movement of his body as he rounded the corner and out of sight. . . . Kreska, here! How had he found us? Had David told him? Oh, no, David, please. . . .

I fought to camouflage my shock as we sat down and Charles gave the blessing, which included Kanapu. We began to eat, that is everyone else began to eat. There was a lid on my stomach that wouldn't let any bites through. Should I tell them about Kreska? Not now.

Not with Kanapu's trials coming up, it wouldn't be right. I'd tell them on the way home. The wind was beginning to blow-dry the mud to dust.

"You're not eating, dear." Emmaline questioned me, "Are you right?"

"It's just the excitement."

Jessica looked disappointed when I insisted she stay with me after the lunch had been cleared and the boys wanted her to go to Kanapu's trials with them. No way would I let her out of my sight with Kreska here. She was sullen and bored with packing away the food, but she brightened again as we neared the hillside location for the trials and ran to Kanapu without even asking me.

There was a small, roped-off clearing, then a planned obstacle course ran up the hill. Dozens of poles with flags flapping in the wind had been staggered every ten feet or so; also narrow passageways had been built with sawhorses, and several gateways. At the highest point was a narrower gateway that couldn't be over eight feet wide, behind which was a small pen. It was a long course. A hard course.

I kept searching the crowd for another sight of Kreska. I tried not to be too obvious, I didn't want him to know that I knew he was here. We'd made such progress. Jessica could overcome her speaking barrier any day now. I was sure of it. I tried to listen to Emmaline's rambling chatter, then Charles motioned us to join them.

I sat on my heels and patted Kanapu's head. "Good luck, you wonderful animal, you," I told him.

"I wanted you to see some of these other dogs," Charles said, pulling up toward a giant white dog with the long hair of a sheep dog, but a head like a mastiff. "Musterers breed and train their own packs of dogs. They're their main source of conversation over a beer at night. Without the aid of a studbook or record, they can trace a good dog's ancestry back for many generations. You can always accept their word as truth; they'd stake their life on it. This is a komondor. They were bred in Hungary as guard dogs. Gad, he's a beauty. He must weigh six stone. Look, girls, see how his coat is corded. This happens naturally and gradually from the time he's a wee pup until it's so thick that tough wolves and coyotes can't tear through it. Best protective dog there is. Hello, Cappy." He stooped to scratch the ears of a tiny dog much like a miniature Kanapu though it was all black. "This is a skipper key, means 'little Captain.' He's a wee one. They're Flemish, used on canal boats. Great hunters." Charles stiffened as we approached the next dog and its owner, a short man with balding hair and a prominent nose. "This is Bess, a favorite huntaway bitch, Kanapu's only competition. She's seven years younger." The dog looked like Kanapu, the same black-and-white coat and sharp collie nose, but she was much more skittish.

"Hello, McGregor," Charles said, "I wish you luck, but not too much."

"Did'n think Kanapu would crack it again, Crookshank. He shoulda quit a winner, I'm thinkin'."

"We'll soon see, McGregor. They're callin' the dogs to their proper places now."

Jessica and I joined Emmaline and Barth on the sidelines. Quint was there, too. "Won't Barth be directing Kanapu?" I asked Emmaline in a whisper.

"They'll only take calls from one man," she whispered. "That's always been Charles. Charles weaned him as a wee pup. There's an intangible bond there."

Two men carried a large box onto the clearing, and a moment later ten mallard ducks squawked and marched in formation all around the arena. The tiny black skipper key ran in after them. He barked and nipped at their feet keeping them reasonably together, all but one, who outwitted him at every turn. He gave up and let the ornery duck have its way and concentrated on directing the rest of the ducks into the small doorway of the box. He succeeded in bandying four of them inside before the whistle blew.

"He'll learn in time," Emmaline said. "Kanapu and Bess are the only other collies trained for this."

The ducks were freed to march again more scattered than they'd been before. Bess came in next. She was good, very good. Her control was smooth and effortless. She used the same quick, darting motions I'd learned to accept from Kanapu. I held my breath as she got the ninth duck into the box, then the whistle blew while the tenth duck still skirted the area out of reach.

Kanapu came in in a low crouch, his eyes boring holes in the down backs. He never darted unless it paid off. It was most effective. The ducks responded and obeyed, all but the stubborn one. Time and again Kanapu would have to leave the nine and nip the tenth back to the group. He worked in circles and squares.

"They've left the door to the box down by mistake," Emmaline said, putting her hand over her mouth in alarm.

Kanapu zoned in on the box. He sniffed for the opening and joggled the door with his nose. When he found he could move it, he worked his nose underneath the bottom edge and raised it up to the catch. The crowd cheered. Back he went for the ducks and scuttled them into the box. That is, nine of them were in the box; the tenth squawked and scrambled just outside his reach. With a final poke at the boxed ducks to make them stay put, he made a magnificent lurch at the errant duck. He caught her tail feathers in his teeth, dragged them to the box, and stuffed her in with the rest. He bumped the door until it fell shut just as the whistle blew. Charles couldn't contain himself. He ran out onto the field and Kanapu jumped into his arms.

"That's some dog!" Barth said. The crowd still cheered, as they moved toward the base of the hill and the obstacle course.

Emmaline smiled as she watched me put on my sun hat against the glare of the sun. I had to hang on to it with both hands in the wind. Jessica and Barth sat on a log just in front of us. I was much too apprehensive to sit down and I knew Emmaline was nervous for Kanapu. There was still no sign of Kreska, but I knew he was there somewhere, watching us with his glassy eyes. I was sure now who had paid the shearer to drop the knife in the machine at the shed. He wanted us to live in fear until we didn't live at all. Emmaline looked at me with concern.

There were at least ten dogs in the obstacle test. They were given three sheep to herd through the limited zigzag, uphill course. Their owners called commands from the side: "Come to left. Comebye to right." One after another they failed. The big white komondor almost made it, but one sheep got hopelessly away at the last narrow gate. He came back down the hill panting from exertion. The officials added a rooster to the three sheep for the next contestants.

"That's not fair," I complained.

"They always do this to the two best dogs. Makes it a real challenge," Emmaline explained.

Bess came next and she was beautiful to watch. She obeyed McGregor's every command with perfect precision, darting from one sheep to the other, keeping the rooster ahead of them toward the last gate and the pen. Where the other dogs had shown the strain on the hill, Bess was still bounding like a young puppy. One sheep, two sheep, three sheep into the pen, then the rooster flew to the top of the gate, and poor Bess turned herself inside out trying to coax it down.

"That's halfway into the pen," Emmaline said. "She'll get an almost perfect score for that."

Kanapu worked in top form. You could see he loved every minute of it. "*Kanapu* means 'bright' in Maori," Barth said proudly.

Partway up the hill, Kanapu's movements changed. He was responding more slowly to Charlie's commands. Emmaline reached over and took my hand. "Come now, boy, watch that rooster," she coached. "There's a good boy. Easy now."

Kanapu was limping on one leg, but he wouldn't stop. The wind whipped the dust, making it difficult for him to see, yet he still had the sheep under control at the last gate and the rooster with them. One went in, then two tried to cram in together. Kanapu gave a good bite at their heels and they squashed through, the rooster in their dusty wake. Cheers went up from the crowd again.

Kanapu turned to look for Charles, "Here I am, boy. Good old boy." Kanapu staggered and fell as he followed Charles's voice. The crowd became hushed, as the small black-and-white dog fell and then rose, only to fall again with each try. Charles was running toward him as the dog fell for the last time and didn't move.

Barth ran up the hill toward them, Quint behind him.

Jessica turned to face me, her face wet with tears, and in her eyes was that terrified, remote look that I'd foolishly thought I would never see again. . . . Death still stalked the little Kiwi.

CHAPTER SIXTEEN

I thought it best not to join the sad little crowd on the hillside. Jessica sat down on the log again and buried her head in her arms.

"Doc Andrews is with them now," Emmaline said. "He's a fine veterinarian."

"Emmaline," I said in almost a whisper, "if Kanapu is . . . if he is—" I couldn't bear to say the word. "Would they automatically perform an autopsy?"

"No, not on a dog. I don't think so. There'd be no reason. A dog dies of old age just like a human."

"Emmaline, I have to convince Jessica if Kanapu dies that he didn't die because of her."

"But how could she . . . ?"

"Remember her other pets? How everything she loves comes to harm? Just telling her that Kanapu died of old age won't help. Besides there's something else you must know—Kreska's here."

"So that's what's been fizzing inside you all afternoon."

"I didn't want to spoil the day. I wanted to wait to tell you after we got home, and I didn't want Jessica to know."

"I see it all clearly now. Jessica does look boggled. I'll go up to Charles. Give us a wee breathing space. Kreska. It's just hateful to think of."

Emmaline climbed briskly up the hill, and I sat

down next to Jessica and put my arm around her. I saw Emmaline reach them; she turned and shook her head at me. "Death is hardest for those who are left, Jessica. Kanapu's not suffering now, but we are. You're going to have to hold up for Barth's sake. He'll need your friendship, and tears won't help or bring Kanapu back." She didn't move or respond in any way. I was glad she kept her head buried so that she didn't see them carry Kanapu away. Barth came back down the hill with Emmaline. I could see her talking to him as they came, probably about Jessica.

Barth stood at the side of the log and kicked at the dirt with his shoe. "It's all right, Jessie. He did himself proud and he wouldn't have had it any other way. He was a champion. They gave Grandfather his blue ribbon." His voice was choked and unnatural.

I saw Charles coming toward us. I left the children and went to meet him. "The doc thought I was loony, but he'll do an autopsy on Kanapu tomorrow."

"Thank you, Charles. My heart is aching for all of you."

"If you learn one thing in the outback, it's that life goes on and death is only another marker on the way. But he was one helluva dog, wasn't he, Marla?"

I nodded. I couldn't speak.

"Emmaline said you saw that fellow, Kreska?"

"Yes, while we were having lunch."

"How do you suppose he knew where you were?"

"I wish I knew. I do know David trusted him in spite of all I told him."

"Mighty risky for David to do a thing like that."

We reached the others. Jessica had her chin on her hands, staring up at the hillside, listening to whatever Barth was telling her. "I don't suppose anyone feels like staying on?" Emmaline asked.

"If the kids don't mind, I'd like to go home," Charles said.

"I'll stay on for a while, if it's okay with you, boss," Quint said.

Charles hurried us through the people along the way that wanted to stop and offer a few words of consolation, and it wasn't long before we were driving back toward the station. We rode most of the way to the house in silence.

My mind was churning. I must get Jessica away from constant reminders of Kanapu. It might be different if Barth were able to stay, but he'd be gone in a few days and she'd be missing another friend. If David hadn't told Kreska where we were, then could he find us anywhere we might go? At least here we had the protection of friends. But look at poor Kanapu, he'd had protection, and if the autopsy showed. . . . No, I mustn't think . . . not yet.

Jessica stared straight ahead, her eyes glazed with pain and guilt. I was sure she felt Kanapu would still be alive if she hadn't become part of his life. How was I to prove to her that she was wrong?

The lights were ablaze in the house as we drove up. Grandfather McNaughton was waiting on the porch. "I know," he said quietly as we filed into the house. "Doc Andrews called me. Sorry, laddie," he said to Barth. "It was a good way to go, with dignity and accomplishment. I will I have it that way when my time comes. Just picture Kanapu barkin' his wee heart out to greet me. Then we'll just keep one another company till the rest of you get there."

Barth dropped to his knees and buried his head in his great-grandfather's lap.

"Go ahead, laddie, cry it out. 'T ain't no shame to cry for a lost friend."

Jessica pushed past me and ran up the stairs.

My heart weighted down my whole chest. Barth would learn to accept Kanapu's death, but how deep had Jessica retreated into her trauma? "Can I talk to you and Charles in the kitchen?" I asked Emmaline in a low voice.

She nodded and motioned to Charles. I followed them and laid the borrowed sun hat on the table.

"All the way home I've been trying to figure out what we should do," I told them. "With Kreska here, everything's changed."

"You know we won't let him hurt you," Charles protested.

"It's not that I'm worried about myself; it's Jessica. She would sense my fear. You can see she's already retrogressed. It might take weeks to bring her anywhere near where she was this morning. No, we must leave tomorrow, early, some way that we can't be traced for a time at least."

"You poor wee girls all alone . . . and our not knowing. . . ." There were tears in Emmaline's eyes.

I swallowed hard before I could speak again. "If I can just reach Jessica. Help her to talk. She can bring the truth out in the open and the danger will be over. Can we come back to you then? I want so much to come back to you."

Emmaline encircled me with her arms. "Of course you'll come back and oh, the times we'll have."

Grandfather McNaughton wheeled his way into the room. "Barth's gone to bed," he said. Charles told him about my seeing Kreska and Jessica's guilt over Kanapu's death.

"Marla wants to leave in the morning. She feels it's best for Jessica," he finished.

Grandfather Mack looked at me with his kind eyes and drew his bushy gray brows together. "Where would you go, lassie?"

"We'll move from place to place with no set pattern. Jessica responds to scenery. It's my best chance to reach her. She *can* be reached, I'm sure of it. It almost happened here."

"You said she'd sense your fear if you stayed with

us. Can you camouflage it better in strange surroundings, still not knowing, always wondering if you've
been followed?" Charles searched my face for an
answer.

"It should be safe with people all around us. I'll
create an atomosphere of game-playing. Jessica likes
the challenge of a game. If I can carry it off, it will
almost be like hide and seek, and somewhere along
the way, Jessie will talk to me. I know it. I feel it."

"What if something happens to you?" Charles said
bluntly.

"I'm taking that risk no matter where we are; that's
why I must reach her before that can happen. It's the
only chance for either of us." I looked at each of
their concerned faces, imploring them to understand.

"How can we help?" Charles asked.

"I've thought and thought. Kreska will be checking
our every means of escape. He may have others help-
ing him. Remember the police are convinced there is
more than one involved. I wondered if we made three
airline reservations for a trip tomorrow morning, do
you suppose the airline would keep the first one a
secret, the one we'd be on?"

"Paul Anderson would do that," Emmaline told
Charles. "He owes us a favor."

"Can he be trusted not to take a bribe?" I asked.

"He can accept a bribe to reveal the second trip,"
Charles suggested. "I'd trust Paul completely not to
divulge your actual departure."

"We could use our real names for the flight, but
from there on I'll keep changing them. I can be Jessica's
aunt, or her sister or—"

"Should David know?" Emmaline questioned.

"This is all according to our original plan. David
left it completely up to me. He knew I'd be out of
touch; it had to be that way."

"I'll call Paul Anderson at home now," Charles
said, picking up the receiver of the phone. "He usually

has the morning shift." A surge of relief swept over me when Charles found him in. I could tell from their conversation that Paul agreed to help. He was sure there was space on the 7:00 A.M. trip for us, then the trip at 2:00 P.M. would be listed as our official departure and the trip at 10:00 P.M. revealed only under bribe.

A charge of adrenaline dispelled the heaviness in my chest. In spite of the danger the challenge of intrigue was taking hold. Suddenly I wanted to share it with Jessica.

"I'm going up to Jessica now," I told them. "I hope you know how much I love you." I hurried from the room. We would have to be up early for the airport.

There were only a few minutes left before our plane took off for Christchurch. Charles, Emmaline, and Barth had insisted that they bring us out to the airport. "If anything goes wrong there, I want to be on hand," Charles said flatly. "No tears now, Emmaline, you ought to know better."

"So I ought," she answered as she sniffled into her handkerchief. "Promise you'll call, Marla, or come back if you need us."

"I'll call you tonight," I assured her. "We must know what Doctor Andrews finds out about Kanapu."

"Doc said he'd tell us this afternoon. Oh, and by the way, McDougall called this morning. He just brought back a litter of Queensland blue heelers from Australia. They're priceless, but he wants Barth to have the pick of the lot. I'll let Barth train him during his summers at the station. Guess you'd better get on, girls," Charles said over the noise of the plane revving up its engines.

Jessica was standing by the gate with Barth. "Come on, Jessie," I called. "It's time to go. Get your ears all better, Barth. We'll be back."

He nodded.

I held Emmaline close for a moment without daring to speak, then took Jessica's arm.

We were completely alone and on the run again. The realization hit me full force after the plane landed at Christchurch.

Christchurch was larger than Dunedin and completely flat, completely populated, and completely English. The homes we passed on the bus to our hotel had small neat hedges or two-foot stone walls surrounding their formal gardens, still colorful with late-blooming chrysanthemums and stately asters. Because of the lack of hills, there were bicycles everywhere. Children waited on corners for school buses, the little girls in trim navy uniforms with white straw sailor hats, the boys in navy suits and white shirts.

From our hotel window I could see the River Avon that wound through the city proper, weeping willows dipping their trailing branches along its edge. There was a small picturesque bridge leading to a modern Civic Centre built at one end of the large park. The emerald grass was trimmed so perfectly and so short, it looked like pictures of Wimbledon. It was a park for nannies and prams, cricket and lawn bowling.

"Jessie, it's only eleven o'clock. Come on, we're going shopping. We'll find a place to have lunch somewhere along the way."

Jessica was withdrawn and indifferent. I bought several things for her right off the hanger. I knew they'd fit, especially the tailored navy coat with the brass buttons. The jeans I made sure were right. When we found the plaid pants suit, I didn't even have to ask her to try it on; I couldn't stop her. Encouraged, we found a bright red ski jacket and red boots that didn't take much coaxing for her to buy. I bought her a tote bag just like mine.

We wandered through the not quaint, but old-fashioned City Centre, our arms loaded with our purchases. We stopped to look in a jeweler's window.

Jewels sparkling against the black velvet dominated the display, an overwhelming reminder that we were not really on holiday. Jessica stiffened.

"We'll take a taxi back to the hotel, and I'll wrap up your old things and send them to a charity."

I dropped my bundles on the bed and made sure the lock and the chain were on the door. "Let's have dinner in our room tonight, Jessie, and go over the maps and brochures we picked up at the travel bureau. I think we should move right along for a while. . . ."

She shrugged, only half-listening, pushing the packages around on her bed, looking in some then closing them again, until she came to the red boots. She drew them out slowly and ran her hand over their glossy surface, then very carefully and deliberately she slipped them on.

At eight o'clock I put through a call to the Crookshanks. It wasn't easy; the telephone dial was wrong-end-up and started with the nine. After several tries I got the hang of it. Charles answered. "No doubt whatsoever, Marla, Kanapu died of heart failure due to the strain and his age. No sign of poison or drugs. The pressure of the course was just too much for him. Most dogs give it up when they're six, Kanapu was twelve."

"Will you tell Jessica? Just a minute and I'll put her on the phone."

I made her listen while Charles repeated what he'd told me.

"Now go take your bath." I told her. "We leave on an early plane for Mount Cook."

CHAPTER SEVENTEEN

The man at the airline reservation desk studied our tickets to Mt. Cook.

"Is everything in order?" I asked him.

"Oh, yes, Miss Dawson," he said, looking over at Jessica. "I just thought I'd mention that this might be one of the last clear days the pilots can fly all the way through the alps to the fjords."

"That would change all our plans. But we've read so much about Milford Sound we wouldn't want to miss it." I tried to affect a slight British accent.

"Then you'd best go straight through and not stop at Mount Cook. I'll change your reservation if you like."

"Do we still take the same flight?"

"Yes, you'll just continue on and change to a smaller plane along the way."

Jessica wore her new plaid pants suit. The red tote bag hung from her shoulder as mine did, and she carried the new ski jacket over her arm. I'd brushed her brown hair out straight and let it hang. The change was unbelievable, she looked twelve years old. There was nothing I could do about the dreadful glasses. I could only hope the rest of her appearance was so altered she couldn't be described as the same girl. I wore my one investment on our shopping trip, a beige turban that covered my blondness, and dark glasses.

It was a gorgeous day as we winged our way over the Canterbury Plains toward the New Zealand Alps. One of our purchases had been an Instamatic camera for Jessica. She'd read the instructions carefully and had ten rolls of film stowed in her tote. "If you can capture that blue sky packed with those icy-white mountains. . . ." She nodded and practiced looking through the viewfinder.

As we approached the formidable peaks I began to hold my breath, hoping any minute the pilot would gain the needed altitude to soar over their tops. Before long I realized we were to fly through them, not over them. I hadn't planned on this . . . no one had warned me this was a hazardous flight. The frosted, rugged sides of the mountains seemed no more than a few feet from our wing tips. The plane banked sharply to miss a jutting piece of mountain. Jessica snapped picture after picture of the jagged peaks and the glaciers. We stopped at a tiny field and transferred to a smaller plane. Once we were airborne again, the flight became a claustrophobic nightmare for me, confined as we were between massive mountains. I took deep breaths and concentrated hard on the skill of the pilot as we threaded our way. He must be able to fly this awesome sky path blindfolded, I told myself. The thought settled my stomach somewhat, and I was gradually able to appreciate the spectacular majesty surrounding us. The lakes had that intense blue of unfathomable depth, and rivers gray with volcanic ash wound like heavy wire in and out of the deep crevasses. Fortunately Jessica didn't show any fear of flying.

We would have so much to show and share with David when we returned. When we returned to what? A house filled with danger? To a David torn apart with an unhappy marriage? I wanted to sort my thoughts, but as in a game of solitaire, the cards had a mind of their own and I couldn't seem to win. Jessica was the only key, and though I knew our relationship had become closer, I knew that one false move on my part could separate her from me forever. Above all else I must keep her trust.

The pilot circled as we reached the fjords, where stark mountains thrust themselves straight up from the deep cobalt water five thousand feet into the sky. They extended on both sides of the bay as far as we could see, with the water a blue boulevard between them. Shafts of noon sun streaked their glazed white sides with glory. Directly below us an exquisite, modern hotel was cradled in the base of the V that formed the origin of the fjords. A green carpet of lawn sprawled in tiers in front of it to the edge of the water. There couldn't be anything more beautiful anywhere in the world, I thought; there couldn't be. We landed smoothly at the minute airport.

"Swallow and your ears will pop, Jessie; mine did."

It was only a short walk to the hotel. Our luggage would follow in a station wagon. "We'd better check in and find out about the boat tour. There was only one listed for the afternoon."

Jessica nodded and tucked the camera into her tote bag.

Our room had a spectacular view. Jessica walked slowly to the window, the forlorn sag apparent again in her thin, little shoulders. I had learned to read her inner despair by the set of her shoulders. This was the pattern now: brief moments of interest, then the burden of her unreal existence would wrap her again in its insidious cocoon. Her enjoyment of the flight had been packed away with her camera. I fought my own depression. "We have an hour before the bus will take us to the boat, Jessie. We'd better see if we can get a quick bite of lunch in the dining room."

We were following the hostess toward a table for two when a familiar voice called to us from a table nearby. "Over here, dearie, over here. I can't believe it's really you." Mrs. Pilgrim's eyes were owlish rounds of delight as we turned toward her table. "Sit down, sit down, there's plenty of room. I always ask for a large table. These are friends," she told the hostess. I smiled a weak smile. We were trapped. "Marla, isn't it?" she chirped. "I never forget an unusual name. My bird training, you know. Who is this sweet little girl?"

"Rosemary, my niece." I lied. "Rosemary this is Mrs. Pilgrim, whom I met on the plane from America."

"What a pretty name, but I thought you said you had no relatives when we were on the plane? Oh, never mind, I do get confused. Are you on vacation from school, honey?"

Jessica looked at me, then nodded.

"Rosemary is recovering from a severe case of laryngitis," I explained. "She's not to use her voice for several days."

"You're too thin, child," she informed Jessica. "The food's good here, girls. It'll put a little weight on both of you in a hurry. I've gained five pounds in the week I've been here," she twittered. "I'm going on the boat trip right after lunch. I've been here a whole week and this is the first day I've stirred out of the hotel. I've only seen the birds out of my window."

"Mrs. Pilgrim is a member of the Audubon Society," I told Jessica. "They study birds. We're going on the boat trip too," I added reluctantly. "I bought our tickets at the tourist desk when we came in."

"Now that's nice. That's real nice we'll be together. What's the little girl's name? Rosemary? She'll like the boat trip. It's windy today, but I understand they're good, sturdy boats."

Jessica and I decided on soup and salad, which we found delicious.

"Mrs. Pilgrim, Miss Dawson," the hostess said, "your bus leaves in ten minutes for the tour boat."

As I stood up to leave, Mrs. Pilgrim edged near. "But your passport said Creighton." I tried to stare her into silence, but she elbowed me and winked. "Incognito, huh?"

Mrs. Pilgrim hovered close beside us every minute, clucking away like an old hen. She had an odd aroma about her, a mixture of perfume and mothballs, overpowering on a warm day. At one point Jessica held her nose behind her hand. "Maybe she's molting," I whispered in her ear.

The bus was full. We were jostled along the narrow, dirt road half a mile to the small dock. The boat was bobbing in the choppy water. It was about fifty feet long, old, but as Mrs. Pilgrim had said, sturdy. A strong smell of aged brine emanated from ragged, whiskered, ancient nets. Boarding was difficult from the unsteady ramp. Two of the crew practically lifted Mrs. Pilgrim's bulky figure onto the boat. She almost stabbed one of them with her trusty umbrella during the process. We were to have a two-hour scenic ride through the fjords.

The deck rolled like the moving walkway in a fun house and the wind blew my hair with frenzied fingers. I should have worn my turban, I realized. "Breathe deeply of that good salt air," I told Jessica. "Isn't it great?" Mrs. Pilgrim fortunately didn't like the wind and went inside to save us a seat.

The sea-worn captain came up beside us, a short, stocky man with close-cropped, metal-gray hair under a squashed captain's cap. His weathered, bare, calloused feet looked as if they'd never known shoes. "You're a ruddy Yank," he said with a broad smile revealing large, crooked teeth.

"Yes." I smiled back.

"Call me Alf. How do you like our New Zealand?"

"I love it. It's an amazing country."

"You'll be right, then," he said, pleased, nodding his big head happily.

"I've never seen so many sheep."

"Aye, but there're plenty of cow cockies too."

"Cow cockies?"

"Aye, dairy farmers," he explained.

"Do you run this boat all year?" I asked.

"No." He took off his cap and held it tightly in one hand while he scratched his head with the other. "Come fishin' season I head for Tauranga on the east coast of North Island. We catch the big 'uns there." A mischievous twinkle came into his sea-blue eyes. " 'Course I get up to Times whenever I can."

"Times?"

"Aye, spelled T-H-A-M-E-S."

"What do they do in Thames?" I knew he expected me to ask.

"Rice."

"Rice?" I asked puzzled. "Do they raise rice in New Zealand?"

"They rise rice 'orses for 'orse rices in Times." He laughed from somewhere down deep inside, showing his full set of crooked teeth.

"Oh." I laughed back at his classical Kiwi answer, conscious that the muscles around my mouth had become stiff. We clung to the railing to keep our balance.

" 'Ope the passengers don't grizzle 'fore we get back to the quay," he said with sudden concern. "I'd best hoist myself topside and check things out. Tike care, you two."

Jessica and I strained our heads back as far as we could to look up at the sheer side of the mountain beside us, radiant with sea-reflected light. The sight was blinding in its brilliance. Jessica took off her glasses to wipe the salt spray with a Kleenex. What a pretty little girl she was without the rimmed monstrosities, her long hair billowing around her face in the wind, the collar of her red jacket pulled high.

The boat tossed even more as we cast off from the dock and started out through the narrow hall of stark mountainsides. I didn't want to go inside, but I thought it might be safer until the water calmed down. "We'd better go in, Jessica. We'll be soaked and so will your camera."

"Thought you'd catch your death out there," Mrs. Pilgrim scolded, waving us to the seats she'd saved by the window. She had her umbrella braced between her legs, and her round body looked like a chicken on a nest.

Jessica climbed up on the wooden bench on her knees, with her camera steadied and ready on the window sill. I curled one leg under me so that I could see out and braced my foot hard against the floor to keep from sliding from my seat. "That's Mitre Peak, that tallest one," Mrs. Pilgrim chirped, pointing. For the first fifty minutes we tossed in the unrelenting, rough water, anesthetized by the awesome beauty of the scenery.

"There, did you see it?" Mrs. Pilgrim screeched suddenly in her myna-bird voice. "I'm sure it was a sachelwing. Rosemary, catch a picture of it, child, if he lands somewhere." Her plump hands fluttered. "Oh, how I wish we'd see a kea. They look like a large parrot, but their feet stick out in front like skis. They live all through fjordland and drive the ranchers crazy. They're nuisance birds. They even let the air out of tires."

The wild water looked like flowing blue chiffon over a black lining with bursts of sea foam lace. "Look, Jessie, over there. . . . I think it's . . . they are . . . seals. On that rock, three of them." She raised her camera to get a better slant. Mrs. Pilgrim smiled that knowing little smile when she'd caught my attention. I'd said "Jessie" in my excitement, not Rosemary. Fine Mata Hari I'd make. The people made a big stir about the seals. I hoped everyone wouldn't rush to one side of the boat, not in this turbulent water.

The boat made a U-turn to go back at last; beautiful as the setting was, the churning water had put a strain on the ride. Jessica poised her camera against the window again and snapped a picture of a waterfall that cascaded, like multiple strands of pearls, hundreds of feet down a rocky precipice. People were oohing and aahing all around us. I hoped it was my imagination, but Jessica looked a little green.

"Zip up your jacket, Jessie, and let's step outside into the fresh air."

There was no one else braving the wind, which almost blew the hair from our heads as we braced ourselves against a metal post. The salt spray wet our cheeks. Mrs. Pilgrim had tied a vermilion scarf on her scant, speckled, gray hair and followed us. She pushed her plump body up tight against us and the strong scent of her unnatural perfume was sickening. Without any warning, Jessica broke free from us and ran toward the railing across the tilting, sea-soaked deck.

"Jessie, wait . . . please, Jessie, I'll help you. . . ." My voice was lost in the wail of the wind. Jessica leaned over the railing, her body heaving with nausea. I hurried toward her as I tried to keep my footing.

"Look out!" I heard Mrs. Pilgrim screech behind me, just as the full force of something metal crashed into the back of my knees. I pitched sideways, headlong across the slippery deck toward the open railing.

CHAPTER EIGHTEEN

My purse flew from my shoulder. A scream of terror and pain tore at my throat. Miraculously I hooked one arm around a post and grasped the railing with my other hand just as the rest of me slid over the edge. My body swung out helplessly over the churning water as the boat lurched and rolled in the angry white-caps. My mind focused on one prayer: *Dear Lord . . . help me. I can't die. . . . What would happen to Jessica?*

The boat dipped and the waves tore at my hair, my clothes. I felt my hand give on the slippery bar and I struggled with all my strength to tighten the hold with my almost paralyzed arm that clung to the post. . . . The corroded metal tore through my jacket sleeve. My shoulder was being torn apart. In only a matter of seconds I'd be swept into the dark icy water beneath me . . . only a few seconds. . . .

The wind swallowed my screams, the salt water blinded me; the added weight of wet clothing was pulling my arm from its socket. . . . I was numb with pain.

"Marla, Marla," I heard an hysterical voice crying. "Please . . . Marla . . . hang on, someone's coming. . . ."

Massive arms grabbed my waist, and the hard surface of a rain slicker crushed against my face. Suddenly I was no longer bearing my own weight, but was lifted up and into a merciful oblivion.

I woke inside the cabin. Jessica had her head buried in my lap. People were clustered around me, curious and concerned. Mrs. Pilgrim's shrill voice was pleading with everyone who'd listen, her hands plucking at their clothing to make them listen. "It was all my fault. . . . Oh, the poor dear. I fell over that cleat and right into her . . . right into her. . . . See my stockings are all torn at the knee. It was the umbrella that struck her. . . . I couldn't help myself . . . it was so rough out there. . . . Oh, dear . . . oh, dear. . . ."

My head spun in and out of focus as if I were under-water. The room was swimming; it was hard to breathe. There was a roar of crashing waves in my ears. I knew if I closed my eyes again, I'd vomit. The pain in my arm and shoulder was unbearable. Someone had wrapped a blanket around me; even so I shivered convulsively. Jessica was sobbing. I started to put my hand on her hair, then pulled it back when I saw the nasty, bloody bandage on my hand.

"It's . . . all right . . . now . . . Jessie," I managed to say haltingly. "Shhh, don't cry." I closed my eyes again against the pain, the nausea. The boat seemed to be rolling less now. How long had it been since . . . ?

I winced as two thin child's arms entwined themselves around my neck. I heard a strange little voice say, "Oh, Marla, Marla. . . ."

It was the same voice I'd heard just before the strong arms had pulled me to safety. I opened my eyes in wonder. Jessica stepped back before me, her eyes red with crying. She pushed at the glasses on her slippery, little nose. I made no effort to control my tears.

"Jessie." My voice was choked with love. "Jessie, my darling, nothing hurts now."

CHAPTER NINETEEN

My clothes clung to me like a damp shroud, and the ruined sleeve of my jacket was a mess. The doctor at the hotel was white-haired, cheerful, and kind. His small office had a warm, safe feeling. He let Jessica stay close by me, seated on a high stool so that she could watch him treat my injuries. The pain in my shoulder spasmed again. I gritted my teeth. Concentrate on Jessica. I reminded myself. Jessica talked, my Jessica.

"A narrow escape you had," the doctor said as he wrapped my arm with gauze and tape. "You're fortunate your shoulder is only strained and not dislocated."

"It was frightening," I admitted.

"Someone said Mrs. Pilgrim fell over a cleat and right into you?"

"She's feeling very bad about it," I answered.

"Knowing Mrs. Pilgrim"—he smiled and shook his head at the thought—"I'm sure she is being vocal about how bad she feels."

I winced as he moved my shoulder. "Do you know Mrs. Pilgrim well?" I asked.

"No, I treated her for a slight eye infection yesterday when she arrived." I sat forward suddenly, almost jarring a bottle of antiseptic onto the floor; the movement brought tears of pain to my eyes. The doctor put out his hand to restrain me. "What did I say to upset you?"

"I thought Mrs. Pilgrim had been here at the hotel the entire past week."

"No." He frowned in concentration, giving his answer careful thought. "I couldn't be wrong. She had just gotten off the bus when I took care of her. Told me all about every bird she'd seen on the five-hour bus ride."

My heart froze within me. *Who was Mrs. Pilgrim?* I really knew nothing about her; the memory of how she'd snatched my passport in Auckland flashed before me. It was obvious she'd lied to us at lunch about being cooped up here in the hotel for the last seven days. There was the chance, of course, that she was slightly senile, but how could we be sure? I'd been trying to convince myself that her fall on the slippery deck had been an accident, but now. . . . I wished I could call David, but he might not be in condition to talk and I couldn't explain to anyone else. I needed help. They would expect me to call the Crookshanks, and the last plane was gone now anyway. Parker? But he said he'd be gone for a few weeks. Geoff James. He'd be outside the family . . . he'd offered to help . . . Jessica liked him. I'll call him tomorrow, there's no time now. Jessica read the alarm in my eyes.

"Doctor, is there still a bus leaving Milford Sound this afternoon?" I tried to force down my panic.

He looked at his watch. "Yes, the afternoon bus to Queenstown should be leaving in forty-five minutes." He looked at me with serious blue eyes. "You can't be thinking of leaving, Miss Dawson, your arm should be kept immobile for at least two days. I was about to recommend two days in bed."

I found it hard to focus my eyes on his; the pain-killer he'd given me must have been a strong one. He looked like Tweedledee and Tweedledum both at the same time but I didn't dare let him know. "I'm sorry, Doctor, we must leave. I'll sleep on the bus, and Jessica—" oops, I blew it again—"will take care of me. I promise I'll rest when we get to . . . when we stop."

"I really don't think—" he tried to insist.

I started to get down from the table. "Doctor, we must—"

"All right," he said, shrugging his shoulders, "I'll put some extra tape on your shoulder and strap the sling to your body, but I can't be responsible for. . . . I'll give you some pain pills to take for a few days. You can take two aspros when you need them after that."

"Of course, I understand, but please hurry, Doctor, we must catch that bus. And may I ask a favor please; if anyone, or Mrs. Pilgrim in particular, asks about us, please don't tell her that we've gone."

"I won't say a word," he answered, "but do you need help?"

"No." I hesitated. "It's just that Mrs. Pilgrim has

become a nuisance and we'd really like to be free of her." I knew this sounded petty, but at least it was part of the truth. "Come, Jessie, we have to hurry."

Jessica did our packing under my direction. She helped me get painfully into dry slacks and a cardigan sweater, which I had her button over my bad arm. My hair looked like dried seaweed. She tucked it into the beige turban for me. Though I knew Jessica understood why we were running, I felt from here on we should put everything out in the open. I told her my thoughts about Mrs. Pilgrim.

"She's evil, Marla," she said in that wonderfully strange voice. "Birds are entangled by their feet and man by his tongue." Ariki Meri could have been in the room.

I was unsteady and in constant pain, but somehow we managed to purchase our tickets. There were fifteen minutes before the bus was to leave. We edged cautiously around the corner and into the lobby, searching for any sign of Mrs. Pilgrim as we braved our way to the ticket window. I had a sudden inspiration for Jessica to write a note to be delivered to Mrs. Pilgrim right away, saying we would meet her for breakfast tomorrow morning at ten o'clock, as I was under doctor's orders to rest until then. I'd checked carefully that both the morning flight and the bus left at nine A.M. We asked for help with our luggage and boarded the waiting bus. I hemmed Jessica in at the window on the backseat, this way no one could surprise us from behind. Right up until the time it started out through the mountainous canyon, we searched the bus to be sure Mrs. Pilgrim wasn't a passenger. The road was so narrow, I wondered if there could possibly be room for two buses going in opposite directions, a thought made more thrilling by the fact that they would be driving on the wrong side of the road. My eyes were heavy with the relaxing effect of the pain pill, but I assured Jessica that I could be alerted instantly if she should need me.

The terrible helplessness of my injured arm and hand engulfed me. We must go somewhere to hide until I was able to defend myself again. Once we were well on our way, Jessica drew Barth's birthday book from her tote. I closed my eyes to the scenery, and to the pain, and to consciousness.

Someone was gently shaking my knee. "Marla," Jessica's tiny voice called softly. I opened my eyes to find the bus had stopped.

We'd reached Queenstown. Fortunately, there was a red phone booth like all those in New Zealand. Jessica dialed the number I gave her and held the receiver for me while I called on ahead for reservations at a motel. I gave our names as Mrs. Crowly and Mrs. Shane. For the time being Jessica would be a married woman and so would I. When we arrived at the hotel Jessica could stay out of sight and I'd sign us in. The motel bus met us, and we were soon bolted and chained into our room. I didn't even undress. Jessica pulled the blanket up over me and hesitatingly gave me a brief kiss on the cheek. It was the last thing I remembered. . . .

CHAPTER TWENTY

I awoke from a devilish nightmare in which Kreska and Mrs. Pilgrim clawed at each other in bird costumes. . . . Elizabeth Blandish held me painfully by the shoulders, making me watch. . . . There were feathers flying everywhere . . . and blood. . . . I opened my eyes to find Jessica sitting on her bed, fully dressed and patiently reading her book.

"Hello," I said.

"Hello," she repeated, with more confidence than yesterday.

So I hadn't dreamed it all. Jessica talked. I thrilled with the realization. "You must be starved, Jessie, shall we order breakfast here in the room?" She nodded and ran to get the menu from the desk. I spent the entire day in bed, taking my pain pills, dozing in and out of reality. Jessica promised to keep the door locked with the chain on and not to leave the room while I napped. I suggested she try to catch up on her schoolwork and reminded her of our promise to Geoff James. She enjoyed the TV with the volume turned down low, though I assured her nothing could keep me awake. By the following morning the pain was almost gone and I was ravenously hungry even though my mouth was parched from pain pills. I suggested we have breakfast in the dining room.

Jessica accepted her new freedom of speech with shy restraint. It was hard for me to keep from asking her the multitude of questions that were so important to both of us. Her father must be inhuman to be so indifferent to this child. I kept reminding myself of the lessons Uncle Mitch had taught me about the unspoken power of love. I could almost hear his gentle voice saying, "Be still, Marla. There are times when you should let love speak for you. Love always knows the right words, we don't. Love will always answer you in its own perfect time." It was my turn to be patiently silent, while Jessica relearned how to communicate, how to trust. I enjoyed her archaic manner of speech. She didn't speak in the vernacular of a child, but from a combination of books in which she'd lived, a touch of Dickens, an odd expression from Twain, and all the people she'd been listening to during her silence. In many ways my accident on the boat had been a blessing. I looked around the dining room, which was only partially filled as we were breakfasting late. Queenstown was a resort town for New Zealanders and this was off-season. Suddenly I was anxious to see more of it.

"Would you like to explore a little of the town?" I asked Jessica.

"Yes," she said, adding a nod by force of habit.

"I don't feel like taking a tour. Climbing off and on buses wouldn't be much fun in this condition. But we could just wander around town, get you some more film and things. When we get back to our room, I want to call Geoff James, Jessie. He offered to help; maybe he can figure out what we should do next. What do you think?" She nodded agreement.

Geoff's phone rang and rang, but there was no answer. "I'll try him again later."

We wandered down the crooked, hilly streets of cobblestone and brick. It was still odd to have the sun in our eyes from the north. The quaint, alpine village was nestled at the foot of one of the Remarkables, a section of the alps overlooking a vast lake. The water had a textured look like blue denim patched with dark shadows of gray clouds. There was no snow here as yet.

Our danger hung over us like a malignancy. I took long, deep breaths of the clear, clean air, trying to relax.

"The earth mother was here," Jessica said. Our Mother Nature had other faces, I realized.

As we passed a field of grazing sheep, Jessica ran instinctively to a small wooly lamb not far from us. "Oliver Twist," she called, "Oliver Twist. . . ." The lamb skittered away at the sound of her voice. The helpless weight of rejection was in the sag of her shoulders again. "Barth said rabbit skins could be poisonous for dogs," Jessica said from out of nowhere.

It was her longest sentence yet. It was easy to see where her mind escaped to. We walked on in silence.

My helplessness swept over me again, and I questioned whether or not it had been wise for us to leave our room. Now I would have to bluff it through for Jessica's sake. We came to the entrance of the shopping mall. We'd read that Queenstown had once been the center of one of the greatest gold discoveries of the last century. The small shops on both sides of the one-block-long mall had the flavor of the old gold rush days. A large, historical wheel decorated the entrance, and Jessica asked if she could take a picture of me standing in front of it. As I posed she took several steps backwards. "Look out!" I cried too late. She tripped over a stone marker and sat down hard; her glasses flew from her nose and hit the rock.

"Jessica, are you all right? We can't both be cripples."

She nodded, rubbing her backside, then she began to search the ground for her glasses. "I think they landed over there," I said. She found them and held them up for me to see. Both lenses were cracked.

"Don't worry about it, Jessie. We'll get some new ones somehow."

I started to brush her off with my bandaged hand, then gave up. "Let's ask about an eye doctor in this camera store." We bought more film for her camera, then the proprietor took us back outside.

"Three doors down," he said, "past the beauty parlor."

We thanked him and followed his directions.

"Here it is," I said. "Doctor Wingate, optician."

"The frames are damaged too," Dr. Wingate informed us in his high-pitched voice. "Would you like to choose new ones?"

Most of the frames were outdated. Jessica tried one pair of pale gold that used to be called pixie rims, then timidly put them back and picked out a pair of sturdy frames almost as grotesque as those she'd broken.

"No," I said, making her put the gold pixie rims back on her nose, "it's time for a change. Do you like these, Jessie?"

She studied her new image in the mirror for several minutes without a word. She looked up at me at last. "Yes, please, Marla."

Dr. Wingate said he'd rush the glasses and have them by afternoon. He gave her some temporary, weak magnifying glasses to wear until then.

"I must get my hair done, Jessie. Let's go back to that beauty shop we passed and see if they can take me." Fortunately they weren't busy. Jessica was intrigued with the shop. She'd never seen a hair dryer or women in curlers. After my hair was clean and shiny, I talked Jessica into having her hair cut to shoulder length with bangs.

"Those pixie rims are going to demand a new Jessica," I told her.

It was a dramatic experience for her to watch them snip off her long hair, but any misgivings about my decision disappeared when the girl was through. She looked darling; the braids were gone forever, and so was the old Jessica. When we left the beauty salon, she actually smiled at her reflection in a store window as she lingered over a yellow dress on display. We bought it for her, and a pair of navy sandals with a shoulder-strap bag to match. I wrote a check of my own for an orange jacket to replace the one I'd ruined on the boat. David would understand my expenditures when he saw the change in Jessica.

It had been a happy day so far, and we seemed closer than ever, but there'd been some anxious moments. I'd been startled by a round, gray-haired woman entering the shoe store; another time I'd looked back to see someone quickly turning a corner by the small postal office, as though avoiding being seen.

Jessica had shaken her head. "We didn't know him." So she was watching too.

I tried to convince myself that we couldn't have been followed, but my subconscious constantly needled me with doubts, the ache in my shoulder a very real reminder. If I only knew how many more Mrs. Pilgrims could be involved in this treacherous affair! With a million dollars involved there could be any number, with faces I didn't know, faces I'd be least likely to suspect. My reasoning told me professionals could trace us anywhere; there just weren't that many tourists fitting our description. I had to free Jessica from this ever present danger. Had our shopping sprees been a gift for her future, or because I wasn't sure there would be a future for either of us?

Hugging her new box of treasures, Jessica mimicked Emmaline's voice, "Would you like a wee cuppa tea?" Her mouth still found it difficult to smile, but her eyes had come alive and there was humor in them.

"That's not like you, Jessie. You never seem hungry."

"Ariki Meri says I have a moa's stomach. They eat nothing but air."

We found a small bakery nearby.

"We'd better get back and pick up your glasses before they close," I said, checking the clock by the cash register when we'd finished.

We hurried back up the street to Dr. Wingate's office.

"They're ready," he beamed. He disappeared into the back of the shop to reappear almost immediately, the glasses in hand. "Here, let me adjust them. There, now see what a pretty girl you are?"

I bent over to put my face next to Jessica's so that I could see her in the mirror. She wore a look of wonder that squeezed my heart. "Jessie," I marveled, "you're absolutely beautiful." Two giant tears slid out from beneath the new gold pixie rims, happy, splashy, wonderful tears. But I saw something I hadn't seen before that made my heart stand still. It wasn't just Estelle. . . . Jessie and I looked alike. There in the mirror . . . except for the difference in our ages and our coloring, we were almost twins. . . .

CHAPTER TWENTY-ONE

"I want a record of this day, Jessie. Stand by the big wheel and I'll take a picture of the new you."

"Please don't fall over that rock," she reminded me, setting her box on a nearby bench. She straightened the jacket of her pants suit, then adjusted the purse on her shoulder. As she turned to hand me the camera we both realized what a ridiculous thought it had been. How could I possibly take her picture with one arm in a sling and a bandaged hand?

At that moment a familiar, deep voice greeted us with, "Good God, what happened to you?"

My heart did a cartwheel. "Parker? Is it really you?"

"The question is, is it really you? What happened?"

"I had an accident while we were at Milford Sound. I'm fine now. But how strange . . . that you should be here in Queenstown."

"Not strange at all. I told you I'd be away a few weeks on a project."

"And it was here in Queenstown?"

"My father and I have designed another motel here. I called you at Blandish House. David said you were traveling with Jessica and he didn't know where to reach you. It seemed odd. I hoped you'd be back by the time I was. This is too good to be true." For the first time he stared at Jessica. "I can't believe it. Is it Jessica?" He gave a low flattering whistle.

She nodded. "It's me, Parker."

He looked back and forth to both of our faces. "There've been many changes since I saw you. Jessica, you're talking!" He put his hands on her shoulders. "When did all this happen? How long have you been here in Queenstown?" he asked.

"Two days, while I've been recovering." I was uncomfortable under his searching gaze; I wasn't ready for all of his questions. "Parker, I want a picture of Jessica with her new hairdo. I tried, but. . . ." I looked down helplessly at my bandages.

He laid his cane on the ground, blew the dust from the lens of the camera, and told Jessica to smile. The best she could do was a crooked, self-conscious, not-quite grin. It was going to take time; her eyes sparkled, however.

Parker stood with his feet spread apart; the khaki walking shorts and blue-knit shirt open at the neck flattered his healthy tan. He had such vitality, his body, his skin. . . . The sun sparkled the fine hair on his strong arms. I had to look away. David's slender figure flashed before me.

"What made you decide to travel?" he asked after handing Jessica back her camera.

"I thought the change of locale would be good for Jessica. We made up our minds in a hurry. We're doing her schoolwork en route. It was all perfect until I fell over a cleat on the boat. The water was so rough from the wind. Wasn't it, Jessie?"

She'd listened with a puzzled frown. I could tell she thought Parker deserved the whole truth. I knew we needed help. I'd been praying for help. I knew now Kreska was definitely one of them. Suddenly Parker's broad shoulders were the most beautiful sights I'd ever seen and they were here. . . . I sank down on the bench and raised my eyes to his. "Parker, I've been talking

a lot of nonsense; there's so much I need to tell you."
Jessica stood close and put her arm around my shoulders. "I hardly know where to begin. . . ."

He sat beside me and took my bandaged hand in his. "Maybe you'll find the truth won't be as hard as all the cover-up."

Telling the Crookshanks everything had helped, but pouring it all out to Parker was different. He strengthened me, renewed my faith in myself; his remarks were so down-to-earth, so natural.

"What else could you've done. . . . What a dumb, brave thing to do. . . . I'm glad you love the Crookshanks. God, if I could get my hands on that Mrs. Pilgrim. . . ."

Jessica looked at me with a question in her eyes. "What is it, Jessie?"

"I didn't know about the man . . . at the *pa* in the steam."

"You know everything now, Jessie, I've held nothing back. Except . . . Parker, why didn't you tell me about my resemblance to Estelle and Jessica?"

"I knew you'd ask me that. It was such a shock when I first saw you in San Francisco. From a distance I thought you were Estelle in a blond wig. Her death, the amulet, the endless suspicions were all unreal. I never saw Estelle's body; she was cremated the next day while I was in the hospital because of my knee. I couldn't even go to her funeral." The muscles in his cheeks had tensed. "Then I got close enough to see the color of your eyes. After we'd met, and I knew you had no knowledge of your resemblance, I realized David had never told you you were related to the Cavenaugh family. He had to have a damn good reason."

"That just can't be true. If I were a distant cousin or something, wouldn't Uncle Mitch have told me?"

"He might not have known. Depends on how far back all the secrecy started. We're struggling with probability versus credibility. I was sure David would explain after you'd arrived. That day at the thermal village, I had no way of knowing whether he'd told you or not. You had no need to confide in me, not with David around. It was a rotten thing not to have told you about his marriage."

"David has a problem."

"He married one."

I felt enough had been said. "We should get back to our motel, Parker. I'm beginning to feel a bit shaky again."

"I'll call you a cab. I flew down here in my plane."

"Please don't. It's only a few blocks; we'd rather walk."

"I'll walk with you then. I don't want you out of my sight."

We walked most of the way in silence. At the door of our room he turned and cupped my chin in his hand. "I want the two of you to have dinner with me tonight. If you're up to it. There's a wonderful restaurant at the top of the mountain with a fabulous view."

"It would be a place to wear your new yellow dress, Jessie."

She nodded and hugged the box again.

"I'll pick you up here at your door at seven." I could tell that he waited until he'd heard our bolt snap in place before he walked off.

I fell into a deep, troubled sleep to the sound of Jessica's television program. When I woke, she had the light on and was still watching.

"Jessica, what time is it?"

"The six o'clock news came on five minutes ago."

"I'll shower first if you don't mind."

"Won't you get your bandages a wee bit wet?"

"I forgot again." I was tired of being helpless. It'd been almost three days—stretching it a bit—since the accident, I reasoned; the doctor had said only two days of rest. "Jessica, come help me out of this strait-jacket."

We unwrapped my bandaged hand first. It still looked wounded, but not too repulsive. It was a struggle for Jessica to pull the tape loose from my arm and shoulder. I bit my lip to keep from crying out. At last I was free. I tried moving my shoulder gently; it was painful but bearable. I'd have to favor it for a while.

I managed to slip into a long pink-and-green silk print and laid out my pink shawl. Jessica and I took turns zipping each other up. Jessica's new hairdo didn't have to be touched. She must have sat up like a poker on her bed all the time I'd been asleep to protect it. Her dress was beautifully tailored with tiny, self-covered buttons and a designed gold belt. I removed the price tag from her navy coat just as Parker called from the lobby that he was on the way up. I no longer felt the need to call on Geoff for help.

Parker had changed to gray slacks and a navy blazer. The appreciative fire in his gray eyes sparked a sudden warmth throughout my body. I was shocked by the intensity of my reaction to seeing him. What was happening to me? He asked Jessica to take his left arm, which maneuvered his cane, and I put a trembling hand on his right sleeve. I made a decision to forcibly leave my torturous fears behind me for now. Tonight was for pleasure.

The taxi left us at a small platform at the base of the mountain not far from the mall.

"Look above you," Parker said, pointing upward. A cleared path straight up the tree-covered mountainside revealed a rustic restaurant perched like a bird's nest on the brink of the mountaintop. Parker stepped inside the small waiting cubicle to telephone the restaurant, and moments later we could see a gondola start its long descent down the clearing.

"This is a popular spot for skiers in the winter time." Jessica looked at me. "As a fish begins to nibble from far below, so the ascent of a hill begins from the bottom."

"A quote from Ariki Meri if I ever heard one," Parker said, studying her.

How could I tell either of them that my heart sank into my shoes? The thought of going up that gigantic alp at a forty-five degree angle was bad enough, but riding in that box, suspended by two cables, was too much. The gondola nudged the cement dock where we were waiting and opened like a giant clam shell for us to enter. Parker helped Jessica in and turned for me. I moved quickly to hide my shudder as I climbed in beside her.

"I think there's room for all three of us on this side," Parker said as he joined us. "I want to share the view with you as we ascend." He had timed it perfectly. An unseen hand had spilled buckets of paint in every glorious color across the water while the sun dipped from sight. First the unforgettable church window, now this; we had so much to thank Parker for. I stole a glance in his direction as he talked to Jessica, his handsome face close to hers. "Lake Wakatipu is fifty-two miles long," he told her.

"Lake Wakatipu? Isn't that the Breathing Lake?"

"How did you know? Don't tell me—Ariki Meri again. New Zealand floats on legends."

I suppressed a gasp as the cables jerked over the first of the support towers that staggered up every few hundred feet. "Queenstown is a beautiful city," I forced myself to say as we watched it diminish in size the higher we rose. Lights blinked on in the houses and I pictured the families in them. My heart couldn't be pounding all that much with fear. I thought of David and felt a stab of guilt. But why should I feel guilty about David? He was married. Parker was staring at me when I turned toward him. He wasn't smiling; his brows were in a straight, serious line. I felt that warmth again, and my lips parted slightly.

"We must be at the top," Jessica said as we bumped the upper platform and the cab sprang open.

The lovely lodge boasted a room full of people. The fire in the large brick fireplace cast its festive light across the low wooden beams. Candles glowed on the tables. Parker had arranged for a table at the window for us. Jessica enjoyed the gypsy violinist who wandered from table to table. I wasn't sure what I was eating; the food seemed to have a magical quality about it. Hans, the maitre d', was a friend of Parker's and catered to us like royalty, especially Jessica.

After dinner, as Parker and I sipped our coffee and listened to the nostalgic music, Hans came up to our table again. "Come, little princess," he said to Jessica. "I will show you the kitchen and let you meet the cooks who lovingly prepared your food." She looked at me for permission. I nodded, wondering if Parker had arranged this too.

"I can't get my resemblance out of my mind, Parker. Why would David keep it a secret?"

"I wish I could help, but I'm as puzzled as you are."

He reached across and took my injured hand in his, turning it over to expose the remnants of the ugly cut. He bent down and brushed his lips against it. "The thermal pits, now this. When will it end, Marla?" My heart couldn't hold an even elevation.

"I wish I knew," I said almost in a whisper.

"How did you accomplish the miracle with Jessica, her talking?"

"When I was in danger on the boat . . . she—she tried to help me."

"Do you really think Mrs. Pilgrim fell on purpose?"

"I don't know, but, Parker, she lied deliberately about having been in Milford for a week when she'd only just arrived."

"Could you have misunderstood her?"

"She said it twice, almost to emphasize it."

"Then she must be one of them. She'd be a clever guise, all right."

"It's a fact that someone at Blandish House is involved too, Parker. That's even more frightening."

"And you think it's Kreska?"

"Doesn't he seem logical? He's had every opportunity. I must find a way to free Jessica from this nightmare."

"There's only one way," he said, his mouth in a grim line. "Either the amulet was lost forever or it wasn't. If it is still hidden as you suspect and Jessica knows where it is, then it must be recovered and returned."

"But if it is in those caves? How can I ask her to go back into that den of horror?" I didn't mention what the thought of going down in those black depths did to me.

"I was there, remember? I know full well what you'll be asking of Jessica, but I'll go with you . . . help you, Marla; it's the only way. I know the caves. I worked the boats there five summers. Even if Jessica thinks she knows where the jewels are hidden, there's the chance she wouldn't be able to pinpoint it. There'd be a million places it could be, that's why the mystery was never solved even after the police searched so extensively. But it's worth a try. Ask her, Marla. It must be done right away. You're both in deadly danger."

"David would never let us go to the caves."

"David be damned."

"Parker, please don't. . . ." I took my hand away.

"David got you into this. I can't forgive him for that."

Jessica came back to the table, clutching a small paper bag. "For our breakfast," she said. She looked at our faces with a puzzled expression.

"Why don't you two look through the souvenir shop on the balcony while I pay the bill," Parker suggested.

We were admiring the hand-crafted jewelry when he

joined us again. Jessica held up the little wooden cross
that Grandfather McNaughton had made her.

"That's a real treasure, Jessie. Let me give you this
to keep it in." He handed her a small carved jewelry
box with an inlaid top of native paua shells. "And
this for Marla, I think." He chose a delicate teardrop
of New Zealand jade on a silver chain.

"Parker, I couldn't—"

"You must," he said. "It was made for you." He
fastened it around my neck, and I thrilled to his touch.

Hans insisted Jessica and I keep two of the beautiful
menus as souvenirs. "My friend, Parker, has fantastic
taste in women," he said in parting.

Spellbound, the three of us looked out over the tiny
lights of the city below us. We waited for the gondola
to appear. I searched the starlit sky for the familiar
Big Dipper, but it was nowhere to be found. There
were vast, black, starless areas I hadn't noticed before.
"It's a different sky, Marla," Parker explained, "those
are New Zealand stars, they're not like yours." The
moon spread a silver path across the lake, an enchanted
path.

Hans called to us from the entrance above, waving
Jessica's paper bag. "Oh," she exclaimed and ran back
up to retrieve it.

Parker came up behind where I was standing and
put his arms around me, holding me close. I felt his
lips kiss my hair, my neck. He turned me gently to
face him. His lips crushed mine.

My arms encircled his neck, oblivious to the pain
in my shoulder. My body pressed against his; I wanted
to meld its length with his. The shadow of David no
longer existed between us. At that moment memories
had no binding commitments. I belonged to Parker.
It took all my strength to push him away. "Parker,
darling . . . please . . . find Jessica for me; she should
be back."

He turned and walked back up to find her.

The gondola was opening beside me. As if in a dream, I started to enter it to wait for them. Then, not wanting to make the ride down the mountain alone by mistake, I stepped back suddenly. At that very moment the jaws of the car snapped shut, tearing my shawl from my shoulders as it started its descent.

Parker rushed up beside me, Jessica just behind him. "It almost crushed you in half," he said in disbelief. We stood there in the disenchanted darkness, watching my shawl being dragged down the mountainside in my place.

CHAPTER TWENTY-TWO

Jessica and I lay in the shadowy darkness of our room, each lost in our own thoughts. Parker had sent us home down the back side of the mountain in a taxi, so that he could investigate the gondola. His nearness was still with me; I could almost hear his voice, feel his touch. I was shaken with the impact of my own emotions, the new meaning in our relationship. I'd thought my heart was forever entombed by David's marriage; now I realized my love for David was just what Andrea had claimed: never physical, never complete. What I felt for Parker involved my whole being. But was I finding real love only to be plunged to despair again? Parker had chosen the restaurant, Parker had had time to arrange for the timely operation of the deadly gondola. . . . There'd been no one else there, or no one

I'd seen. He had his plane in Queenstown, he could go anywhere. Two giant tears squeezed from between my closed eyes and zigzagged down my cheeks. It still could be Kreska following me, checking with Mrs. Pilgrim perhaps? What of my resemblance to Jessica and Estelle? Could I be a distant cousin, but if so why the secrecy? This would have affected Steve too. How was I related to David?

"Marla? Are you awake?"

"Yes, Jessie."

"Are you in love with Parker?"

"I think so. Real love is so precious, I want to be very sure."

"I'm sorry about your shawl. I had a beautiful day 'til—"

"Jessie, Parker could have been involved up there on the mountain. I have to face it."

"Not Parker. You couldn't think that."

"No more blinders, Jessie, no more game-playing. We have to uncover whoever is after us, disarm them forever. We can't wait any longer."

"How, Marla?"

"Can you bear to tell me about the jeweled amulet, about Estelle, the caves?" There was a long silence. I waited, my heart pounding in my ears like an overly loud windup clock. "It's asking so much of you, Jessie, but our only chance is to know the truth about what happened. Now that you can tell about it, you're in greater danger than I am. They could make you tell."

"I promised Estelle."

"Your loyalty is to the living now, Jessie. David needs you and, wherever he is, I know your father needs you too."

"I've thought and thought, Marla, and I'm so frightened. All the time I'm frightened. . . . If anything happened to you I'd die . . . just die."

I crossed over to her bed and put my good arm around her. "I've prayed constantly, Jessie, and the only answer that comes to me is that it's time for truth . . . for complete trust between us. I'm asking you to break your promise to Estelle, as she'd want you to do if she knew you were in danger. Do you know where the amulet is, Jessie, or was it lost?"

There was only the sound of our breathing, then her answer came at last. "Estelle hid it."

My heart lurched. "But where? How did she ever manage to? Parker said the police searched and searched!"

"She hid it before we got to the ledge, while the man was fighting with Parker."

"And she kept the empty pouch?"

"Yes."

"Jessie, do you know where she hid it? Could you find the place again?"

"Yes. It had a special marking. She made sure I saw it, but when we were on the ledge, she made me promise I'd never tell till she came back."

"She can't come back, Jessie."

"I know that now, but when that man pulled me back into the boat . . . and that awful fat woman held me." She hesitated and I felt her stiffen. "I remember it now"—her voice became taut with dread—"that terrible smell; it was in the boat . . . it was Mrs. Pilgrim." She shivered and tightened her arms around her misshapen koala bear. I was glad it was too dark for her to see the expression of terror on my face. It was one thing to wonder if someone were guilty of trying to kill you, another to know. My heart was beating furiously in my throat. "Marla, she's a bad, old woman. She pretended she was being kind to me in the boat, but she tried to search me. . . . She was trying to find the amulet, wasn't she? Everyone was screaming about Estelle after Parker was back in the boat all bloody. Oh, Marla. . . ." She crushed against me.

"Poor baby." I tightened my hold. "Think back

carefully, Jessie. Could you see who grabbed Estelle when you were on the ledge?"

"It was just someone. . . ."

"Could you tell if it was a man or a woman? Could it have been Mrs. Pilgrim?"

"It wasn't her," she said without hesitation. "They were thin arms in black sleeves; she's fat."

"And it could have been a man?"

"Yes, I think so."

"But you're not sure?"

"No."

"Jessie, are you brave enough to go back into the caves with me and search for the missing treasure?"

She didn't answer for the longest time. "I think . . . I could," she whispered. "Marla, is it the only way?"

"The only way we can be free of this ghastly intrigue is to give the amulet back, and it will be up to the two of us. We can't trust anyone. Not Parker, not Geoff, not even David for fear he'll forbid us to go. Do you think you can pretend that you still can't talk when we get back to Blandish House?" I could see the dark outline of her head nod. "We'll sleep now, darling, and say our prayers; then tomorrow first thing we'll go back to Rotorua." I tucked her in, kissed her on the forehead, and crawled into my own bed.

"Aren't we supposed to have lunch with Parker tomorrow, Marla?"

"We'll be long gone by then. Go to sleep, Jessie." My pillow was suddenly wet with tears.

CHAPTER TWENTY-THREE

There were two cars already parked in front of Blandish House as our taxi drove up; one was a police car. I hurriedly paid the driver and he placed our luggage by the door. Jessica used the huge brass knocker. I put my finger to my lips to remind her she was not to talk. We waited several minutes and were about to knock again when Sims opened the door. He'd aged noticeably in the few days we'd been gone; his color was pasty. He looked at Jessica with astonishment, then to me, "Miss Creighton, I'm so glad you are back. It's been dreadful for Master David. He tried everywhere and couldn't reach you."

We slipped out of our coats and laid them on our luggage where Sims had placed it in the entrance hall. "Sims, what has happened? What are the police doing here?"

"It's Miss Andrea," he said, avoiding my eyes. "There has been an accident. . . . Miss Andrea was killed in her car. She's dead."

"Sims, how terrible." I put my arm around Jessica and drew her to me. "Where is Miss Blandish?"

"I'm right here, Miss Creighton," she said in an accusing tone. She was dressed in a severe floor-length dress; the contrast against her pale, thin-skinned face with its high forehead was stark. Perfect casting for a black widow. "It was needlessly cruel not to have been available when you were needed." Her voice was razor sharp. I noticed her thin arms in their black sleeves and shivered inwardly. As she spoke she glared at Jessica from head to toe. "What have you done to Jessica's lovely braids?"

"She wanted a change, Miss Blandish," I said with more courage than I felt. "She wanted to look her age."

Ariki Meri came up behind her. "I think she's wrought a miracle." Jessica ran to her impulsively and hugged her waist. Ariki Meri put her hand tenderly on her hair. "Ariki Jessica," she said softly.

The hatred in Elizabeth Blandish's eyes almost struck me physically. "You are creating difficulties that we cannot forgive."

I ignored her words. "We would like to see David now, please."

"He is with the police . . . perhaps you shouldn't. . . ."

"Now! Miss Blandish."

"Then you must leave Jessica here with me."

"No, Jessica will stay with me." I had taken her by surprise; she seemed stunned at my attitude and made an impatient motion for Sims to take us to the library. We followed Sims. The grandfather clock chimed an eerie eleven as we passed. Andrea dead . . . poor Andrea . . . poor David.

Sims knocked on the library door, and David's voice called to come in. I walked into the room, Jessica at my heels. Two men were standing beside David near the fireplace, one in a police uniform. My stomach tightened as I continued forward. "David, we've just returned. I'm so sorry, so terribly sorry. . . ."

The man in plain clothes stared at me with shrewd, appraising eyes. He wasn't tall, but his military bearing gave him a sharp air of authority. He had a small, thin mustache, which he twisted when he was concentrating. The policeman was short and stocky, with a florid face and sandy hair. He kept shifting from one foot to the other in an uncomfortable manner. I was aghast at David's anguished, haggard eyes set in the dark hollows, the pained, downward twist of his sensitive mouth.

"Marla," he said, "thank God. I've tried to reach you ever since—"

"Sims told us there was an accident . . . about Andrea. David, how did it happen?"

The man in plain clothes cleared his throat.

"I'm sorry," David said. "This is Marla Creighton. Marla, Miss Creighton, is Jessica's companion. You remember my sister, Jessica, I'm sure. They've been touring the South Island. This is Detective Inspector Saint Johns and Constable Mollaire."

"You knew nothing of the accident?" St. Johns asked, looking directly at me.

"I just explained," David said, "they've been traveling, and I couldn't reach them."

"Had you planned all along to return today, Miss Creighton?"

"Why no, Inspector, we were not on a planned schedule. I'm so grateful we decided to come home."

"How long have you been away?" The inspector's cool eyes never left my face.

"Almost two weeks," I answered.

"Not a very long time to see the beauties of the South Island. Had you planned to stay longer?"

"Well, I . . . that is, Jessica completed her study outline and we thought it best to turn in her work and begin a new series of lessons. We can always go back again later. Jessica's teacher at school, Mister James, has been giving us the necessary material to help her pass her grade. He. . . ." I was angry with myself for talking so much; the man's eyes were rattling me.

"Mister James of the Merrimont School?"

"Yes," I said.

The inspector was not through with me. "Where were you yesterday, Miss Creighton?"

"In Queenstown."

"How long had you been there?"

"Two days," I answered.

"Did you attempt to reach them in Queenstown, Mister Cavenaugh?"

"Why yes," David started to say, then hesitated. "That is I tried so many places. I'm not sure. . . . Obviously I must have missed Queenstown."

"Strange, it is such a central location for travelers, I would have thought it would be the first place you would have tried."

I realized with a sick feeling how difficult it would be to explain why we hadn't used our right names. I spoke quickly before he could ask where we'd stayed. "David, why are they questioning us? It was just an accident, wasn't it?"

"Andrea had gone into town shopping," David began, running his fingers through his blond hair. "She didn't return for dinner. Early the next morning they found her mangled car where it'd missed a curve and struck a tree." His voice broke.

The inspector spoke again, "It was not an accident, it was murder."

"Murder!" I gasped. Jessica came up beside me and put her arm around my waist. "But who would . . . are you sure?"

St. Johns nodded, distracted as he looked long and hard at the two of us side by side. "The autopsy revealed a blow on the right side of her head as the cause of death, a fact the murderer hoped to conceal by demolishing her body in the car. Her forehead struck the windshield, but not with sufficient force to kill her."

"I called Andrea's mother in London," David interrupted. "She said that she was too ill to make the long trip and we were to go ahead with the funeral. It's scheduled for eleven tomorrow."

"What can I do to help, David?"

"It's all taken care of, Marla. Auntie made the arrangements."

"You're close friends, aren't you?" the inspector asked, studying us as we were talking.

"Marla's brother was my roommate in college in the States. I knew Marla then."

"Before you were married?"

"Yes, before I was married!" he said in an irritated tone.

"Just checking all the details, Mister Cavenaugh. Remember I pride myself on being a very thorough man."

"I want you to find the person responsible for this," David told him, "and you can be as damn thorough as you wish. However, do not intimidate Miss Creighton, I warn you. She is an innocent victim in all of this."

The close resemblance between Jessica and me registered in the detective inspector's next words. "You haven't told us everything, Mister Cavenaugh, have you? Miss Creighton is more than just a friend."

David looked at me and then at Jessica. "This isn't the time—"

"The resemblance is startling, David." I implored him. "Jessica and I both need to know; are we related?"

My question shook Inspector St. John, and for a brief moment he lost his cool approach. He had evidently assumed I knew all about it. His eyes demanded an answer from David.

David nervously brushed his hand through his hair. He walked to the bar and poured a stiff drink, which he consumed in one swallow, then turned to face us again. He stared right at me. "Marla is my half-sister." His voice shook with emotion. The impact of what he said stunned me to silence. Bitterness entered his voice. "My father had an affair with my mother's younger sister. She never let him know Marla existed."

His words shredded my life to a nothingness. I shook my head as though to ward them off.

"I should never have brought you here. . . ." David's voice broke. "You need never have known. . . ." I walked over to one of the chairs and sat down; my legs no longer wanted to bear my weight.

David was my half-brother . . . and so was Steve. I'm glad he never knew, I thought, as a pain of amputation went through me, as though half of me that had belonged to Steve had been sliced off and given to David.

"Why did you bring Miss Creighton over here, Mister Cavenaugh?" the inspector persisted.

"Can you look at Jessica and ask me why?"

"Granted she has changed. How old are you now, Jessica?"

I held my breath; would she forget and answer? Jessica looked at him with complete innocence and silence.

"My sister doesn't speak, Inspector. I'm sure you remember."

"Of course, Mister Cavenaugh, of course I remember. However, she's a very changed little girl since the last time I saw her." The constable shifted again and looked at the floor, his red face a hue brighter.

What was Jessica thinking? She was my half-sister. I was more than a stand-in for Estelle. . . . My love for David had been natural. No wonder God had stopped me from twisting it into something more. Jessica was trying to tell me something with her eyes; when I couldn't respond, she walked over to where I sat and put her arm across the back of the chair as if to guard me.

The inspector pressed on with his questions. "Did your wife know you were related to Miss Creighton?"

"No one else knew, other than my father."

"Didn't your wife question the resemblance?"

"She never met Estelle. It wasn't noticeable before with Jessica. It must be the change in her hairstyle, the new glasses."

"How did you explain your obvious affection for Miss Creighton to your wife?"

"She knew how close I'd been to both Marla and her brother, Steve."

"And she did not resent this?" David glared at him without answering. "Sims was forced to tell us that you threatened to kill your wife. I believe he said both Miss Creighton and Jessica were there at the time."

I looked over at David. This was taking an even uglier turn. I realized with sudden clarity that David had told the truth of our kinship to destroy the inspector's suspicions of me, but in doing so he'd implicated himself even more as the most logical suspect.

"Andrea made a vicious remark. I answered her in anger. I'd been drinking. . . ."

"Are you always quick to anger when you've been drinking?"

I found my voice to say, "Inspector, what are you implying?"

"I have a murder to solve, Miss Creighton. I must search all possibilities. Did you hear anyone else threaten to kill Mrs. Cavenaugh?" There was nothing I could say. Either I helped incriminate David, or I jeopardized Jessica's safety by telling my suspicions of Kreska. The inspector shrugged his shoulders as if he realized that by forcing the exposure of my family ties with the Cavenaughs, he'd created a tense personal situation that would block any further questioning. He cleared his throat and motioned to the unhappy constable that he was ready to leave. "I will want to talk to both of you again after the funeral," he said and marched briskly from the room.

David shut the door behind them, refilled his glass, then walked back across the room to me. "That first day I saw you, Marla, I knew you had to be family. Father hired an investigator to find out who you were. Your mother's maiden name turned out to be Kathryn Blandish."

Emmaline had said there was something between Aaron and Charlotte's younger sister. "But she died in England."

"That was a family lie. She visited my mother when Steve was a year old. The family disowned her after she went back to the States."

"And you've known all this time."

"Father made me promise not to tell you. He knew what it would do to Steve, to both of you. But Steve's dead now and I need you . . . Andrea's dead. . . ." He took a long swallow of his drink. "I killed her."

"David, don't say such a thing." I felt Jessica's hand grip my shoulder.

"I killed her," he repeated. "I never loved her. I never gave her a happy moment. She had to find love any way she could. That's why she went after Parker. It wasn't Parker's fault. I believe that now. When he refused her, she went after someone else: the doctor, the lawyer, the Indian chief. . . ."

"David. Jessica's here." I didn't want her to listen to such accusations. Parker and Andrea . . . no, I wouldn't believe it.

Jessica walked over to David and put one small hand on his arm. "David, I'm sorry . . . about Andrea," she said haltingly.

He stared at her unbelievingly, then tears poured down his cheeks. He held out his arms and she clung to him. "Jessica," he said chokingly, "Jessica, oh, thank God, Jessica. . . ." His eyes met mine and my throat began to swell with tears. "I knew you could work a miracle."

"It just happened," I said, choked with emotion.

"We'll never be separated again," he said. "I promise, it will always be the three of us."

Tears remained static in my eyes. My hand went instinctively to the jade teardrop hanging at my throat.

CHAPTER TWENTY-FOUR

As Jessica and I walked down the quiet hall toward our room, a chilling thought blotted out everything else and shook my mind until my teeth chattered. Andrea murdered! They were closing in, they were everywhere—but why Andrea? All this time I'd been thinking only of myself, of Jessica. Andrea hadn't been a danger to decoding Jessica unless . . . unless she'd seen or heard something that had made her a threat. With David indisposed most of the time she must have spent many hours alone with Kreska. An ugly thought crystalized: Was Andrea one of them? There had to be one of them here in the house; had it been Andrea? The ugliness of the thought spread like a virus. Had it been Andrea and Parker? I was breathing harder than my climbing the stairs demanded.

By the time we reached my room, I'd made a decision. We paused at the door. "Jessie," I said in a low voice, trying to keep its tone controlled, "we can't wait until tomorrow to go to the caves, tomorrow might be—" I caught the words before they tumbled out. "David is in danger now too. We must go today. There was a one o'clock bus listed in the tour folder; we can just make it."

Her eyes stared at me through her glasses in disbelief.

"David needs us, Jessie. Andrea's murderer must be

caught. I know what I'm asking of you, but tomorrow the police may not let us go." I didn't add tomorrow Parker might be the one to stop us, though the thought was more menacing than the police. "Do you know where the necklace is? There's no use in our going, Jessie, unless you're absolutely sure."

She nodded grimly.

"Okay, it's settled. We'll leave a note under David's door not to worry about us, then we'll ask Sims to drive us into town." I thought hard for a minute as we entered my room. "We'll tell him we have to pick up some things we ordered and that we'll take a taxi home. He'll just have to accept that."

I blocked from my mind everything but what we were about to do and slipped the flashlight from my bedside table into my purse. The wire Dutch had used to hold my window open caught my eyes. I untwisted his handiwork and bent the wire over and over to slip into my jacket pocket. "We'll keep our ski jackets on. Jessie, get your boots; they're in your case."

"It's not raining," she said.

"I want you to wear them for warmth."

As she searched for her boots I noticed her pick up her bear, then tuck him back into the suitcase again. As I looked around the room, my eyes focused for a moment on the initialed dresser set. E.C. Suddenly the realization that I had lost a sister too washed over me. As I closed the door behind us I had the odd feeling Estelle knew every step we were taking.

We found Sims in the library. He frowned down his long, English nose when I asked him to drive us into town. Actually I didn't give him a choice. I told him we'd made a previous commitment and we had to meet it.

"Yes, of course, Miss Creighton, I can be ready to go in just a few minutes."

"Thank you, Sims. Jessica and I will meet you at the car."

Fortunately we saw no one inside the house as we walked through. Miss Blandish was no doubt lying down with a migraine. We'd seen no sign of Ariki Meri, and I was grateful. I knew my words would stumble. She had a way of demanding only truth. David had said only his father knew who I was, but now I suspected both Ariki Meri and Elizabeth Blandish knew too. Dutch was nowhere around the grounds. We waited at the side of the car until Sims appeared and helped us into the back of the large black limousine.

Before long we'd passed through the iron gates and wound our way down Blandish Hill toward the city. The landscape flashed by as I tried to sort out my thoughts and plans. I was taking on a grave responsibility in what I was about to do. Jessica was my half-sister; didn't this increase my responsibility, or at least justify my decision? How could I love her more than I did? She had already become a part of me. I'd no way of knowing what psychological effect going back into the caves might have on her. True, she'd changed remarkably in the past few days, but was this only on the surface? She'd just had the shock of learning of our relationship. Could I plunge her into a deeper trauma by exposing her to the site of the tragedy she'd experienced? But I had no choice; the thought of what they might do to drag the truth from her now that she could speak conjured dreadful visions. A million dollars in jewels could turn men into animals.

The pressure of coping grew heavier and heavier, like the weight of sandbags across my shoulders. And what of my own reactions? Could I be sure I wouldn't panic once I was inside the caves? The palms of my hands were damp, and my mouth grew so dry I couldn't swallow. What else could I do? David had to be freed from suspicion; freed from the evidence that incriminated him irrevocably. The police would be on Kreska's side. He worked closely with them; he would have every opportunity to bribe his way to the precious talisman once he knew its hiding place; if he found the amulet and said nothing to the others Jessica would still be threatened. There would have to be witnesses. Would I ever have the chance to meet my real father?

We stopped at a red signal in the City Centre on Queen Street. "This will be fine, Sims. We'll find our way from here." I pulled Jessica out of the car with me and onto the sidewalk. "We'll take a taxi home, Sims," I called over my shoulder, and before he could protest, we lost ourselves among the shopping people.

We rounded several corners and passed the variety of downtown shops. I hailed a taxi and asked the driver to take us to the tour bus station. We hastily bought our tickets and found the bus marked WAITOMO. The driver was already in his seat as we crawled in directly behind him. The bus was to leave in ten minutes. It was a miracle that we'd made it. I felt a deep sense of relief when the folding doors whined shut.

For the first hour Jessica fought the fatigue brought on by the long, shattering morning. We didn't talk about the shock of being related. Evidently she too felt a need to adjust her thoughts to this incredible change before putting them into words. Finally she fell asleep, lulled by the rocking motion of the bus, her head on my shoulder. Parker would have my note by now and I tried to picture his reaction. Had he guessed that David was my brother and didn't want to be the one to tell me? It would explain his anger toward David. David was my brother. Why did I feel like crying? I needed a brother.

Tears blurred my vision as more lovely, hedged pastures streaked by, some with sheep and others with bright, clean cattle enjoying the long afternoon shadows. A jarring flash of red against all the tranquil green caught my attention in the driver's side mirror. Then my heart almost stopped beating as the red became a small sports car. There was another car between it and our bus on the narrow road so that I only caught snatches of it as each bend exposed it briefly. It's only a coincidence, don't be a fool, I told myself, yet I shivered as I remembered that panic-stricken moment when Parker and I were forced off the road and death had seemed inevitable. All either of us had known for sure was that it was a small red sports car. I sat up straighter, trying not to wake Jessica, and stared into the mirror, tense and frightened. No one could know where we are, I scolded myself, we left in such a hurry we didn't even know. . . . Yet wasn't this our logical move? Logical or insane? What was I leading Jessica into? But what other choice was there?

"Is anything wrong, Marla?" Jessica asked.

"Sorry, Jessie, I'm just tense. This won't be easy for either of us," I spoke in a low voice close to her ear so the driver couldn't hear.

"The caves are really pretty," she said bravely.

I squeezed her hand. "I'm sure this is the only way we can make everything right again. You understand I plan for us to go through the caves with our tour group first and you'll point out the hiding place? Later, when the caves are closed for the day we'll go back and find the amulet." I didn't dare tell her she couldn't go back with me, but I knew I had to do the final, dangerous part alone. No way would I endanger her with this; I'd already lost one sister there.

"I understand. I wish Parker were with us."

"Not right now, Jessie."

"David will worry about us."

"I'm sure he will. But he has Andrea on his mind." I didn't mention that he was probably quite drunk by now.

"I never liked Andrea." It was a child's simple statement of truth.

"I really didn't know her," I answered half to myself. "I wish now I'd tried to know her better. There should be honesty in marriage. David should have told her

about our being related. It might have made all the
difference."

She shook her head. "She wouldn't have let you,
Marla. She didn't like girls."

Jessica knew much more than I realized.

"How do you feel about Kreska, Jessie?"

"He's creepy."

I nodded my head in agreement.

"Do you think we'll ever see Mrs. Pilgrim again,
Marla?"

"That's a terrible thought. I honestly don't think
we will. She'd have no way of knowing where we are
now. She doesn't have wings like the rest of her friends."
I was rewarded by an almost-smile.

We talked away the time, still not delving into the
newness between us, as the red sports car danced in and
out of the mirror like a well-tied lure on a fishing line.

"We are approaching Waitomo, folks," the bus driver
announced over the loudspeaker. "The caves are just
ahead. *Waitomo* means 'water entering the hole' and
stems from the way the Waitomo River disappears
abruptly into a limestone cliff just below us now. We're
at the top of the caves."

We drove through the oval entrance sign and parked
beside other buses waiting there. The way we had to
park blocked my view of any other cars, making it
impossible for me to keep track of the sports car. Had
it gone on?

"This way, Marla," Jessica took my arm. I hesitated
for just a moment, then we started up the dreaded
gravel path together.

CHAPTER TWENTY-FIVE

People from another tour bus had joined ours, bringing our group to almost sixty in number waiting at the entrance of the caves. Our guide herded us to one side to allow those returning from a completed tour to exit into the late afternoon sunshine. They emerged slowly, shielding their eyes from the sudden glare. It would be dark when we came back out, I realized.

I purposely avoided putting my arm around Jessica, hoping the surging crowd would camouflage the trembling of my body. We inched forward as the outcoming people thinned to reveal a giant, black hole in the side of the hill, the entrance to the caves. I wanted to run, but my feet were buried in sand like a bad dream. Inevitably we were swept through the menacing opening by the tide of bodies, and the world of air, earth, and sky dissolved into a shadowed and clammy crypt. Jessica hugged my side, and I kept her hand fast in mine. The young tour guide waved his electric lantern for us to stand at attention while our eyes adjusted to the darkness and he prepared us for our walk down into the earth. I noticed a darker hole off to our right that looked too small to walk through. . . . Surely they didn't expect . . . ?

"Duck your heads, please." The guide's voice rose above the incredulous mutterings. "The ceiling will be quite low for a short way."

It was like a living nightmare as we entered the ridiculous opening and crouched through the narrow passageway, breathing the bottled air. I fought down the panic that threatened to engulf me. *Oh, please, Lord, let me see this through for Jessica.*

We broke out into a larger area, and I noticed mine was not the only sigh of relief. I took a deep breath of larger space and looked around. The brochures had not prepared me for this magnificent, medieval, limestone cavern. Stalactites hung from the ceiling everywhere, and stalagmites rose from the floor to meet them. We were like ants walking through a giant chandelier of limestone, which was porous and oddly textured and of the palest green—almost white and luminous. The guide's voice rambled on. "Stalactites and stalagmites are formed by the slow drip and evaporation of water containing dissolved limestone. They grow at a rate of one-half inch a year, so you can see this cave has been here a while—about twelve million years. There's one stalactite on ahead twenty-two feet long and four feet around."

His facts were mind boggling, and there was comfort in the knowledge that the caves had remained intact through all the volcanic earthquakes New Zealand was subject to. I looked down at Jessica but couldn't see her expression in the dim light.

We followed the guide's voice and the light of his lantern along the steeply descending path. "Watch the bridge ahead," we were warned. "You'll be crossing a shaft that goes straight down eight hundred feet. Hold on to the wire ropes at all times, please."

I changed hands with Jessica so that she could walk in front of me and we'd each have our right hands free to hold on to the wire railing. The people behind us urged us on to the small suspension bridge, which swayed sickeningly with our weight.

"Don't look down, Jessie. Don't look down." Speed, I thought. Cross as quickly as we can. I heard someone

not too far behind say, "Hey, don't push!" Was someone trying to reach us? The thought shuddered through
my body. I scanned the crowd back over my shoulder,
but saw no one I recognized. In near panic I loosened
my grip on the wire and pushed Jessica forward to
circle the couple ahead of us as if rushing past the slow
figures on an escalator.

"You had better keep that little girl hanging on,
lady," they admonished me.

"Sorry . . . please forgive us, excuse me. . . ." We
pushed and threaded our way until an extremely heavy
man blocked our progress completely. I was breathing hard from the exertion. As we tried to urge his
gross figure forward I made the mistake of looking
over the edge. The shaft dropped straight down into
an empty blackness that wanted to vacuum me into its
depths. Waves of nausea from the black void swept
over me and my knees almost buckled in their weak-
ness. Jessica must have sensed my reaction; I felt her
pull me back from the drop-off.

"Marla," she whispered. "Marla!" Her frightened
voice brought me back to reality. With new determination I elbowed the fleshy side of our roadblock with a
sharp jab. He winced and squeezed to one side, mut-
tering a few obscenities as we passed. If he's that mad,
he'll be more difficult for someone else to pass. I
prayed. We could see the guide at the far end of the
bridge now; just a few more unsteady steps and then
we were on beautiful, solid rock.

We collected in an enormous area with a cathedral
ceiling. The guide began his spiel: "This is a phe-
nomenon. Note in the upper left corner over there
the almost perfect formation of a pipe organ." Our
eyes followed his arm; there was no questioning his
words; an awesome sculpture of an immense pipe organ,
even to the bench from which it might be played, was
surrounded by massive icicle candelabra. I would not
have been surprised to have heard its rich volume fill

the room. A sanctuary formed by nature hundreds of feet beneath the earth, an architectural fantasy. No wonder Parker had chosen to work here during his summers.

As my eyes wandered over the enchanted room I noted a sickening fact: There were niches everywhere, vertical, horizontal; thousands of them. The limestone caves were one big cubbyhole desk. If Jessica's memory had miscalculated in any way, our whole plan was hopeless. I looked down at her; what a flood of unhappy memories must be closing in on her. There was still no one I recognized among the people around us, yet I knew we were being followed. If we could just stay far enough ahead of them. . . .

It was so hard not to press on past the guide, just listening to his monologue drone on and on. Spots of turquoise and aquamarine moss began to appear here and there as we descended deeper and deeper. In the dark recesses of the cavern roof we could see strange, cold spots of light. "You are beginning to see the lights of the glowworm larvae," we were told. There were long, shimmering threads hanging from the tiny lights; in the glow of the guide's lantern, the threads seemed like miniature silver chains of beads. "The beads are actually globules of acid designed to paralyze and trap insects," the guide explained. The delicate threads took on an ominous quality as he talked. "The larva is about one inch in length with the purest light known to man at one end, eighty-eight percent light and only twelve percent heat.

We moved cautiously down the steep, winding passageways that corkscrewed into the ground; the air was increasingly heavy, and it was harder to see. The guide spoke again, "The lights will get dimmer from now on so that your eyes will be accustomed to the dark when we reach the boats. I must also ask that you do not speak, not even whisper, as two things make the glowworms turn out their lights: They are other light and noise. Once their lights go out, they won't turn them on again for at least four hours."

Jessica and I followed just behind his words, which had silenced the crowd following in our steps. It was growing darker and darker, and the lack of air choked my throat closed. I suddenly remembered the strength in Parker's arm over mine on the airplane, the strong, rough pressure of his lips. . . . Parker, oh, Parker, I almost moaned out loud. Even if Parker were guilty, I loved him.

I was jarred back into the present when I noticed people disappearing abruptly ahead of us. We must be coming to another stairway, I reasoned; then the sound of slapping water and the foreboding scrape of a boat against a dock seeped through the eerie darkness. Jessica and I held on tightly to the stair rail and to each other as we crept down the narrow, hazardous steps. I gasped as I thought one of the threads of acid brushed my forehead. Someone said, "Sh!" The air was fresher as we reached the bottom, but there was a strong odor of constant dampness. There was no sound from the shadowy forms the guide helped climb into the long boats. Jessica and I stepped to one side to let others board first. It was impossible to see clearly even the person standing next to you. When the third boat drew up, the guide motioned for Jessica and me to climb into the front seat. A stocky man climbed in beside Jessica, gesturing all the time for his wife to take the seat behind us. Our guide leaped onto the small pointed bow in front of us. He stretched up and grabbed one of the all but invisible guy wires, which were stretched across at fairly close intervals so that he could maneuver the boat quite smoothly with the current. He was short but strong, and the muscles in his back bulged against his shirt as he manipulated the heavy load of people through the black water. Estelle must have been sitting right where I was now, looking up at Parker. We were passing through a long corridor with thick blackness for a ceiling. I wondered if we could be at the bottom of the shaft with the bridge, and suddenly looking up was as bad as looking down had been. The sound of the water resisting the thrust of our boat was magnified by the silence of the people. No one wanted to be responsible for turning out the glowworms for four hours after all we'd been through to get here. A glow in the distance seemed to be drawing us toward it. When I came back, would there be cannibalistic people threads there waiting for me?

As we penetrated the lighted opening, the darkness overhead was exploded by the sight of thousands of weird, cold particles of light, reflected vividly in the water like a maze of unfamiliar constellations, like billions of stars. What a spectacle! I caught my breath and stared with open mouth at the splendor of it. I was so engrossed in the awesome beauty around us, I didn't notice any details until the boat had traveled the entire length of what must have been a city block, surrounded by diamonds and their ethereal threads. Then, as the guide turned the boat around with the wires, Jessica pinched my knee awake. I was suddenly very alert. There weren't just curved walls in the wide tunnel; hundreds of columns rose from the water to the ceiling. Jessica shook my knee hard. There was a broad shelf off to our right. When I turned to look at her, her face was contorted by a spasm of pain. She regained control in time to point one finger so that it couldn't be seen by anyone else. I strained to see where she was directing me. There it was, just as she had remembered; two hundred yards before the shelf, a column different from the others because of a perfect H formed by crevices in the limestone near the edge of the water, yet it could have been missed so easily if you didn't know it was there.

Just as the cathedral cavern had been peppered with thousands of holes, niches, crevices, and shelves, so was this tunnel. No wonder the police had failed; it would have taken years of meticulous searching to find the amulet even with all their equipment. There were foot- and handholds available for climbing everywhere. Fortunately the glowworm lights were eight or ten feet above the water; it was their reflection that made them appear solid all around us. I shuddered at the thought of touching them, realizing it would not be long before I would be back here by myself; alone in this cold, star-spangled mausoleum.

CHAPTER TWENTY-SIX

We pressed our bodies tightly against the porous wall behind the colonnade and held our breath. Through the lacy openwork of limestone we could see the people from our tour group ascending to the entrance of the caves; they glanced high at the organ silhouette if they looked back at all, just as I had hoped. Our group was the last of the day; this would empty the caves until tomorrow. No one would wait for us; I'd told our bus driver we were meeting friends and returning home with them. The retreating people climbed back above the noise level where they could speak again; the sound of their voices wafted down to us as if from another planet.

I thought back to when we'd climbed off the boat onto the shadowy dock and I'd nudged Jessica on ahead to mingle with a family with three children while I followed closely behind her, faking a few words with the man next to me as though we were together. Anyone searching the dark to find us couldn't have identified us easily; they would have to check the outcoming people to be sure we were still inside. This is what I was counting on to give us the time we needed.

Jessica would rebel when I told her I couldn't take her with me. She'd pointed out the H column that should be all I'd need to find the talisman. The thought of being on my own in that clammy hole was unbearable, but the thought of endangering her was worse. She was so small, she'd be well hidden. She'd be frightened, but safe.

I swallowed hard before I could speak. "Jessie, I want you to stay here. I must do this alone. I can't be responsible for something happening to you because of my hairbrain scheme."

She stared at me for a full minute, then her body grew taller and she stood very straight. "You can't do this alone, Marla. You'd never find it." I couldn't believe the tone of her voice. She spoke with authority.

"What do you mean?"

"I mean that the H marked the column, but the amulet is farther around."

"Oh, Jessie."

"Also, Marla, you couldn't handle the boat without me to hold the light."

"Then we won't go back."

"They're waiting for us outside, aren't they? We can't give up now. You know it's the only way."

Tears flooded my eyes and it hurt to swallow.

"We'd better hurry," she said, pulling my arm.

My hands shook as I took the flashlight from my purse. Dear God, this wasn't what I'd planned, but she was right, I had no other choice. Jessie had to be with me. It was now or never. We groped our way back down the familiar passageways, the light shaking an unsteady path ahead of us. It was so quiet, my heart-beat hurt my ears.

"Makes you think of Indian Joe, doesn't it?" Jessica whispered.

She was enjoying this. There was no fear in her voice. Suddenly it had all become an adventure to her.

"Jessie, I—"

"Don't slow down, Marla," she scolded.

My legs were so wobbly I wondered if they could bear my weight. I shivered repeatedly as the clamminess of the caves increased. It was colder without all the people around us. Jessie did have a warmer slack suit on than I did and her boots helped too.

"The stairs"—even the whisper hurt my throat—"they must be just ahead." I held the flashlight steady on the steps while Jessica climbed down through the swatch of light, then I followed.

Once we were on the dock, I threw the beam of light across the boats. They did vary in size; the smallest was about fourteen feet, the largest about twenty. "We'll take this little one." I held it tightly to the dock while Jessica climbed in. "Make sure the oars are there."

She nodded her head.

I crawled up on to the bow and flashed my light up at the wires, then making a conscious effort not to look down at the ebony water, I timidly tried to stand erect. Would I be able to reach the wire? I was surefooted in my tennis shoes. Slowly I stretched up straighter and straighter until at last I felt the cold metal with my fingers and grasped it firmly with one hand. If I'd known about the wires, I would have brought gloves.

"Here, Jessie, put the light on the seat, then untie us."

She obeyed without hesitation. I held the wire rigidly with both hands as she loosened the rope, then cautiously maneuvered the boat out into the cavern and pointed it toward where I thought the tunnel would be, grateful to find the empty boat quite easy to handle.

"Keep the light shining directly at the wires in front of us, Jessie." We had only gone a short distance when I realized the current was getting stronger each boat length. The guy wires were a blessing; it would have been next to impossible for me to row. Even so, I began to have difficulty keeping the stern of the boat from getting ahead of us and we were coming dangerously close to the wall. I felt a jab of pain on my ankle, accompanied by the sound of ripping cloth, as we struck the side. I tried my hardest to move my hands faster, but I knew we would strike and scrape our way from here on. I thought of having Jessica push us away with one of the oars, a ridiculous notion for they were too heavy for her to handle.

"Sit . . . on floor. Hang on . . . seat. . . . Doing . . . my best." My words came out broken and strained from my exertion. Perspiration ran down into my eyes. The heavy wires cut into my hands; I could feel the blood slither down my wrists. I closed my mind to the pain. The banging of the boat echoed and reechoed through the chamber; there would be no mystery now as to our whereabouts. The noise would roar clear to the top. *Dear Lord, we must be getting close.* How long would the boat hold together with this beating?

"The lights, they're just ahead, Marla. They don't seem as bright."

"The . . . noise."

Jessica was right; as we entered the tunnel there were noticeable patches of dark in the ceiling that had not been there before. There were still a myriad of lights to see by, however. "Save . . . flash 'til . . . there," I coughed. How old were the batteries? I wondered. A foolish worry at this point. At least the wires were closer together here and the water seemed more calm; I could manage with a minimum of effort.

"Marla, that one. I think it's that one."

I pointed the boat in the direction she indicated.

"The other side. Go around it."

She flashed the light over the pillar. There was the deeply creviced H, down low near the water. I looked around desperately for a place to tie the boat, trying at the same time to hold us still.

"Can you throw the loop over that jagged point, Jessie? Over there near the small ledge." She took the loop in both hands and leaned over the side as I pressed harder with my legs to bring us in closer. "Careful, Jessie, don't lean too far."

She threw the rope, but missed.

"Try again. I'll get us in closer yet."

This time the loop held around the jutted piece and I felt the pressure lessen on my hands. As the captive boat stabilized I sank down weakly on the bow and hugged Jessie to me.

"We're going to make it," I whispered against her hair. I assessed our position while I rested. We could start on the ledge, then climb the rest of the way to the ten- or twelve-foot column with hand- and foot-holds.

"Jessie, give me that piece of rope on the bottom of the boat." The words came with difficulty from in my narrowed throat. I tied one end around her waist, making sure the knots were secure, left an eight-foot slack, then tied it around my own waist. There was still an un-wieldly twenty feet of rope left, so I tied a loop at the very end and pressed it down on the same jagged piece of limestone we had used to moor the boat.

The ledge was noticeably smaller than the one Jessica had shared with Estelle, hardly big enough for the two of us; but I was right, there were handles to hang on to everywhere, sharp and biting but available.

"You go first," I nudged Jessica, "so I can see you every minute."

"Marla, your hands!"

"They're fine. Go slowly, Jessie."

I watched her edge out toward the pillar, then with the flashlight in my jacket pocket, I reached out to follow her. We were forced dangerously close to the black water in certain areas, and my shoes were soaked. The porous limestone had a living, breathing quality to it that was almost sensuous, like a brutal, would-be lover, as it tore at my clothing and hair. If David's aunt could see us now, what would she say? "My dear, how theatrical!" The excess rope between me and the hook slipped into the water, its wet weight dragging at my waist. Several places I found a handhold but no place for my feet. I tried moving higher. . . . There, that was better. I could see Jessie moving ahead steadily, grateful that she was so agile. A brittle lip broke off and splashed below me, and the sound ricocheted off the empty walls like a cannon shot. How many hundreds of years down the drain, I thought crazily. Jessica looked back at me, a startled expression on her face. The cave grew darker.

I tried to wedge my foot in her direction, but this time the rope completely stopped. It was caught. I couldn't move.

"Marla, are you coming?" There was near panic in her voice.

"Just hang on," I called as I freed one hand and tugged at the rope in the water behind me. The slack had caught somewhere under the dark river. I managed to turn my body enough to maneuver the rope out from my side and I jerked and twisted it, half sobbing with the effort. My hand that clutched the limestone niche to steady me was numb. I had to try again . . . harder. I gave as violent a twist as I could manage, a last desperate try. . . . It broke free!

"Jessie," I called, "I'm loose. I'm coming."

Then I saw the entire picture of what I'd done as our boat whirled before it floated on past us with the current, the rope with which it had been tied stretched in the water straight behind it like an accusing finger. In freeing the line around my waist, I had also destroyed our only means of escape.

CHAPTER TWENTY-SEVEN

"Was—was that our boat?"

"Oh, Jessie, how could I have . . . I released it when I freed myself. Go on ahead, I can follow now."

The rope between us grew taut several times as she moved on around the column and out of sight. I struggled to keep up with her. There were more footholds and handles the further I moved, and soon she was in sight again. She was at least two feet lower than I was and dangerously close to the dark water. She waited, watching me climb toward her.

"Don't worry about the boat, Marla. After we find the amulet, we can find a ledge and wait until the first tour comes through in the morning."

I nodded at her calm reasoning, knowing full well that when we didn't come back out of the caves, whoever was after us wouldn't hesitate to come looking for us. They'd know where to look and they wouldn't wait for morning. "Have you found the spot, Jessie?"

"I—I think it's there." She pointed to a deep slot just past where she was holding on. It was one of thousands all around us, but it did have an odd, almost question-mark shape at the opening.

"Can you get past it," I asked as I reached her, "then I could get on this side?"

She crabbed her way over beyond the slot. I moved ahead with her until we were on each side of it. Nothing mattered now but to get the precious talisman and try to hide before they could find us. I found a large double indentation down close to the water that I could wedge my whole left leg into and around, which freed my hands.

"Let me have the torch, Marla, I'll shine it on the spot for you."

"Jessie, what if the hole goes right out into the river?"

She shook her head. "They dragged the river again and again. It would have been there; it was too heavy to float."

I took the wire from my pocket and bent the end into a hook; when the rest was straightened out it was over five feet long. It was good sturdy wire; it would hold a heavy object. I wished it were longer now. I wrapped it once around my wrist so that I couldn't lose it, then carefully edged the hook end into the crevice. It caught several times as I inched it down, but each time I was able to maneuver it free. At last it was down its full length and it touched only space.

"It's not long enough," I moaned.

Jessica had watched my every move intently. She freed one hand and pointed to the water under me. "What about the rope?"

"The rope? But how?"

"Tie it on to the end of the wire."

"It might work." I fished up the wet piece dangling into the water beneath me, shivering as its wetness soaked my jacket. The damp knot resisted being undone, but I finally managed to tie it to a looped end of the wire. Down . . . down . . . down went the wire, then foot after foot of rope. Suddenly the rope slackened in my hand as the wire hook hit bottom.

Jessica's eyebrows rose in expectation as I bounced the hook up and down, then slowly they lapsed into a frown as I felt nothing on the hook and shook my head in discouragement.

"Could it be another hole close to this one, Jessie?" She looked carefully over the area. "The boat bumped here. I saw her slip it right in there."

I tried a few more times, then began to retrieve the wire slowly. It caught. I jerked it once, then twice. Then, although it was coming up without real resistance, it was definitely heavier, as though it had snared something along the way. I grabbed the end of the wire as it came into view. It was weighted down. We'd snagged something for sure. My heart was beating so rapidly, it was making me light-headed. The cold water had seeped up through my shoe and pant leg, gradually paralyzing my leg. Slowly . . . slowly now. . . . The hook appeared buried deeply into a thick gold chain tinged green from being imprisoned. I tried to control my trembling as I eased it up to the edge of the hole. Then the heavily jeweled piece broke free, and I held it in my hand.

Though it was encrusted with lime, the jewels glowed through with an intense iridescent light. It was a small diamond-studded cross enclosed in a circle four inches in diameter; ringed with rubies, emeralds, and sapphires, and bordered again in diamonds. It was breathtaking, like a shimmering, miniature shrine in the beam of the flashlight.

Jessica stared at it as though hypnotized. "It is beautiful," she whispered at last. "I didn't know it was a cross."

I broke myself from its spell and reluctantly zipped it into the large pocket of my ski jacket to keep it safe. I could no longer trust my shaking hands. "Better switch off the light, Jessie." The sounds of our voices had turned out so many of the glowworms, less than half of the tunnel still sparkled. What were we going to do now?

"Marla, you look sick." Jessica's voice sounded worried and faraway. "Hang on, please hang on. Can you get back to the ledge?"

"Let me rest a minute, then I'll try." I wanted so badly to close my eyes, but I knew I didn't dare. My cheek felt hot against the clammy, damp limestone. Jessica was strangely quiet. "Jessie, are you all right?" I struggled to read her face through my half-closed eyes.

"I've been praying," she said simply. "Marla, I remembered something from Barth's book." I waited for her to go on. "It was telling about the baby Jesus in the manger. Only, Marla, it wasn't really a manger; it was a cave in the side of the mountain where the shepherds kept their sheep and cattle warm where the baby Jesus was born. They said it was a limestone cave, Marla, like ours."

A warmth crept over my body as I watched a radiance light up her face. "Limestone, Jessie?"

She nodded and suddenly a miraculous thing happened. Jessica smiled! It was a dear, beautiful smile, full of wonder. Tears coursed down my cheeks unheeded. *Lord, You've been with us just as You promised,* I said silently. *All this time You've been with us.*

We both heard it at the same time . . . the sound of another boat forging toward the tunnel.

"Don't stop praying yet, Jessie, not until we know who it is. . . ."

CHAPTER TWENTY-EIGHT

We could see the guy wires bend from the pressure of unseen hands propelling the boat toward us. The eerie swishing of the bow through the water preceeded it. Part of me wanted to call out "Hurry, hurry"; another part wanted to blend into the limestone to which we clung. Suddenly the boat swung into clear view. I thought my eyes had tricked me as I recognized the energetic figure manipulating the boat.

"Geoff," I called in a hoarse voice. "Geoff, over here. How did you find us?"

"Good God, what a sight. Are you all right?" He moved the boat in our direction, then found as I had that the wires didn't come that close and there was no place to tie the boat.

"Over there by the ledge," I waved an arm toward the errant boat hook.

He talked as he tied the boat: "Saw you in the crowd when I came out with my school kids," he explained, "but couldn't reach you. I waited, but when you didn't come out. . . . Come on, girls, climb back around here. I'll drive you both home and get you warm again."

"In your red sports car?" Jessica asked in childlike anticipation.

Red sports car! There had been no shock on his face at hearing Jessica speak. He knew! "Jessie, wait! Stay where you are!"

He turned his face toward my words. The transformation that came over his amiable features was terrifying. His eyes hardened to knifelike slits and the warm, friendly smile on his mouth melted into a drawn, vicious snarl.

"Don't be a fool, Marla."

"You mean more of a fool." It was so painful for me to talk. "I never once suspected you, Geoff."

"This could all have been avoided," he hissed, "if **you had died on the road that first day, or in the** steam pit."

"And Andrea . . . did you . . . ?" I thought back to the looks she'd given him, but then Andrea looked at every man that way.

"She was convenient, but expendable."

It hadn't been David. . . . It wasn't Parker; oh, Parker; oh, darling.

"If I give you the cross, will you let Jessica go, Geoff? You couldn't hurt Jessica."

"Don't trust him, Marla." Jessica's voice was firm. His eyes narrowed again.

"I'll throw the jewels in the water," I threatened.

He laughed. "You bungling amateur. I'd know right where to look after I'd taken care of you." He turned unexpectedly and pulled a tarp from the back of the boat. The familiar round body of Mrs. Pilgrim rose with it. "I'll need you now, Birdie."

"Oh, Marla." It was a little girl's frightened voice.

Another chill shook my body. No, I couldn't let it happen—I hadn't found my family only to lose it forever. It took all my strength to cry out, "Jessie, scream. Put out the glowworms." I didn't have to tell her twice. Her shrill voice, magnified by the echo, pierced the tunnel like a flock of banshees, and blackness surrounded us almost instantly.

"Damn you!" came Geoff's voice out of the dark. "Birdie, get the torch."

"Little bitch!" came her high-pitched, hawkish voice. We could hear her scrambling around in the boat.

"Jessie," I whispered, "untie the rope around your waist quickly. . . ."

"It is," she whispered back.

I worked to release mine when the beam of light hit me. Part of our rope was floating dangerously near their boat. *Dear God, don't let him see it!* But my prayer was too late. He reached for the rope in the water and with the second try caught it and began reeling me toward him off the ledge. In seconds he could pull me into the water.

"Hold the light steady, Birdie. I've almost got her."

Jessica looked white and petrified beside me in the light. As the rope came loose from my waist I whispered something to her. At the same time as I gave the rope he was holding a violent jerk, Jessica thrust out her tongue full length with a guttural scream and rolled her eyes like a Maori warrior. The whip of the rope toppled Geoff backward against Mrs. Pilgrim, knocking the light from her hand. We heard it splash in the water. I was nauseated by the stream of filthy words that reached us.

"I'm going to crawl out there," Geoff told Birdie. "I'll kill that bitch if it's the last thing I do."

"Not in the dark, Geoff. Don't be a damned fool. I can't handle this boat myself."

"Any better suggestions?" his voice sneered.

We could hear him clawing his way toward us. I was weak and shaking from the cold. I hardly felt the fear for myself. Jessica might be able to climb to safety. If I can just stall him, struggle with him . . . anything to save Jessica. . . .

"Jessie, if you love me, you'll climb out to somewhere you can hide 'til David can find you. . . . Do this for David. . . ."

I could hear Geoff's hard breathing as he grew closer and closer. . . .

CHAPTER TWENTY-NINE

A sudden explosion of light exposed Geoff clinging to the side just a few feet from us. He turned his head into the limestone from the glare. Mrs. Pilgrim put one fat arm across her face and sat down in the boat. There were many voices. More than one boat. David was in the first boat, Parker propelling it on the prow. Kreska and the policemen were in the second boat. I recognized Inspector St. Johns and Constable Mollaire. They pulled their boat in next to Geoff's, and the metallic clang of handcuffs told us what had happened.

"Marla, Jessica, are you right?" It was David's voice.

"They're safe 'til we reach them." Parker maneuvered the boat with practiced hands. He used the heavy oar to bring it up directly alongside of us. David reached up for Jessica. She was crying as he lowered her into their boat.

"David, grab the oar. Marla's mine." They changed positions and Parker reached out his hands to me. There was something familiar about that gesture, something to do with a window and quiet water. I fell into his arms without hesitation. Parker crushed me to him as we sank to the wooden seat. I let my body blend against his, and once again that surge of physical strength generated a healing warmth over my entire being.

"Parker, I love you," I whispered against him.

"Marla, my love, my dearest love, don't ever do this to me again."

David used the guy wires to bring us back toward the dock.

"Jessie? Jessie? Where is Jessie?"

"I'm here, Marla," she called from just behind us. "She's sick, Parker, awful sick. She has been for hours."

I looked up at David's lithe figure on the bow. His head was averted as he concentrated on guiding the boat. There was a buzzing in my ears that wouldn't stop. My throat had a closed, swollen feeling.

"She's on fire with fever," I heard Parker say as though he were under the boat.

Parker swung himself onto the dock, then gently lifted me out beside him. Jessica jumped out. I saw the pain in Parker's eyes as he realized his knee wouldn't permit him to carry me up the stairs.

"You carry her, David. I'll take Jessica. Careful now."

David swung me into his arms, and I buried my burning face into his jacket. "There's an emergency phone at the office, isn't there, Parker? Call Doctor Newton. Tell him to be at the house when we get there. Plan to spend the night, Parker. She's not through this yet."

I coughed uncontrollably from my first breath of fresh night air; I'd drunk too deeply of it like a thirsting man on the desert takes his first drink of water. The stars were extra bright in the black sky, and I thought with pleasure no human cry could put them out either. . . .

Parker held me all the way home; Jessica slept beside me. David drove silently. He'd hardly said a word. We'd exchanged a long look of loving understanding, and it had been strangely satisfying.

I must have slept a good portion of the way; it seemed only minutes until I was being carried from the car up the stairs to my room at Blandish House. I could hear familiar voices all around me: Sims, Miss Blandish, Ariki Meri . . . not Andrea . . . never again Andrea. Andrea was dead . . . Steve was dead . . . Uncle Mitch, all dead, even Kanapu, poor Kanapu . . . everything was dead all around me. . . . "Jessie!" I tried to scream.

"She's all right, darling." It was Parker's voice. "Just lie back; the doctor's with you now."

I didn't want to open my mouth, my throat hurt so, but he was forcing me to. . . . I fought him. . . . It was a poisonous stick he was using; didn't they know. . . ?

"Parker," I moaned. "Oh, Parker, where are you?"

"I'm here, darling, right here. You're just bloody sick, and he's trying to help you."

There was a sharp pain in my right arm. It didn't make sense . . . nothing made sense . . . someone should turn the thermostat down . . . there, that coolness on my forehead . . . there, that was better . . . there . . . I was floating . . . floating in and out of danger . . . just a spectator at a cockfight . . . I'd seen it on TV . . . no it was real, I could feel the stickiness of the blood on my hands . . . it was painful blood . . . my blood hurt . . . my hands, won't someone help me? "Parker, my hands. . . ."

"Marla, thank God you're awake. You gave us a terrible scare."

I reached up and touched his cheek. It was real. The black stubble of his beard caught on something. He turned my hand over and kissed the bandaged palm. He was bleary-eyed with fatigue. I tried to smile, but the sides of my mouth didn't want to move. Nothing about me wanted to move. It was as though I'd been sandbagged.

"You've been terribly sick. The shock and the virus combined."

"How—how long?"

"Three days."

"Jessie?"

"She's fine. She's sat with me for hours beside you. Hello, Doctor. She's awake."

"So I see. I'm Doctor Newton. You've had the Port Chalmers flu, much worse than most. We couldn't get the temperature down." He turned to Parker. "She's through the first of it, but she'll still have to be watched twenty-four hours a day. We'll put a nurse on 'round the clock. She'll probably doze on and off for another day or two. The less she talks the better; her throat needs time to heal. Limit your visits to short periods of time."

"The cross?" I asked Parker when the doctor was gone.

"The authorities are taking care of the details."

"David?"

"He's making an effort, Marla. Your father's flying in tomorrow night. Close those gorgeous eyes. I won't leave you until the nurse gets here."

"I love you, Parker."

"And I love you."

Suddenly two small arms were around my neck. "The doctor said I could see you. You're awake."

"Easy, Jessie, she's still weak," Parker cautioned.

"Marla, my father's coming home."

"Wonderful."

"Come on, Jessie, let's let her rest. You'll see her when she wakes up again."

Ariki Meri came up beside Jessie. "You are a wonder, child. I cannot believe all you have done."

"I'm fine. Just tired," I whispered.

I felt myself slipping away again. . . . Where was Miss Blandish? Everyone was happy, Parker said, but Miss Blandish. She needed to know I wasn't a threat. Parker said everything was straightened out; what was bothering me? It must be my illness . . . but something was still not right. Geoff hadn't been at the house for the pitchfork . . . he hadn't slashed the bear. Kreska had been in the house both times. He'd been in the boat with David and Parker. . . . They trusted him. Jessie was no longer in danger, but evil was still a guest somewhere in this house. . . .

CHAPTER THIRTY

My eyes seemed able to focus for the first time. When I'd awakened before briefly, I'd been aware of a starched white uniform floating about the room like an apparition. This time the ceiling stayed in place above me and the lampshade wasn't wavy. Someone was sitting beside my bed. A man I didn't know. I studied through half-closed eyes his silvered blond hair, the aristocratic nose, the mouth both sensual and sensitive. His blue-green eyes were bright like those of a young man, though he must have been past fifty. He had the high structured forehead of an intellectual, his brows arched in a permanent attitude of appraisal. Something about him was familiar; it could be the nose . . . David's nose.

"Mr. Cavenaugh?"

His eyes darted quickly to my face. "You're awake? But how did you know?"

"I knew . . . you were expected." It was an effort to speak, my throat felt constricted. "You have . . . David's nose."

"David has mine," he said, smiling. I felt strangely comfortable with him. "You've given everyone a scare with your illness."

"I love Jessie."

"You're all she talks about. How can I ever say thank you for all you've done."

"Just show her that you love her. Be with her; she needs you. Dreadful about . . . Andrea."

"Murder is despicable."

"Is David . . . ?"

He searched my face, trying to understand. "David is bitter, but he's been sober. That's a start."

"He's needed you too."

He frowned just like Jessica.

"You need each other."

He didn't move or look away. Suddenly he reached over impulsively and took my hand in his. "I didn't know you existed. Kathy visited us in England. Charlotte told David stories of her torment over my affair with her sister to win his sympathy. God, how she had to have sympathy." I waited for him to go on. "She begged me to continue our marriage on any basis for David's sake. The fact that we had two more children was to ease my conscience, but nothing more. I never saw Kathy again."

"Poor David."

"David told me he hated me for what I'd done to his mother and always would."

"If he hated you, he must hate me too." I hadn't meant to say the words, they just came out. If David hated me, if our friendship had been a fraud, could his hate be strong enough to want me dead? I turned my face into the pillow to hide my emotion. Aaron Cavenaugh tried to pull his hand away, but I held on to it tightly. My need for him would last forever.

"I made David promise he wouldn't tell you. I didn't want your life torn apart. Then Elizabeth wrote me that you'd arrived and had taken Jessica away. She guessed who you really were, of course. The letter didn't reach me until the day before David called about Andrea."

I had a spasm of coughing. He handed me the glass of water from the table. "I'm sorry," I gasped.

"I'm the one who's sorry. I've tired you. Rest a while and I'll come back later and we'll talk. I have a feeling we'll always have a lot to talk about. You're very like your mother."

He left the room and I was alone. I picked up the book David had left on my table, one he'd enjoyed. A scrap of paper fluttered onto the bed from between the pages. David's bookmark? Then I recognized Sims's large, sprawled handwriting. It looked like a hastily written telephone message:

CALL BIRDIE—MILFORD NO LATER THAN TUES. A.M.

His telephone call must have been interrupted and he'd hidden the note in David's book. At the same moment the full implication of what I'd read struck me, I looked up to see Sims staring down at me—the telltale note still in my hands.

He was not the same man. His face was distorted with anger. "How unfortunate that you found that just now."

"Sims . . . in the house . . . the bear. . . . Was it you?"

His long nose quivered, his nostrils flared. "Our plan was all so perfect, so near completion. I persuaded Estelle to steal the pouch to claim it as her rightful inheritance. She never knew its real value, and Daddy was covered by insurance anyway. I was her best friend, you know." There was a sick sneer in her voice. "It was a cinch cracking the safe, but she eluded me in the caves, the little witch. Yes, I slashed the bear. You turned out to have more lives than the cat. It died easy. That fork shouldn't have missed. Damn you! She was so near to cracking and spilling it all to Geoff."

"Did you pull Estelle from the ledge?"

"I was after the pouch, it was Geoff did her in. One of the few times he killed it by mistake and not for pleasure."

"You were frightened . . . that first day . . . you thought I was—"

"It was uncanny . . . the resemblance. . . ."

He picked up the pillow next to mine. The realization of what he was contemplating spread over my scalp with icy bristles. He knew my illness had destroyed my ability to scream; it was all I could do to talk in a hoarse whisper.

"You still haven't committed murder, Sims. At least this would be on your side," I begged.

"I'm wanted for murder in England," he smirked. "The man I'm impersonating here wouldn't hand over his papers easily. Your nurse is having coffee with Annie. The rest of the family is occupied. With Geoff and Birdie both in custody, I've got to get away quick, and you won't prevent my leaving. You've been very sick—touch and go—they'll think you had a sudden relapse. . . ."

He raised the pillow over my head. "Make it easy on yourself, don't struggle." The pillow pinned my hands back as it crushed over my face. . . .

CHAPTER THIRTY-ONE

The agony of losing my breath convulsed my body, but just when I thought I'd lose consciousness, the weight of the pillow lessened and was pulled to one side. David was fighting with Sims. There was a fury in David's blows I hadn't realized he was capable of. Sims was a vicious opponent despite his age. He grabbed the dressing-table chair and swung it. David dodged, and it only grazed his side. He jumped full length at Sims, and the weight of his body knocked them both to the floor. He struck Sims time after time with his fists.

"No, David, no," I groaned, too weak to stop him.

Suddenly Parker had David by the shoulders, pulling him from Sims, who was lying very still and crumpled on the floor.

"He tried to kill Marla," David said, trying to get back again to Sims.

"Marla!" Parker called to me.

"I'm okay," I half-choked. "David's right . . . he's a killer."

"Father didn't know he was to tell the nurse when he left so that Marla wouldn't be alone," David told him. "I just happened to go into the kitchen and saw her. My God, that was close, Parker. When I saw him holding that pillow over her face, I didn't know whether I was too late or not."

Parker pulled the semiconscious Sims to his feet and shoved him out the door in front of him.

David came over to me. I raised his bruised hand to my lips. "If ever . . . a girl needed . . . a big brother. . . ."

"Kreska warned us something like this could happen, but we didn't suspect Sims."

The nurse came sheepishly into the room. "I can't believe what happened. I'm so sorry, Mister Cavenaugh. I think she should rest now. She looks peaked."

The following morning the nurse brought me a mirror and I brushed my hair myself for the first time. I looked like a ghost in turquoise pajamas. Elizabeth Blandish came into my room soon after. Her lavender dress was oddly out of style, as though she hadn't worn it for many years. The change from her usual black was revolutionary, her paleness no longer stark, but more fragile. Except for the rigidity of her features, she was almost beautiful. She came and stood by the bed. "I've come to ask your forgiveness," she said stiffly.

"I don't understand."

"I've been lying in my room with one of my head-aches for days on end, trying to right things in my mind. We do tend to deceive ourselves, don't we?"

I nodded, at a complete loss as to what to say.

"Because of David's hatred for his father, I thought his mind was twisted." She blurted the words out as though they were poison she'd been hoarding. "As if the pain of losing his mother and finding his father unfaithful wasn't enough, he lost his sister too. Then came Andrea. She tried to compromise Parker, David's best friend, and we believed her. Jessica was a constant reminder of Estelle's death. . . . It was destroying David. And with Aaron estranged, David was all I had. I thought when I saw you that David would be driven over the brink. Instead Jessica and David both responded to you. Jealousy is a sickness."

I reached out and put my hand over hers. It was still bone cold under my touch, but I didn't find it repulsive.

"Let me finish, please," she begged. "I can accept you now, Marla, and—and when I think what a sacrifice you were ready to make for Jessica. . . . I want to change. It won't be easy, but we do what we can."

"We're a family now," I told her. "It will take getting used to for all of us." She left the room without another word, just as Jessica had done when she was in the process of defrosting.

Parker came in with Leon Kreska, who looked immaculate as usual in his brown suit. There was a black stripe in the brown tie that matched his hair. Now that he was properly cast in my mind, I could accept his image. He did his part well. "If only David had told me you were an investigator. For the IDSO, is it? I can't seem to remember the words."

"The International Diamond Security Organization," he said. "David couldn't tell you, he was sworn to secrecy. Sims's papers and background were faultless, even to his description by his former employers. He was an artist at machination, a foremost British safecracker.

"Geoffrey Storch, alias Geoffrey James, was a qualified teacher; it was one of his less colorful skills. He worked with Birdie Potts, alias Mrs. Pilgrim, between London and the States in smuggling and credit cards. Storch is a first-rate con man, hit man, you name it. Birdie worked in girls' schools as a part-time, sadistic matron. She used her hobby of bird-watching to great advantage. She was suspect from the beginning because she was on the plane when the agent was killed transporting the amulet from London. With her background we knew she was involved, but we could never prove it."

"She was a dreadful woman," I said.

"I was following her on your flight to New Zealand. When she sat across from you—and you were obviously a relative of the Cavenaughs, which they had neglected to mention to you—you became suspect too. Then Parker connecting up with you cinched it. I still had misgivings about him." He paused. "Nothing personal, Brandt. You could have taken the amulet to be with Marla."

"Why did you attempt to steal Marla's purse?"

"Your Mrs. Pilgrim bribed that Fijian to grab your purse for her," he said to me. "She must have paid him plenty; he wouldn't tell me a thing. Birdie gave my man the slip in Wellington; when I'd traced her to Milford, you'd both gone. Fortunately I rechecked Storch's bio and when I found he'd taken a leave of absence from the school for no apparent reason, I figured he was after you."

"And Andrea?"

"I found witnesses to his affair with Andrea. She must have discovered his connection with Sims. David told me you were in Dunedin."

"I saw you there."

He looked surprised. "I didn't know. Storch bribed a shearer there to create trouble at the Crookshanks's and drive you away from their protection. Both Storch and I went to Christchurch hoping to find you after we found you'd slipped past us in some way. How did you camouflage your flight?"

When I told him he laughed. "It worked. I'll have to remember that. Storch bribed that airline reservationist to steer you on to Milford Sound, where he had Birdie waiting. Birdie called Storch when she found you were on your way to Queenstown."

"I found the attendant unconscious after Storch had knocked him over the head in time to operate the gondola when you came out of the restaurant," Parker added. "I was going to tell you about it the next morning, but you'd gone."

"You did pretty well for an amateur, Marla," Kreska said.

"Will you be leaving Blandish House now, Leon?" I asked.

"Yes, I have another assignment waiting for me in Istanbul."

"Good-bye, Leon. Thank you and good luck."

"Good-bye. If you ever want to join the force, let me know."

He even had a sense of humor, I thought. It was there in his blue-glass eyes, I just never noticed it.

The next day I was able to sit up in the floral rocking chair by the window. Jessica sat at my feet, David on the bed, and Parker stretched out on the floor with his hands behind his head. Jessica opened Kreska's music box every now and then and the delicate strains of the Viennese Waltz escaped. She was still too quiet, but she smiled easily now.

"I called the Crookshanks this morning, Marla," Parker told me. "I knew they were worried about you. Barth's ear operation was a success. They said to give you a 'wee bit of love' from all of them. They wanted you and Jessie to visit soon to recuperate. I told them maybe after our honeymoon."

"Something's changed with Father," David said. "He plans to stay here at home for several months. That's the first time since Estelle—"

"Marla will make a difference," Parker said, looking at me in that special way. "And he can't seem to see enough of Jessica."

"I'm thinking of taking that engineering job in Fiji, Parker."

"That should be a good move."

"David, you never mentioned this."

"The offer came while you were sick, Marla. I told them I'd consider it. Pretty right of them after all the other times I've turned them down."

"When would it begin?" The thought of his leaving was painful.

"Soon." He walked over by me and looked out of the window. "Even Auntie is trying. She wants Ariki Meri to make Blandish House into the museum she and father have always wanted. Auntie can keep house for me in Fiji. We all need a change. Jessica could go to school there too."

"I'd like to go to boarding school when I go back," Jessica said.

"Like one in Canterbury Plains near Dunedin?" I winked at her.

She smiled. "Maybe."

"One thing still bothers me, Jessica," David said. "Could you have talked at any time if you'd wanted to? There were times when I. . . . I'm sure Marla would like to know too."

Jessica looked up at me, and something registered between us.

"No, David, if Jessie wants to tell you, that's fine, but I don't ever want to know." I started to giggle uncontrollably. "It's . . . just that it's . . . so much . . . a part of . . . the intrigue." I gasped. "It would spoil it . . . knowing. . . ."

Jessica was giggling now too, then the sound of her full laughter filled every corner of the room and we doubled up with happy tears.

"It's easy to see what a bloody future we have to look forward to, David," Parker said with a grin, "with these two around."